Balance
Samantha M Thomas

Contents

To the overwhelmed.

Find yourself a Felix and let him lead the way to self-care.

Chapter 1
Felix

My jaw clenches tight enough to crack a molar. The questions the fucking media are asking Antionette are out of line, but I know better than to interject. She has to learn how to deal with the vultures if she's going to make it as a team principal.

That doesn't mean I don't want to punch every single one of these fuckers.

Antoinette Bailey came onto the Formula 1 scene like a tornado. One of my favorite people, Sydney Davis, hired her on a hope and a prayer, and I should know better than to question her methods, but this one I don't understand.

Antoinette isn't ready. The media is starting to eat her alive. Most days, her back is straight, her shoulders are pulled back, and her head is held high, exuding confidence. Today is not one of those days. She's slumped back in her chair, her hands in her lap while she holds the microphone, and it shows every ounce of her uncertainty.

I grip the microphone in my hand tighter, trying to think of a way to interrupt that wouldn't look ten times worse for her. But then she shocks the shit out of me. She straightens her shoulders, rolls them a little, and plants her feet on the ground.

"It sounds to me like you're asking if a woman can do this job. Is that what you're asking?" Her tone is the utmost professional, but it's the undercurrent that pulls me in. Willful in her challenge, she's not letting them walk all over her. Calling out the dumbass question and putting the reporter on the hot seat.

It's really fucking sexy.

Fuck. No. The thought shouldn't even be in my head. She's a colleague. Nothing more, nothing less, and that's how it should stay. Lord knows neither of us need any controversy around us.

Been there, done that. Have the kids that barely talk to me to show for it.

Not putting myself in that line of fire again, even if this particular woman is intriguing as hell.

"Uh— Umm, no, that wasn't what I meant." The bumbling idiot backtracks.

"Hmm, it sure sounded like it." She grins, and I damn near choke trying to keep my laughter in check. "Let me help assuage your worry. I am very capable of doing this job. Last year was hard for our team overall. There was a lot of change, and we were never able to get our footing. Considering I only had about half a year to get things going, it was a tough challenge that I wasn't able to improve upon. The great thing is that it's a new year, and we've already seen a drastic improvement in testing and with the drivers. I'll be honest; I expected to be answering questions about last year. What I didn't expect was my gender, and therefore my ability, to be called into question."

My lips roll together to stop the smirk from tipping up. Goddamn, she's more than intriguing; she's a dynamo. I watch with amusement as she stares down the kid who asked the question. He smartly backs down, but another takes his place just as fast. I see the cocky smirk on his face when he asks her if her lack of experience is affecting progress.

"You know, I thought we were here to talk about the cars and the upcoming season," I coolly say into my microphone to head him off. "It would be lovely to stay on task." I can almost feel the heat of Antoinette's stare boring into the side of my head, but I don't dare acknowledge it. Instead, I look at every single reporter, making sure they know that I see what they're doing and I won't stand for it in one of my press conferences.

I may be the team principal for Legacy Racing, but I'm the most experienced on the grid and everyone knows we play by my rules. If they want to get on my bad side, they won't have a job next week.

Am I choosing to ignore the fact that I'm feeling this way because of a certain spitfire sitting next to me? Absolutely. I'll live in this delusion a little while longer and focus on the questions now being directed at me.

Forty-five minutes later, I place the microphone on the chair I vacated and walk out of the press conference at a fast clip.

"Felix!" She calls from behind me, but I don't turn around. The Legacy hospitality area ahead in the paddock is within my sights.

"Hey!" Her voice sounds closer.

"I've got shit to do, Antoinette," I grumble.

"Yes, I know, dear King of the Grid. I wanted to say thank you for back there. I had it handled, but I appreciate the support." She's nearly jogging to try to keep up with me.

"No thanks needed." I desperately cling to my indifferent attitude, hoping she doesn't read any more into my actions. I'm not the nice guy. I'm not the helpful support system she wants, and she needs to remember that.

She sighs loud enough that I almost stop to look at her. The temptation is there, sure, but then I remember everything I went through seven years ago. The drama almost cost me my career, and that's not something I'm willing to gamble again. It's the only thing I was able to keep, the only thing I have left.

God. What a depressing party of one I am.

"It's okay to be nice once in a while. You know, smile, take a compliment or appreciation from a colleague." I can hear the smile in her voice. Her dangerous, beautiful, blinding smile.

Grunting, I keep my pace until I'm steps away from the doors that will separate me from her.

"Fine, Felix. I'll take the hint. Good luck in practice tomorrow."

I don't breathe until the sliding doors shut behind me and the air conditioning washes over my overheated body. Slumping against the side wall, I watch Antoinette pause, look up at the sky, and blow out a steady stream of air, before straightening herself back up and heading toward the Empress garage just down the pit lane from us.

That was too close. I know better than to insert myself into anyone's business, especially Antoinette Bailey's.

"Sooooo, are you just going to stand there all creepy-like, or are you going to head back to your office?" Julie, my assistant, asks from the front desk.

"You know, I think I'll stand right here and see if I can figure out Empress's tactics for this Australian race." I add an extra level of sarcasm that doesn't go unnoticed.

"Uh-huh. And would those tactics happen to be in the form of the delightful Toni Bailey?" she asks with a playful twinkle in her eye.

"Don't you have work to do?"

"Careful boss, or I'll jump ship like Susie did." She smirks so I know she's joking, but it doesn't sting any less. Sydney hijacked my last assistant. If it had been anyone else, I would have fought to keep her, but Sydney needed the help more than I did.

My eyes narrow before her tinkling laugh fills the small reception area.

"God, you're so easy to rile up. You need to lighten up majorly. Maybe in the form of a certain brunette."

"Julie, I will say this once: if you ever talk about my companionship or lack thereof again, you can go take a walk and get a job at Guardian." I use one of the bottom three teams as an example.

"Duly noted." She sobers and nods.

Sighing, I attempt to refocus. "Any messages?"

"Nope, but Eric wants to meet about the weather this weekend."

"Send him back." *Fucking Eric and his goddamned weather reports.*

As I walk upstairs, a little guilt creeps in at threatening Julie. I'm a hard-ass, sure, but I've been trying to soften my image lately. Clearly, it's a work in progress.

Plopping down behind my desk, I think about the conversation I had with my ex-wife last week.

Stephanie and I split on amicable terms. We've stayed friends, and she's really the only person I don't have to act a certain way around.

She encouraged me to turn over a new leaf at work. Attempt to be more friendly and *nicer* to my staff.

Day one into the new season, and I'm failing miserably.

A knock at my door means it's time to deal with all the parts of this job I dislike. The tedious details that go into every race weekend. The small stuff that

I'd rather leave to other people but still need to sign off on.

"Come in," I mutter.

***

The view of the track from my hotel room usually calms me. Tonight, it's doing the opposite. Pulling the glasses off my face, I rub the sides of my nose with my finger and thumb.

Legacy is a powerhouse in Formula 1. It has been for as long as I've been a team principal here. My confidence is waning this year, though. Our cars have not performed in our testing like we're used to, and our engineers have been working overtime to figure out the problem.

But we're not where we should be, where we *need* to be.

I have no doubts that Sydney put together a stellar team this year. Sawyer Joseph seems to have gotten his shit together since last season, and the addition of Alejandro Suarez is a good one. Antoinette knows her shit, although I'll never tell her that, but they've got all the necessary tools to make waves this year.

And Legacy's stuck in my version of hell.

The gin and tonic in my hand does nothing to soothe my nerves. Tomorrow is Practice One and Two, the true test to see if all the changes we've made over the last two weeks even made a difference. For the first time in over a decade, I feel unprepared.

It feels as if there's a new wave of Formula 1 coming. Old drivers who have dominated are no longer on the grid, with more and more rookies coming in to take their places. A changing of the guards, if you will. My drivers are young, untested, and I'm worried that combined with our car problems means a failed season.

I can't have a failed season.

At forty-eight years old, I have always felt I had many more years to give to this team. But a disastrous season would mean accountability, and I could be the first on the chopping block. It's a cutthroat world. Lots of money to be made with wins and the championship race. If you aren't making money, you're cut faster than you can say Formula 1.

I haven't been under this amount of stress in years, and I need to find a way to manage it before it consumes me.

A brunette—curvy and head-strong—pops into my head, and I groan out loud.

Antoinette is not who I should ever think about in any context besides racing. She's a rival, a competitor, and that's all she'll ever be.

Slipping the glasses back onto the bridge of my nose, I look at the track again.

This is the year I need to focus and evolve. This is the year I need to completely ignore my attraction to Antoinette Bailey.

Chapter 2
Toni

I know better.

That's all I can think as I walk back to the hotel after a long-ass day with the media and meetings with my engineers.

I let the reporters get under my skin, and I know better than to take the bait. Stay indifferent because they'll grab onto any sound bite they can get.

Now, there's sound bites of me asking if I can't do this job because I'm a woman all over the internet, in the opposite context of which I used it. I'm counting down the seconds until Sydney, my boss and owner of Empress Racing, calls me and gives me an earful. It'd be well deserved.

Like clockwork, my phone buzzes in my hand.

"Hey, Boss," I answer in a clipped tone.

"You okay? That was fucking brutal. I already called that asshole's boss, and he's kicked off the circuit for now."

"What?" I ask, confused.

"That reporter that implied your fucking gender had any bearing on your capabilities won't be there for media days anymore," Sydney reiterates.

"You're not . . ." I pause, trying to wrap my head around things. "You're not mad?"

"Why would I be mad?" Her tone is patient.

"Because I took the bait, and now there are sound bites fucking everywhere," I say, surprised it's not obvious.

"Please." She huffs out a laugh. "There are so many worse interviews out there. This won't even be talked about by tomorrow. Besides, you're a badass, and everyone knows it. Just go out there tomorrow and be the kick-ass team principal we know you are. Don't think a minute more about that dumbass."

I blow out a steady breath, my shoulders slumping in relief.

"I forget how awesome of a boss you are sometimes," I murmur.

"Well, try not to forget. I have a reputation to keep after all." She giggles.

"I'll see you tomorrow, Sydney," I tell her before hanging up the phone as I walk into the hotel elevator.

The elevator shifts as it begins its ascent. I let my eyes fall closed, taking the solitary moment to try to remember why I wanted this job to begin with. It was a chance to prove I was more. I'm a damn good engineer, but this pushes me to the next level. Last season, everyone balked at Sydney hiring an untested engineer for their team principal. I was in a weird place. My boyfriend at the time was controlling as fuck, and the Formula 2 engineering job I had was full of egotistical rich men who didn't listen to a word I said.

Life is completely different now. I'm stronger, more independent, and I need to remember that I can handle all of this. Reporters are always going to be difficult, but I need to remind myself that I'm above the petty bullshit they try to pull from me.

I need to be more like Felix Karlsson.

Felix. His short, salt-and-pepper hair and thick black-framed glasses flash in my head.

Not my usual type, but there's no denying he's a beautiful man. The problem is he's a certified egotistical know-it-all. Not that he doesn't have a right to be that way. He's the gold standard in this job. And it made it easier to keep him in the "asshole" box I created for him in my head. But dammit, I wish he wasn't so fucking attractive. Sleep doesn't come easily as I wrestle with the pressure and need to not show it getting to me in front of anyone. But I manage to grab a couple of hours before heading back to the paddock for practice.

***

My cheeks are flushed as I head back to the hotel after a drink with Sydney and her right hand woman, Daisy. It's been a good fucking two days. Our cars are performing well and our drivers even better. We're in pole position tomorrow, and it feels like the biggest "fuck you" to the reporters from a few days ago.

It's the Australian Grand Prix, the first race of the season, and I'm beyond ready for it. Empress is a force this year, and I'm ready to shut up the haters.

What's surprising is Legacy Racing. They've struggled all weekend but somehow managed to have both drivers in the top ten for tomorrow's race. It's almost disappointing that they aren't doing better, though. I always want to go against the best team, and yet the best team feels drastically worse this season.

I'll take it, though. I'm not one to look a gift horse in the mouth.

The warmth of the day clings to my skin as I peel off my damp clothes. I take a quick shower before throwing on an oversized T-shirt and shorts for bed. The temperature has dropped a little since the sun set, so I grab a water and make my way out to the balcony that overlooks the track.

It's mesmerizing.

The lights are still on—a glittering representation of a new year and a fresh start, in more than one way.

It's only been a few months since I dumped Brad, and it finally feels like I'm out from under his control. Free to kick ass and make a name for myself. Something he was against from the get-go unless he got some pretty wild perks. It took me too long to realize he was bad news, but all that matters is that I'm done with him. It's now time to prove to myself that I don't need to rely on a man for my self-worth. Something surprisingly hard to work through, if I'm honest.

A throat clears from the balcony next to mine. It's far enough away that I'm not right next to him but close enough that the outline is one I recognize.

"You ready for tomorrow?" Felix asks in his professional tone.

"As ready as I'll ever be."

Silence wraps around us, but I get the feeling he's working up to say more, so I wait him out.

"You're doing a good job with Empress. It's like a night-and-day change from last season."

His praise shocks the shit out of me. "Uh . . ." I clear my throat. "Thanks."

There's that self-worth I was thinking about. I don't need Felix's praise to remind me I'm doing a good job.

But it doesn't hurt.

A heavy sigh comes from him. "I'm just trying to . . . I don't know, say good luck tomorrow, even though you guys look great and probably don't need it."

The backhanded compliment is overshadowed by the undercurrent in his words. *He's giving me a true compliment.*

I don't think I've ever heard a compliment come out of Felix Karlsson's mouth in the almost year I've known him.

"Are you okay?" I ask with curiosity in my voice, instead of just graciously taking the compliment he offers.

"Fine. Why?" he clips.

"Because you're never nice to me, and that's now twice this weekend alone." I cringe at my lack of tact. He's so cultured and refined, and it's never been clearer how opposite of that I am. It's hard to be in this world when I didn't grow up in it. It's not only a boys' club but a rich boys' club—something I lack in spades.

"I've recently been told I should be nicer." The way he reluctantly says it has me cackling. "It's not that funny," he grumbles.

"It's a little funny," I counter.

"How are you feeling about tomorrow?" He side-steps the conversation instead.

"Good, actually. I mean, there's a lot that can still go wrong, but I feel more hopeful than I did all of last season. How about you?"

"I am feeling . . ." There's that sigh again. "Jaded, I suppose. We've got a lot of work to do already this season, and I'm not hopeful that any of it will make a difference."

He may give off a harsh demeanor most of the time, but I don't think I've ever heard him defeated before. It's unnerving.

"Anything I can help with?" My people pleasing tendency is front and center before I can reel it in. Of course I can't help him. We're competing against each other. It's all trade secrets and "if I tell you, I have to kill you" crap.

"Want to trade cars?" He chuckles.

"Sadly, I don't think that's an option. I have wine over here if you want to grab a drink and decompress," I offer—stupidly, I might add. I have no idea what I'm doing. This isn't me. I just got done self-lecturing about not needing to rely on men, and yet here I am, dangerously close to crossing a line.

"That's probably not the wisest decision. Thank you for the offer, though. I think I'm going to call it a night. I'll see you bright and early out there, Antionette."

I watch as he moves to the door to go inside. It's then I realize he's only wearing pajama bottoms, no shirt. The outline of his body against the lights of the track is drool worthy, and I'm momentarily shocked into silence. *Who knew he had* that *body underneath those button-up shirts and suits.*

"Umm, yeah. Uh, of course, you're right." I stumble on my words. "I'll see you tomorrow."

He goes to walk inside but stops before turning back to me. "It was nice talking to you out here. Thank you for that." Then he turns and heads inside without another word, the soft hiss of the door sliding closed his only goodbye.

Stunned. That's probably the best word to describe how I feel. I'm not sure who this Felix is, but I want to know more about him. I know it'll all disappear tomorrow, but a girl can dream, right?

Sighing, I slump back into the chair and stare at the track lights. This is dangerous territory, and I need to call it quits on this line of thinking immediately. First, getting involved with a colleague is bad-news-bears, not to mention he's older, has kids, and probably doesn't even see me as anything other than a pain in his ass. One moment of weakness, of vulnerability from him, doesn't change what I know him to be. It's best I remember that.

People always show you who they really are if you're paying enough attention.

This is supposed to be my fresh start, my time to figure out who I am. I was with Brad for so long that I lost the ability to think beyond what he wanted for me and for us. I made a vow to myself when we broke up that it was high time I be the person I wanted to be. No outside influence, no narcissistic men trying to tell me I can't do something. It's a year to kick ass, take names, and channel my inner Sydney because that woman is a proven badass.

Felix can't factor into any of that.

I need to be able to stand on my own two feet, as hard as that feels when reporters are saying such misogynist things.

As I take a deep breath, the lingering scent of fuel and hot rubber from the track seeps into my soul.

This is my time.

This is when I become *the* Toni Bailey, unstoppable force in Formula 1 and best team principal on the grid. I want to be the team that drivers are begging to be a part of.

Nothing will stand in my way.

Chapter 3
(Transcript)

Interviewer: So, Felix, can you tell us what went wrong today?

Felix Karlsson: Everything went wrong today, thanks for asking. We have a lot of work to get done on the cars, and we need the drivers to step up as well. It's the first race of the season, though, so we've got time to make adjustments.

Interviewer: We saw Johnny Rousell take that bad spill into the barriers, almost taking out Suarez. Any update on the car and if it'll be ready for the China Grand Prix?

Felix Karlsson: Johnny's fine, though you didn't ask. We'll be ready for the next race; no need to worry about that.

Interviewer: Next question is for Toni. How do you feel winning the first race of the season? It seems like you put on a master class of progress.

Toni Bailey: Well, all the praise can go to Sawyer for a stellar drive. He took pole position in qualifiers and never looked back. The cars look great out there—they have great pace—and the drivers are on board for all the changes we've made this season. I'm looking forward to seeing what the season holds.

Interviewer: Do you feel confident in your transition from Formula 2 Engineer to Team Principal in Formula 1 this season? Last season seemed like a rough changeover, but if today was anything to go by, things are running smoother.

Toni Bailey: Well, Tom, I think coming into a team with a lot of change halfway through the season would be a challenge for even the seasoned team principals. I'm sure you could ask a hypothetical for Felix, and he'd give you the same response. During the off-season, the team and I came together for the common goal of winning, and it's showing on the track. That's the best we can hope for.

Interviewer: Well, Felix, do you think, hypothetically, the transition would be a hard one?

Felix Karlsson: Hypotheticals are for the busybodies who are prying for a story. I congratulate the entire Empress Racing team on a great race, and hopefully we'll give them some more competition in China. Are we done here?

Interviewer: I wanted to ask what that . . . argument after the race was about between you two. I assume it was about the almost crash but wanted clarification.

Toni Bailey: Felix and I were just discussing the FIA's decision. Nothing more, nothing less.

Felix Karlsson: There was a little more to it than that, Ms. Bailey. I believe you told me to get my drivers under control.

Toni Bailey: And I remember you saying that our win was a fluke.

Felix Karlsson: And then I told you to call me next race when you managed to drop off.

Toni Bailey: And then I said f—

Interviewer: Oookay, well then. That's certainly interesting. I think we'll call it today. Thank you both for talking to us.

Chapter 4
Felix

It's been the week from hell. Everything that could be going wrong is, and I'm on the verge of firing everyone. I won't because that doesn't accomplish anything, but the temptation is there nonetheless.

Getting heated with Antoinette after the race because of an almost crash was stupid. It only served to blow off steam. Being that close to her, seeing her passion, was not good for my willpower. Arguing about it in our debrief with the media after the fact was stupidity of a higher level.

I don't know when everything got so out of control, but I need to rein it all in immediately.

My phone rings, and I pick it up without looking.

"Felix," I bark.

"Oh, someone's in a mood." My ex-wife, Stephanie, tsks.

My shoulders sag, and I huff out a breath. "This season is already a fucking disaster."

"What's going on? You're never this 'doom and gloom' about the team."

"I'm not sure if you kept up with the race last weekend—"

"I did," Steph cuts me off.

"Then you'll know we didn't get any points and had to rebuild half a fucking car in a week."

"Nothing you haven't dealt with before. I also saw videos from that press conference after the race."

I tense up, not wanting to talk about anything relating to Antoinette right now.

"And?" I counter instead of saying anything intelligible.

"You were quite testy. I'm not sure I've seen you act that way . . . ever." That's saying something coming from her since we've known each other for almost twenty-five years.

"The reporters are getting out of hand, that's all," I grumble, tossing my glasses on the desk and massaging the bridge of my nose.

"And it has nothing to do with the very capable and beautiful Toni Bailey giving you a run for your money?"

"As a competitor, sure. I'm not sure what you're insinuating."

"What I'm getting at is I've never seen you flustered or impulsive at your job. It's been, what, a decade? And even through our divorce, you were the perfect professional. Honestly, it was fun seeing you all worked up. I was worried nothing could crack your Tin Man exterior."

"I don't have a Tin Man exterior."

"Sure, Felix. Whatever makes you feel more in control."

"You're annoying as shit right now, you know that?" I sigh.

"I'm only annoying because I know you so well. You aren't used to anyone challenging you, especially at Legacy. You're the king of F1, and you're worried you're losing that—I can tell." Stephanie has always been an intellect, even going so far as to get her doctorate so she could teach psychology at university. But she's never turned the tables on me. Even when we split, she didn't psychoanalyze me.

"What's your diagnosis, Doctor?" I deflect.

"Ha ha. This weekend will be better; I can feel it."

"Considering you aren't the one driving the cars, I'll hold off on my optimism, thanks."

"Well, the reason I called was to check on you and also to ask you to call Emilie. She's nervous about graduating, and I think it would be good for her to hear from you."

"Her and Henrik are still pissed about everything that happened before the divorce. They don't want to hear from me." As painful as that is to admit, I know it's the truth.

"They were kids, Felix. They didn't understand that we could be amicable.

Or that we were already split up. Both of them are learning that there was no malicious intent by either of us and that we simply work better apart. Call her. Please."

"I have a meeting in ten minutes, then I'll call her. Thank you . . . for listening to me but not for psychoanalyzing me." Sitting up straight, I put my glasses back on.

Her tinkling laughter sounds over the speaker. "You would be in a world of hurt if I actually psychoanalyzed you. Let me know if you need anything. Are you still going to be back in Belgium after this race?"

"For a week or so, yes. Thanks, Steph." I hang up and stare out the window. My relationship with Stephanie may be good, but I've never earned back my kids' trust after the scandal. I stayed away because it felt like the most stable approach to things, but who knows if that was the right decision. Stephanie frequently tells me it wasn't.

The meeting reminder pops up with a chime on my computer, and I flip my brain from who I am behind the curtain to the Felix everyone else knows me as.

Time to get this fucking team in order.

***

"Hey." Emilie's shy voice sounds over the phone.

"Hi, Em, how are you?" I cringe at my stilted language.

"I'm good. Watched the race last weekend." Awesome. She watched her father fail even more.

I grunt, unsure of how to respond.

"It was . . . interesting to see you not be on top for a change. Shit, I mean—"

"I know what you mean. Don't worry about it. I, uh, talked to your mother. She said you were getting nervous about graduation." A change in topic feels like the best approach.

"I'm not nervous," she balks. There's that good ol' Karlsson pride.

"It's okay if you are. This is a big time in your life, a scary time. It's normal to get a little freaked out by that," I offer, not sure if that's even what she needs to hear.

"Dad, it's fine. I'm not nervous. It's just a big change, but I'll be good."

My heart, that stupid organ that I pretend doesn't work, thumps steadily in my chest. She doesn't want or need my words. She never has, but it's very obvious she doesn't want my support either. I'd be lying if I said it doesn't hurt. But the tragic thing is that this is my own doing. Steph warned me about this happening, and now I get to watch it in real time.

"You know I'm here if you need anything. Or want to talk." I cringe at my words. I sound like a teenager trying to be a grown-up, not a forty-eight-year-old father who should have his shit together by now.

Her silence is anything but reassuring.

"Yep. Listen, I've got to go, but I'll talk to you later." She hangs up before I can get in a word, and my heart cracks in two.

Father of the Year, I am not.

"Love you," I murmur into the phone even though she's long gone.

A throat clears from the doorway. My head snaps up. Sydney.

"Well, well, congratulations on the win." I smirk, but there's no heat there. Sydney is a good friend, and I'm genuinely happy for her win.

"Thank you. I was in the area and wanted to check in on you."

"Check in on me? Because you think both of my drivers not being in the points is a cry for help?"

She plops into one of my visitor's chairs. "No, the cry for help was the press conference after." Her eyebrow arches.

"It wasn't that bad."

Her burst of laughter isn't reassuring.

"It's just a rough start," I grumble, shaking my mouse to wake up my computer.

She waits me out. The woman is nothing short of a force of nature, and being on the receiving end of it is not something I enjoy.

"Fine, it was fucking awful, and I'm not hopeful things will turn around."

"And?" The arched eyebrow pisses me off more.

"And what?" I snip.

"There's more going on. I know you. You can handle the job pressure better than anyone I know, so there has to be more to it."

"And you're nosy enough to come digging."

The side of her mouth tips up in a smirk, and I know I showed my hand.

"Damnit, I'm losing my touch." I sigh. "I talked to my daughter, and it . . . was what I expected, but it still makes me feel like a deadbeat."

"Why do you assume that?"

"Because the divorce was hard on Emilie and Henrik, and I decided to let Stephanie handle things with them since I travelled so much. Now, if I talk to them, it's stilted and unfeeling. I'm not sure how to change that or if they even want to change it." What I didn't expect to do was info dump on my greatest competitor. *Friend.* Yes, friend too, I suppose.

"Feel free to ignore everything I'm about to say, but have you asked them directly about any of that?"

I don't want to admit that I hadn't even thought about that, so instead, I grunt. As per usual.

"Like I said. . ." She smiles. "Take it or leave it. Just an observation. Speaking of observations. . ."

"Here we go."

"Press conferences have been quite interesting with the two of you."

"Who?" I ask, playing dumb.

"God, I love it when you tell me everything I need to know without saying anything."

"What are you talking about?" Sydney is scary sometimes. She sees too much.

"Toni and you. A very interesting combination if I'm being honest. One I didn't see coming until Daisy and Luka's wedding, but I'll definitely be tuning in from now on." Her smile has only grown.

"You're insufferable."

"And right."

"Nothing is happening. Lord knows I have enough shit going on with this team. I'm not trying to make my workplace more complicated than it needs to be. And she's my damn competitor. Our . . . disagreement after the race was a one-off."

"Oh please. Team principals are the only people who know what you are going through. I know you all talk and go to dinner. You're not fooling me."

I stare at her, hoping she'll back down, but it's a fruitless endeavor. The only thing to do now is shove all thoughts of Antoinette down and act like I abhor her. She's just a new annoying team principal. I'm just keeping the reporters in line; nothing more, nothing less.

Sydney knocks her knuckle on my desk before getting up and walking out as swiftly as she came.

And I'm left reeling that the two women closest to me have seen how affected I am by one Antoinette Bailey. I thought I was doing a good job of keeping things locked down, but no.

That night on the balcony races through my head almost every night. It wasn't only the company; it was the conversation. It fueled something that I haven't felt in a long time. Companionship, *friendship,* someone who relates to me on a baser level. Like Sydney, but on more equal footing.

But after the conversations I've had today, I need to steer clear. I need to nip whatever feelings and thoughts I'm having about the elusive Ms. Bailey and treat her as what she is: a colleague.

Settling deeper into my chair, I tip my head back and stare at the ceiling.

Fuck, this may be easier said than done. But I have to try.

If only to keep up my reputation as this year goes to hell.

Chapter 5
Toni

Two races down, and we're sitting pretty in first in both the Constructors' and Drivers' Championship. The flight back to Austin is the most relaxed I've felt in months. But I don't want to get comfortable yet. The season is long, and we still have a lot of work to do. I don't expect Felix to sit idle and watch his team implode.

My phone buzzes with a message, halting thoughts of the gorgeous, unattainable man.

Brad:

I'm stopping by the house. We need to talk.

Me:

Absolutely not. Write whatever you need to say in an email.

My heart freezes in my chest as the plane taxis.

Brad:

I'll be there in thirty minutes.

His complete disregard for anything I say still pisses me off. At first, I liked how in control he was, until it turned into a nightmare. It's a quick hop, skip, and jump to abusive when you don't know what you're looking for. Now, I can't figure out how to get him out of my life completely. Every so often, he pops up, needing some bullshit thing. It's all an excuse to keep his claws in me, and I despise that I have no leverage.

I did change the locks, though, so at least he can't get in without me. The last time he did this, I had to call the cops before he would leave.

A restraining order is my next step, but all the lawyers I've talked to said he hasn't been physical, so it'll be difficult to obtain. Clearly, I need to figure out a long-term solution as he doesn't seem to be going away.

As I get off the plane, I contemplate heading to our offices here. Vanstone Properties houses the Empress offices as well now, a home away from home when we're not in Europe. If I go there, I'll end up working long into the night, and for once, I just want a night off. I've been going nonstop since Sydney hired me, and an attempt at a relaxing evening is desperately needed.

Instead, I drive around the city, ignoring message after message and call after call from Brad until he gives up and I'm able to head home.

A note taped to my front door sends panic through my veins, but I try to suck in slow, deep breaths as I pull in and grab my suitcase. I hurry through the door, snagging the note with one hand before slamming the door and flipping the lock with the other in a rush, just in case.

Toni,
You can't run forever. You will talk to me again.
And I'll be waiting for you.
-Brad

Fucking psychopath. What did I ever see in him? That's right; as an eager twenty-five-year-old, I loved the attention. Something I wasn't used to getting, he gave in spades. I just didn't realize that attention would turn toxic and have him pulling me away from my entire support system, however small it was.

Six years later, I'm stronger. Well, I *hope* I'm stronger. I know I'm wiser, but that doesn't always translate into action or results.

Crumpling up the note, I toss it in the trash and grab a sparkling water from the fridge. Not two minutes later, my phone rings.

"Toni," I clip.

"I have updated specs on Sawyer's wing. Sending them your way now," Sawyer's chief engineer, Mason Piel, says without fanfare.

Sighing, I grab my laptop bag and set it up on my dining room table. Guess tonight is a work night after all.

So much for relaxing.

***

I've been going incessantly for three weeks straight, it seems. We're gearing up for the Chinese Grand Prix, and I'm looking forward to spending a couple of extra days here after the race to explore. I need a damn break, or I'll crack under all the pressure. The media is only getting worse, and putting on this confident face in front of everyone is wearing me thin.

The need to find a balance in my life has never been more prevalent than right now. Working all day every single day isn't sustainable if I want to make this a long career. Like Felix.

Fucking Felix.

I don't know how he does it. Legacy is down in the dumps, only scoring three points in three races, and he's still as cool as a cucumber, not showing an ounce of concern. He's his usual stoic self, taking all the punches as they come.

I need some of that strength and nonchalant attitude ASAP.

My phone rings, and I answer without looking as I walk back to my office behind the pitlane.

"Yes?"

"You doing okay?" Daisy, Sydney's right-hand woman, asks.

"Kind of." I sigh.

"How can we help? I know it's hard without me or Sydney there, but I'm sure we can help somehow. Do you need food? A drink? A massage?" I'm not even sure she took a breath between each question.

"Umm, as thoughtful as all of that is, I don't really have time for all of that until this race is over. Good news, though: I only have to make it through one more day!" I say with false positivity. Truthfully, I'm exhausted as hell, but race day waits for no man—or woman.

"Toni, take a break. Everyone is working on the cars; there's nothing for you to be actively doing right this minute." Her tone is soft, but there's an undercurrent of demand there too.

"It's too early in the season to not be on top of things," I counter.

Control freak, party of one. I'm honestly not even sure how to mellow out the need for control. I've been so desperate for it for so many years that I don't want to give up an ounce.

But it's already wearing on me. The desire to give up some control is what drew me to Brad in the first place. I forgot how much my need for it took over my life.

"How about this? Go back to your room, order room service on us, and call it an early night. Tomorrow, you can be up early as fuck and triple-check everything."

"Fine. I have a feeling if I don't agree, Sydney will call me and then I'll be in real trouble." I chuckle.

"See, you already know us so well," she teases.

"All right, I promise after I check my email, I will call it a day. How are you doing?" Newly pregnant, she's traveling less but is somehow no less involved. It's a skill, truthfully, and one I'm slightly jealous of.

Daisy and Luka have had their challenges—there's no doubt about that—but their relationship now is incredible. Same with Sydney and Beckett. Witnessing two healthy relationships helps me see how wrong things were with Brad. They show me that there is a man out there who will compliment me as a woman, as a partner. God knows I don't have time for that shit right now, but it's somehow always in the back of my mind.

"I'm doing well, thank you. Drinking my weight in lemonade but finally not puking my guts out. Sorry, TMI there."

I laugh at her candidness. "Hey, I'm just glad you're feeling better. I'll touch base with you guys after the race. Thanks, Daisy."

I hang up and stare at my computer.

This lack of work-life balance is already an issue if Daisy is calling to lecture me. Exploring China after this race is a chance to figure out some sort of solid footing, and hopefully it'll be the start I need to make the season more sustainable. Once my inbox is finally clear, I sneak out the back and text my assistant, Jennifer, that I'll be back in the morning and to not call me unless it's an emergency.

The gorgeous hotel lobby greets me, and I'm already drooling over the prospect of a juicy steak for dinner.

A phone call to order food and a quick shower help me feel refreshed before the knock of room service summons me.

Digging into my food, I let my mind wander. I didn't even know I was interested in this job when they interviewed me, but I wanted to prove to myself that I could do it. The need to show women everywhere and my mother that I'm something *more* is a strong motivator. But damn is this kicking my ass. When we were terrible last year, it was hard, sure, but the expectations weren't there. This year, it's like every race we need to be better, make improvements to stay on top, and it's difficult. I'm not sure how Felix has stayed at Legacy for as long as he has, much less at the top of the grid for just as long. It's admirable, of course, but I'm also jealous that he's able to brush things off so easily.

The half bottle of wine I've yet to drink comes with me to the balcony. The lights of China are mesmerizing. It's like another planet here, and I can't wait to see more of it.

Sighing, I collapse onto the sofa and close my eyes.

"We've got to stop meeting like this."

I shiver at his deep voice. From my balcony, I can't see him. The hotel is curved to allow for privacy, but I guess it was easy to peg me from my exasperation.

"They've got to stop putting our rooms next to each other," I counter instead.

His soft laughter washes over me as I sip my wine.

Silence takes over, but I hear him shuffling around on his side.

"How are you doing?" His voice takes on a softer quality, one I've never heard from him before, and it catches me off guard.

"Umm, good. Great, even."

"You sure? It seems like every time I see you, you're rushing off to do something. I don't think I've seen you slow down and take a breath in almost a month."

His concern triggers my defenses; my hackles immediately go up. "So, working hard is a crime now?"

"No! No, of course not." He sighs. "This job is difficult, especially if you don't have a friend on the grid."

"Who says I don't have friends on the grid?" I snip.

"Equal friends." I can hear the frustration in his voice, but it doesn't lessen the walls I have up. "Someone who understands the pressure of this job," he adds.

My shoulders drop with a release of tension at his words. I've learned very quickly that this is a unique job. It's great to be friendly with staff, but I'm everyone's boss. Well, except Sydney and Daisy's, but even they don't truly understand how much work I do daily.

Drawing boundaries was the first thing I did. I won't ever be best friends with anyone on my staff, and Felix is right. It's difficult to shoulder all of the pressure.

"And you're going to be my friend?" I ask with an equal mix of caution and amusement.

"How about confidant?" he asks.

"Too posh for friends?" I chuckle.

"You're American," he deadpans.

"You seem like a posh man, though." I smirk. I don't quite know where he's from—not England, I know that much, but maybe some Nordic country. Posh still works for his entire vibe, though.

He scoffs before shuffling again.

"Sorry, I'm not too great at this friend thing, I guess." I sigh and take another sip. I'm not sure friendship with Felix is the answer, but he isn't wrong about finding someone in a similar position to talk to.

"You and me both."

I decide to go out on a limb and hope it doesn't bite me in the ass. "How do you do it? I mean, how have you stayed in Formula 1 for so many years? I haven't been here a year yet, and I want to pull my hair out most days."

It's a scary admission. It means I have faults, and this man is the last one I want to know about them.

"I've gotten good at wading through the bullshit. People come and go in this sport. Journalists, drivers, employees. . . But if you want longevity, you need to keep the goal as your focus. Winning is the only thing that matters."

Well, that's depressing as fuck. "And what if I want there to be more than winning?" I ask. I'm showing too much, being too vulnerable.

"Then prepare for a second career at some point." He says it so dully, so nonchalantly.

I always knew he was jaded, but this feels like another level. How can a person be so indifferent to everything life has to offer? I may not know a lot about him, but to boil your entire career, your life, down to winning seems like a life not lived.

"I think I'm going to call it a night. Good night, Felix," I say softly as I stand up.

His sharp inhalation reaches my ears, but I don't wait for a response. This conversation is not what I thought it was going to be. It honestly made me sad for him.

I know one thing for sure as I crawl under the sheets: I don't want to end up like him in this job.

***

China is incredible. It's inspiring and the break that I needed. Eating my weight in food has refilled my spirit and helped me see that exploring these wonderful places we travel to is how I keep my sanity this year.

Being able to completely disconnect from the race and the job is stress relief.

As I stare out to the bustling street, I promise myself I'll take more time for myself. More time to learn what I want my life to look like and how to be the best damn team principal I can be.

I push the ever-elusive and intriguing Felix from my mind, and decide to put my sole focus on myself for a change. He's shown me his priority in life is his career. Who would want to play second fiddle to that?

Chapter 6
Felix

China was a failure once again. No points and nothing but problems with the cars.

As we get ready for the Bahrain Grand Prix, I'm holding an all-staff meeting at our headquarters before we fly out to the race. Something needs to change.

"This year has not started the way we're used to, the way it should have. I know you all are working hard, but we need more. The team needs more. Engineering needs to trace the problems, figure out what and how all of this shit started, and then we need to fix it. Pit crew, you're slow, and we've had too many fumbles this year. Put in the extra time if you need to; we can't afford any more mistakes. Everyone else, chip in where you can, keep pushing. There are no ideas I won't listen to. We need a change, and we need it yesterday. We fly out tomorrow, so let's kick our asses into gear." It's as close to motivational as I get. I'm more of a "hold everyone accountable and push them harder" type of boss.

Scolded yet determined stares meet my gaze before I nod and exit the room.

"Sir!"

I keep walking. I may have asked for ideas, but I meant email me, not flag me down immediately. I have shit to do before hopping on a plane.

He runs up next to me out of breath. "Sir! Hi, I wanted to see if I could run something by you."

I squint at him in an attempt to show my annoyance, but really, I'm trying to remember his name. *Chad . . . Chip? No clue.*

"Email me," I grunt before continuing my path.

"But just hear me out." He borders on begging.

"Either talk to your boss or email me. Those are your options." I cross the threshold of my office before shutting the door behind me, essentially blocking him off. Slumping against the door, I heave a deep sigh before going around and grabbing my suitcase.

No rest for the wicked, especially those of us who run an entire goddamned Formula 1 team that's currently fucking up.

I make it to the private plane, blissfully alone, and spend the entire flight looking at every single spec of our cars.

***

My leg bounces as I watch the laps count down.

Only seven more to go. A lucky safety car at the expense of Suarez at Empress means we got a break. It shook up all the drivers enough that it looks like we may podium and, for the first time this season, Empress may not.

I wonder how Antoinette is handling that.

Not the fucking time to be thinking about her.

The chief engineer for Johnny, Rick Luther, taps my leg, drawing me out of my thoughts, pointing to the screen, and wordlessly showing me that we have to stay steady for two more laps.

I hold my breath, not daring to move until Johnny is on the straight coming into the black and white flag. Movement around me barely registers, but I know the team is losing their minds right now.

The second he crosses the finish line, I rip off my headset and hug Rick. We jump around like school girls; it's a small weight off my chest. We didn't win, but I'll take a third-place podium right now, considering how we've been out of the point more than not this season.

I watch as Johnny parks his car before climbing out and jumping onto the pile of engineers and crew waiting for him.

It was a hard-earned win for everyone and the boost we desperately needed when things were looking so dire.

The trophy presentation goes quickly, and as the Canadian anthem plays for Johnny's win, I peek over and see Antoinette standing on the edge of the crowd.

Her normally determined yet happy face is marred with defeat. I fucking *hate* it.

She faces everything she's been thrown head on, and yet this race is the thing that's getting to her. A stupid crash and a safety car that gave us the chance to be on the podium are the same things that crushed their chance of getting any points this race.

They dealt with that plenty last year, but it's hard to be consistently winning then have it ripped from your grasp. I already heard murmurs that they put in a grievance to the FIA about the Amaro driver that ran into Suarez. It's exactly what I would do, and a sense of pride radiates through my chest at the thought.

Once the fanfare is over, I head back to the hotel.

A well-earned beer is on the agenda after I stayed far too long at the garage debriefing with the crew.

A good result is great, but it's only one race. The work continues, as always.

I settle into a corner table with a view of the whole bar. Luckily, it's quiet. Everyone is out celebrating instead of staying at the hotel.

Except for a certain brunette sitting at the bar that catches my eye.

Antoinette Bailey, of course.

Her shoulders are slouched forward, betraying her usual pride. For a split second, I debate walking over there to check on her but decide not to. Sitting here observing her allows me to look at her unnoticed, unchecked—a rarity with so much attention on us both. She rolls the glass in her hand around its bottom rim, barely anything but what looks to be whiskey left in it. *Not that I know her well, but whiskey seems like a wallowing drink for her.* She looks up at the bartender as he walks past and nods before turning her head down again.

I slowly sip my beer, watching as another glass gets set in front of her. She tilts what's left in her other drink back, swallowing it all in one go before slamming the glass down hard.

Even from here, I can see how disappointed—no—*destroyed* she is at the results today. A novelty for me since Empress still did better today than we've done all year so far.

But I understand it. The frustration. The annoyance. The worry. God, the worry. It feels as if your job is on the line with every single bad result. Nothing you've done before, nothing the team has accomplished prior, matters. All that sticks in your mind is how you fucked up somehow and maybe that fuck-up is bad enough to get you the sack.

The stress is high; there's no doubt about that.

I rack my brain in an attempt to remember what I used to do in my early days in this career in order to get out of slumps like the one Antoinette is currently in.

Stephanie used to force me to get manicures purely so I could sit still for an hour. It allowed me time to think, but for whatever reason, it was always constructive not dwelling on the bad race. I still do it to this day, just less often. Now, it's like my brain is triggered the second I step through the doors of the nail salon, and it goes into problem-solving mode.

Antoinette needs something like that.

But it's not like I can invite her on a spa day. I'm sure she'd punch me in the dick for even mentioning it. Pointing out she has weaknesses won't help her any. Lord knows I'm the same way.

As my thoughts run wild with ideas of how to help her, I keep a keen eye on how many drinks she's consuming.

Two becomes three then quickly turns into five.

My one beer turns into my only. There's no way I'll hinder my ability to look out for her right now. She needs someone to keep an eye on her, to let her have tonight without fear that she'll be the next news story or, God forbid, have an asshole take advantage of her state.

There's definitely no alternate reason I can't take my eyes off of her.

Her short hair barely brushes the top of her shoulders but swishes back when she looks to the ceiling and blows out a breath.

My traitorous dick takes notice and a vision of her on her knees, my hand tangled in her hair, infiltrates my mind.

Fuck, now is not the time to let my dick do the thinking.

She abruptly stands up, swaying in place. I'm moving before I realize I've stood up. Catching her around the waist and holding her up, I whisper in her ear as she jolts at my touch. "Just me, darling. I've got you."

Instantly, she melts into me. An action I cannot look into more for the sake of my own sanity. I'm only helping her to her room.

"Today sucks, Felix." Her slurred words accompany her spinning in my arms. She buries her face into my chest. I breathe in the subtle scent of the track lingering on her combined with something purely Antoinette.

She's intoxicating . . . and intoxicated, I belatedly remember.

"Let's get you upstairs," I murmur into the crown of her head before running my hand down her back.

She fits perfectly against me. Something I need to forget immediately before I make some really terrible decisions.

"Okay."

She steps back only to wobble, so I keep my arm around her waist and lead us to the elevators. I threw down some cash to cover her bill and mine before we left. The bartender who damn near overserved her looked grateful, but it pissed me off more.

"Do you know what floor you're on?" I keep my arm wrapped around her but lean her against the wall in a poor attempt to not seem like I'm greedy to touch her.

"Umm . . . Thirty-two. Room 3287," she says with stunning clarity.

"Good. That's so good, darling. I'll get you there in one piece," I say low enough that I hope she doesn't hear the desire in my voice.

"Where did you come from?" she asks.

"Just right place, right time." She tilts to the side, but I hold her tighter to me. "We'll call it luck."

Her bright smile as she looks up at me changes my entire molecular makeup. It's not only beautiful, but it feels like it's directed only at me. I'm the only one who gets to see this smile from her. My chest puffs out slightly as I feel ten feet tall knowing I made her smile like this.

"Has anyone ever told you how handsome you are?"

Laughter threatens to choke me, but I hold back. "A time or two, maybe." I smile down at her.

"That's a damn shame. I think it's the silver in your hair. Makes you all distinguished and shit. Makes me think you know what you're doing in the bedroom."

This time, she's stunned me into silence. I truly thought she tolerated me—nothing more, nothing less. I'm under no delusion that my thoughts about her are one sided, but this makes me think they may not be after all.

"Is that so?" I offer, not giving away my thoughts.

"Mm-hmm." Her eyes close, and she leans into me again. "Maybe that's what I need. A good lay."

I'm hard in an instant. I want to show her everything she thinks about me is true and then some. Serious relationships may not have been on my radar since Stephanie, but a man has needs. I'm forty-eight, not dead. I manage one-night stands when the need arises.

The things I could show this woman. The things I could *do* to this woman.

My hand clenches tight at my side, my mind begging me to be the gentleman. She's under the influence, and I won't do more than get her to her room safely, but fuck, I wish I could do more.

"Sex is wonderful for stress relief," I say instead of keeping my mouth shut.

"I don't think I've ever had good sex before. All the men I've been with didn't care about getting me off." She pouts, and I think it's the most adorable thing I've ever witnessed.

"That's a damn shame, Antoinette," I murmur.

"Why don't you call me Toni?"

"I, uh, suppose I'm used to a set of decorum." I won't tell her it's because I like being the only man who calls her by her full name. That it makes me feel like I'm something special even though nothing could be further from the truth.

"I like that you're the only one who calls me that. I usually hate my name." Her wistful sigh gives me too much hope. I have to tamp it down and focus on my task.

The elevator stops in the nick of time.

We shuffle through the hallway, and as I follow the room numbers, I realize that she's yet again in the room next to mine. How the fuck does this keep happening?

"All right, darling. 3287, here we are," I say, my voice soft to sooth her as we stop in front of her door. We stand in silence for a couple of moments before I clear my throat. "Do you have your key?"

"Shit, yes. Sorry." She cringes and disentangles herself from me. The loss of her body against mine is visceral and something I'm entirely unprepared for.

She pats her front pockets then her ass, and I have to keep my groan in my throat. I'd like to be the one tapping her ass. Maybe spanking her when she's a brat.

Jesus, Felix. Get a fucking grip.

She digs in her front pockets again and comes up with her card, a triumphant smile on her face. Slapping it against the card reader three times does nothing. I finally grab it from her hands and get the door open.

"Is it all right if I accompany you inside? I just want to make sure you get situated okay." A ruse if ever I've heard one. Even if it is true, I want to spend a couple more minutes in her company before going back to my lonely room.

"Sure," she squeaks.

I observe her tossing her things onto the side table before stripping out of the thin cardigan she had on. The silky green fabric revealed underneath damn near has me falling to my knees.

"Can I get you some water?" My voice sounds lower, more gritty, betraying my attraction to her. The curves she chooses to hide in the name of professionalism are criminal.

"Yes please." Stumbling out of her shoes, she finally gets them kicked off as I hover before we walk farther into the suite.

It's exactly like mine except reversed, so I know where everything is, thankfully. She wanders to the living space and collapses on the couch as I fill up the glass. Rounding the corner of the couch, I see her shirt has risen enough to reveal the skin of her stomach. It should be innocent. It should be just another stomach. Instead, it's inches of skin I wish I could touch, kiss.

"Here's your water." I sit on the edge by her feet. After taking the water from me, she sits up a little, and I drag her feet into my lap. As I dig my thumbs in her arch, she moans mid-sip, freezing my movements.

"God, that feels good." She takes another sip.

I continue massaging her feet. Sometimes digging in hard where there's tension, other times gently brushing against her skin, memorizing it.

It's hell on my libido and my mind.

I'm both confused and aroused, and I can't do a damn thing about it.

Her glass clinks on the table in front of us, drawing my attention.

"Felix," she whispers. Her pupils are blown, and there's a flush going up her neck.

Groaning, I slide my hand to her ankle as she lithely moves to sit up. Maybe she's not as drunk as I thought she was. My hand naturally glides up her leg as she maneuvers to straddle me. The fucking FIA president, the media busting down the door, couldn't get me to let her go right now.

Her weight settles on my thighs, leaving just enough space that she doesn't feel how hard I am for her. There's heat in her eyes. The building on fire around us couldn't stop me from leaning in.

"Tell me to stop," I mutter, millimeters from her lips.

"I'd really prefer if you didn't."

Soft, plush lips greet mine when I press into her.

Everything I've known to be true about myself over the last three decades shatters.

My world narrows down to the feel of Antoinette on my lap. I'm desperate for more, desperate to throw caution to the wind.

But those three decades have taught me a lot of lessons, and this is something I can't fall into. There's too much at stake, mostly for her. I won't be the thing that jeopardizes her career. Not when she's just starting out.

Pulling back from the brief kiss is akin to breaking my own arm. It's the last thing I *want* to do, but it's the thing I have to do.

Leaning my forehead to hers, I breathe her in one last time.

"I need to go," I whisper.

"Need to or want to?"

"Need. I definitely don't want to, darling."

She sucks in a breath at the careless nickname.

"Stay."

"That would be a bad decision." I sigh. "I'm sorry."

I feel her nodding against me but neither of us move.

Minutes or hours go by; I've lost track of time.

What I do know is I need to leave now. I'm in dangerous territory, and I need to be the responsible one here.

Gripping her hips, I slide her off to the side but not before squeezing them tight. Letting her go is torture but one I must endure.

"Good night, Antoinette," I murmur against her lips before pressing a chaste kiss to them.

Nothing but regret sits in my chest as I walk out of her door and turn to the right. The walk is brief, but it's enough to reinforce that something like that can't happen again.

If nothing else, I need to protect her position within F1, no matter what it potentially costs me.

Chapter 7

Toni

It's been a week and a half since the Bahrain Grand Prix or, as I like to call it, the Karlsson Mistake. Drunk Toni is a stupid Toni. I mean, sure Felix is hot and smart and intriguing, but that doesn't mean I can fucking straddle his lap and try to make out with him.

It was a damn good lap, though. His gentleness surprised me, and even though it was technically only two kisses, they somehow felt like . . . *more.*

More is dangerous.

I can't afford to risk my job, and I need to keep that in the back of my mind from here on out.

As I walk up to the garage, I bask in the warm Miami sun. A U.S. race is always nice. It's less travel for our crew, and I've been to Miami enough to get away from the attention if I want to—not just to my hotel room. If this race ends up like the last one, I'll need the distance.

I hope it's not like the last race.

The taste of winning, of excelling this year, makes me want it more, so not getting points in Bahrain was hard. My ultra-competitive personality didn't handle it well.

Or maybe you did since you landed in Felix's lap.

No, bad Toni. Those are not the kind of thoughts I need right now—or ever.

"Hi. We've got engineering in a meeting about the wing on Sawyer's car, and Daisy is running interference with the media. They want you in the press conference, but we're saying no," Sydney rattles off as soon as I'm in the garage.

"Because I suck in front of the media? Or because Bahrain was that much of a shitshow?" I ask.

"Neither. They don't need you every fucking race, and it's getting old that they needle until we give in. Another team principal can take the heat for once. Fuck 'em." She smirks.

"You know, I really love you." I speed walk around the car and head back to the meeting space.

"I know you do! Call me later!" she yells as I enter the engineering meeting late.

I don't say anything. This is my domain, so it's easy for me to pick up where they are in discussions. The hard part is not jumping in and telling them all they're idiots. Sydney and Beckett told me I can't take everything on, and that means making a conscious effort to not overstep in engineering, no matter how much I want to.

It doesn't mean I can't steer them a little, though.

"Did we fix the wing? And is Alejandro's car fucked too?" I cut to the chase since they were on a completely different topic.

"Uh, umm." The one who was talking stutters. I think he's on Alejandro's team, but I can't remember. *I need to be better about knowing the entire team, no matter how big it is.*

"Alejandro's car is showing signs of the same wing issue, but we think that his upgrades are counteracting it more than Sawyer's. We don't have either solidly fixed, but we put in a short-term solution to hopefully get us through the weekend while we work on narrowing down what the problem is," Sawyer's chief engineer, Mason Piel, takes over.

"And if it doesn't get us through the weekend?" I ask.

"Then we're probably going to be spending all-nighters fixing the fucking cars again. We cut off the part of the wing that's causing drag, so it'll have to work, and we'll just hope no one pitches a fit over the modification." His growl of annoyance isn't directed at me; it's at the fact that there's a real possibility that'll be what our weekend looks like, and none of us are happy about that.

"Fucking awesome. Keep working on it, please. Rethinking the wing is going to take time. I need to talk to the pit crew before Practice 1. Thank you all." I turn on polite and charming Toni in the hope it motivates the team.

Instead of heading to chat with the pit crew, I turn left and head to my mobile office. I need to think. I'm giving myself thirty minutes to see if I can problem-solve the wing issue before getting back to my normal job duties.

It's hard to break the habit of engineering.

Thirty minutes later, and I'm no closer to magically solving our issues, but hopefully the team is having better luck. I did a few sketches that I sent their way that may help them in the long run.

My feet seem to have a mind of their own as I step out of the sliding doors and down the stairs. I decide to check my messages on the way, oblivious to everything around me.

Until I crash into a strong body that almost knocks me backwards.

"Oh!"

"Shit. Are you okay?" Felix and I say at the same time.

My hands are smashed between our bodies, and he's holding onto my shoulders.

"Good. Yep, totally good." Except flashes from that night roll through my head, and my entire body heats at the memory.

Clearing his throat, he makes sure I'm stable before stepping back and shoving his hands into his pockets.

"You weren't at the press conference." He says it low enough that if anyone were to pass us, they wouldn't hear. But his tone is accusatory.

"Uh, yeah, Sydney put Daisy on the case so I could get a break this week." God, I sound so immature. Like I can't handle the pressure.

Which, maybe I can't. I'm not entirely sure yet. The show of weakness is one I need to eradicate. Last year was hard, but this year is an entirely different challenge. I've yet to get a full grasp on it, and we're already two months into the season. But who I outwardly show to the world needs to be strong.

We stare at each other for a moment too long, but in his eyes, I see the same want that I feel.

"I kind of missed you telling off the reporters. Adds a little excitement to this shindig." The corner of his lips tips up in a barely there smirk.

His very kissable lips.

I do laugh at his words, though. "I'm not sure I provide as much entertainment as you usually do. I aspire to have control over that room like you do."

His eyes shift between mine. "You have more control than you think."

Is he flirting? Fuck, I don't even know what flirting looks like nowadays. Abort, abort. Get out of this conversation now.

"Umm—"

"Hey, Toni? The pit crew is having a meeting now," Mason says as he passes me to get to the garage.

"Be right there," I call out. *Thank you, Universe.*

Turning back to Felix, I take a moment to really study him. He's just under six-foot tall, and his facial features aren't the only thing that are classic. He always wears a button-up shirt with the sleeves rolled up and slacks. I've never seen him in casual wear, and it has my brain itching to see him a little undone.

His throat clears, my head jolting up to see that damn smirk on his face letting me know that he definitely caught me checking him out.

"And I'm leaving now," I concede. It's easier than addressing whatever this tension, this connection, is with this damn man.

"Good luck later, Antoinette." His game face is on, and if anything, it makes him sexier.

Shit. I damn near sprint to the garage, the pit crew meeting already underway as I round the corner. I don't interject because my mind is firmly elsewhere.

Luckily, it seems all things are smooth in this department at least. Now we just have to make it through practice today.

***

Practice wasn't total shit, thank God. Now we just need to get through qualifiers in good standing, and I'll start to feel less tension throughout my entire body.

Currently, I'm hiding behind the building where my little office setup is. Everyone else is running around the pitlane and garage, but I needed a breather. If I stayed in my office, someone would have found me and needed something.

"Not basking in your car's good performance?"

Felix. So much for taking a moment to myself. My "breather" turns into a sigh when his deep voice interrupts my peace.

"Nope. Sometimes, I just need space from all the hecticness," I say as Felix settles against the wall next to me, his arms folded over his chest.

"I get it. I usually go hide in the Amaro office." He dips his head down toward me, a smirk on his face and his voice low like he's sharing a secret.

"I didn't even know that was an option," I mumble.

"Stephan is a friend of mine, so we sneak off to each other's office when we need a break from our own teams. It's easy to feel like you need to be accessible 24/7 with this setup, but that's just not possible for your own sanity."

"Does that mean I can sneak into your office when I need to get away?" I snark back before my smile fades. "I meant that, like, you're my only friend among team principals." I cringe. I'm only making things worse.

"Hey," he draws my attention. "I knew what you meant, and you're always welcome at Legacy."

"Except when the media sees and starts running wild with stories." I arch an eyebrow at him. There really doesn't seem to be winning with the media.

"You would be right about that." His tone is that of someone who knows firsthand how the media spins tales. If I venture a guess, he's been burned hard before.

"Does this get easier? Or less . . . taxing?" I'm not sure how to put it into words but this need to be the best, to prove myself as competent, is so strong that we're only a couple of months into the season and burnout is on my radar.

"Yes and no. I think, in a sense, it gets easier because you learn to set boundaries. You make sure your team in place can handle things and you make sure you take the time you need away from it all. If you make yourself available at all hours while it's race weekend, it's just not feasible to be your most productive self. But that's a lesson you have to teach yourself, you know? I don't think the job ever gets easier, though." He sighs. "Every year there's a new challenge or a new problem you've never dealt with pops up, and it's like you are a rookie on the job again."

"Feeling a little of that this year?" I ask, not with malicious intent but with the hope that talking will help him in the long run. Just like he's doing for me now.

His laughter is hollow. "To say the least."

"Want to talk about it?" I hold my breath over this tentative friendship.

Felix is an anomaly to me. Of course, I think he's sexy. Of course, I think he's brilliant, but I cannot even begin to surmise how he feels about me. Friendship feels . . . safe.

"Not particularly. I think I need to get my nails done."

"What?" I'm sure I've misheard him.

"Manicure," he clips. "Helps me think."

I nod like I understand his words, but it's all foreign to me. Is this some super-secret team principal shit? Am I in the know now?

"Well, I have a meeting. Come hide out at Legacy if you need it." He walks off like our conversation never happened, like that night in Bahrain never happened, and I'm left more confused than ever.

Chapter 8
(Transcript)

Interviewer: Empress had a great race. Sawyer Bennet looked great. Are you happy with the result?

Toni Bailey: Absolutely. We had challenges in Bahrain, and the team rallied and came together. We're thrilled to have both Sawyer and Alejandro on the podium today.

Interviewer: You seem to be running away with the Constructors' Championship. You going to take it all this year?

Toni Bailey: I'm a "take it one race at a time" person. We have a lot to improve. We need to stay consistent. Ask me again in Vegas.

Interviewer: More problems this race, Felix. Can you tell us what happened?

Felix Karlsson: Well, we lost. I'm glad that Pavel got us some points, but it doesn't help the overall picture. Johnny having engine problems wasn't great, and that's something we need to work on as well.

Interviewer: Is there concern that you won't be able to fix the issues? They seem to be increasing as the races go on.

Felix Karlsson: Nothing is impossible. It can be complicated and hard work but not impossible. We've got to buckle down and be ready for Italy.

Interviewer: Do you think you have a chance to compete with Empress this year? Time seems to be running out.

Felix Karlsson: Empress needs to watch the rearview. You never know who is close behind you, and that could be us in a couple of races.

Interviewer: What do you say to that, Toni?

Toni Bailey: I say you better be looking at your car's schematics if you want to be out of our rearview. Sounds like an awfully difficult challenge for Legacy at the moment.

Interviewer: One more question for Toni. There's a rumor that the wing is off on the car. What is your response?

Toni Bailey: My response is that we took first and third in Miami today. I don't believe we had any issues today. Whoever your source is may have us confused for someone else.

Interviewer: Interesting. Well, we'll be keeping an eye on that on the driver's radios next race, but we wish you both success in Italy.

Chapter 9
Felix

"Come with me." I snag Antoinette's arm as we leave the media tent.

"Please just let me go." She yanks at my arm, but I keep my hold, practically dragging her to the small offices off of the media tent.

Slamming the door behind us, I finally let her go.

"What?" she demands.

"What the fuck was all of that?"

"That was me taking control of shit."

"So you call out me and Legacy in the process?"

"I didn't call you out. You started that, Felix; I just finished it. Bitch at the reporters for asking such ridiculous questions if you're that upset about it." She crosses her arms, going toe to toe with me.

She's right, dammit. I let my emotions get the best of me, which is not something that happens often.

"That was wrong of me; I apologize." The last five minutes of that interview were fucking brutal, and we both fed into it.

"It's fine. I'm fine. I don't need you to check on my fragile little self after every single altercation. I'm perfectly capable of handling assholes myself. And I'm not sorry for hitting back after your bullshit comments." Her scowl is wildly attractive, and I have to force myself to focus on what she's saying instead.

"I know you are, but that doesn't mean it doesn't get to you. Again, I apologize. I know better than to take out frustrations in the media tent." I'm not sure why I'm trying so hard to smooth things over and get her talking to me again.

"Sure. I need to get going." She turns to the door in a huff, which just pisses me off more.

"Toni!' I finally yell in exasperation. She freezes and turns to face me, her arms crossed and that brow arched again. "You are a stubborn fucking mule. It's okay to be affected by those assholes."

"I'm not a fucking mule. And I'm not going to be vulnerable in front of enemy number one. I can handle myself. I don't need you to save me, Felix. You proved your character in there today, and it's best I remember that."

Oh, this woman. I take a deep breath and run my hand through my hair, taking my glasses off once I'm done. "I know you don't need me, and I apologize for calling you a mule, but you are stubborn as hell, woman. I don't like what was said in there. If it's pissing me off, I *know* it's getting to you."

"Listen, I appreciate the gesture, but I need to handle this on my own. I need to be able to take their shitty comments—and yours—and move on. You won't always be here to run interference or 'check on me'." She air quotes.

"I didn't even get to run interference this time," I grumble.

Her shock of laughter has me grinning.

"My point stands. And I've got a meeting with Sydney to debrief that shitshow. Thank you for checking on me, but I'm good, Felix, and we're done here."

Neither of us moves, the tension hanging taut between us like a string pulled too tight about to snap. Neither of us is willing to look away. It's that same stare down that we seem to always do in moments like this. A little bit too long and seeing a little bit too much. Then she's out the door, and I'm left to figure out what the fuck just happened.

***

My house is lonely.

I have a week and a half until I leave for Italy, and I'm at a loss as to what to actually do with myself. Belgium is home base, has been since I've been at Legacy. Luckily, Stephanie kept the kids here as well, so I was able to see them when we were together. Unfortunately, that hasn't happened a lot recently.

"Knock, knock!" the familiar voice calls from the front door. I don't move from my prone position on the sofa, though.

"Dad!" Emilie's voice rings out, causing me to jolt up.

"In here." I manage to get up as they round the corner. Sure enough, Steph is here with Emilie and Henrik in tow.

God, it's good to see them.

"To what do I owe this surprise?" I attempt to inject curiosity and not accusation into my voice, but I'm not sure it works by the look Henrik gives me.

"It's been a few weeks, and you've been all reclusive, so we brought dinner." Stephanie holds up a bag.

Emilie's slightly behind her, one arm crossed over her body holding the other, almost like she's unsure what to do with herself. She's not quite comfortable enough in my space to just sit down, but she's not rolling her eyes and sighing loudly the way teenagers do to let you know they'd rather be anywhere else. I'll take it. What I couldn't handle is her or Henrik very obviously not wanting to be here. Steph's been trying to get us to do more family dinners and things when my schedule allows the past couple of years, but I'm not sure I'm helping the whole vibe she's going for.

"That was very nice of you, guys. Let me set the table."

I hate that I'm not sure how to talk to my kids. I hate that having them in my house makes me so uncertain of myself. But I'm also not sure how to change any of that.

We sit down to eat, and no one says anything of substance until Henrik speaks.

"So, that team principal for Empress is hot."

I almost choke on my food.

Breathing becomes hard as I cough, unable to respond.

"Hen, she's, like, ten years older than you," Steph scolds, but there's a twinkle in her eye.

Are they egging me on together? Is this some kind of lie detector test?

"She's such a badass. I mean, look how much she turned that team around this year already," Emilie says with something close to admiration on her face.

"She does seem pretty awesome. What do you think, Fe?" Steph smirks at me. I shoot daggers at her with my eyes, but all she does is laugh at me.

"The media is grilling her hard. It's annoying to watch. I mean, I know the media are dicks anyway, but I don't know, it feels like they're worse with her," Henrik says before taking another bite.

"They are," I growl under my breath, afraid to give more away.

Emilie is looking at me too hard. It's unnerving.

"How's school?" I ask, changing the subject and hopefully putting an end to this not-so-subtle search the entire family is doing.

"Boring. Fine but boring." She sighs, always more open with her mom in proximity.

"Not long left, though. Then a gap year before you make the big decisions." I try to spin it in a positive, but Stephanie shoots me a look that says "shut up".

"Oh yeah, that gap year, huh, little sis?" Henrik needles her, and I get the strong feeling that I'm out of the loop on something big.

"What am I missing?"

Steph and Hen look at Emilie while I bounce between the three of them, waiting for someone to speak.

"I just . . . don't think I'm taking the gap year," Emilie relents.

"Okay, what are you doing then?"

"Moving to the U.S."

I choke on the bite I just took, pounding on my chest and trying to come to terms with my almost eighteen-year-old daughter wanting to move across the fucking globe.

"What? You can't move! I thought you had a plan!" My voice gets louder and louder, even though I have no right to dictate my daughter's life.

"Felix . . ." Steph warns.

"This is why I didn't want to tell you." Emilie slumps back in her chair, and I see just how far removed I am from the family.

"I'm sorry." And I am sorry for not being more involved. Sorry for pushing them away because I didn't know how to handle the separation from them.

Sorry for being a terrible father. "I'm just . . . shocked. Can you tell me more?" I look over at Stephanie. She nods in approval for once, and maybe I'm on the right track this time.

Emilie hesitates before telling me all about how there's a fashion program there she applied to and got in. She's already looking at places to live, and she and Stephanie have been to visit twice already.

It's amazing how much she's planned and figured out already, but my heart hurts that none of them felt like they could talk to me about it. I would have come with. I would have seen what contacts I have for apartments, for anything she needed.

This feels like just another aspect of my life that I'm failing miserably right now. But maybe it's time to stop wallowing. Maybe it's time to actively figure out how to be more involved in their lives. To try to figure out this shit car situation at work too.

Should I figure out Antoinette as well?

"What were you thinking just now?" Steph points her fork at me.

"Nothing," I snap. I see the way her and Emilie's eyes light up, knowing there's so much more to that "nothing".

"You're screwed now," Henrik mumbles through a little chuckle, that same light in his eyes.

I realize with stunning clarity that talking about my personal life with them might just help us all feel a little bit closer. Hell, Steph already knows—or guessed, really—so what does it matter if it potentially gets my kids to talk to me more?

"I, uh ... Um, the team principal, Antoinette..." I struggle through my words, which is so unlike me. "We've run into each other a few times and—"

"Oh my God, you like her!" Emilie squeals, her voice reaching a decibel that makes me wince.

"I don't— It's not like—"

"Okay. I'm going to grab ice cream, and then you're going to tell us everything," Emilie cuts me off again and bounds into the kitchen.

"I'll help." Henrik joins her.

I look over at Steph with what I'm sure is a look of horror.

"This is going to be good for you. That girl loves the gossip, and you just handed it to her on a nice, shiny silver platter." She laughs.

"No one warns you about teenage girls," I grumble, but I'm secretly ecstatic that Emilie even wants to stay and talk more.

It's been a long time since they felt comfortable enough to have a candid conversation with me, so if it takes talking about Antoinette to accomplish that, I'll fall on my sword.

"It's about time some of that nosiness was directed at you, honestly. Want some wine?" Steph heads to the kitchen as I nod.

I don't know what I just got myself into, but I can't find it in me to care. Emilie is showing interest in me. Even if it makes me uncomfortable, I'll suck it up to try and build our relationship up.

The night is more fun than I've had in years. At the end of it, I feel less disconnected to my children, more informed about their lives. Telling them a little of my infatuation with Antoinette was a small price to pay to be more involved in their worlds. I learned about Emilie's ambitions, Henrik's job prospects once he graduates college, and a not-so-secret relationship Steph has been attempting to hide from the kids and me.

It's a true family dinner, for the first time in longer than I can remember, and one I hope to repeat on my next break.

Chapter 10

Toni

Gearing up for Monaco is stressful. While it's not the fans' favorite race, it is iconic and synonymous with Formula 1 racing. Which means it's a big deal and we need to kick ass.

May is almost over, yet this season has felt like it's taken both years and days to get to this point. I don't know if my body can handle the stress, honestly. Sydney's been forcing me to eat when we're at races because I simply forget.

I need to find a balance, yet I have no clue how to make that happen. The only time my brain has been calm on the circuit is when I've been with *him*. Felix.

What I said to him was true, though. I need to be able to handle this on my own. I need to be able to take the pressure and the criticism, or I'll never make it long term.

When Felix talks about how he manages everything, I listen, though. I got a damn manicure the other day, in the hopes it would help me figure out the problem with the cars, but nothing's working.

"How are you feeling?" Beckett asks from the corner where I'm pacing.

"Oh, great. Heartburn is eating me alive; I've gotten all my steps in by eight this morning. Things are looking up." I grin, but my sarcasm is thick enough that concern leeches from his features. "I'm fine, Beck, really. Just ready to start the race."

"You need a break," he says.

Laughter bubbles up in me. "A break isn't going to happen until summer. I appreciate the sentiment, though."

"Toni . . . You're working yourself to the bone. Sydney and I just want to make sure you're okay. We need longevity, not short term because you're wound so tight you crack. No one wants that."

"I know." And I do. "I'm working on it. I promise. After this race, things will settle down." A lie every single adult tells themselves when they are drowning.

"I'll hold you to that." He nods once before heading off to find Sydney.

We have to perform well here. Last year was a shitshow, and we can't have a repeat. I can only hope the wing issues with the cars are fixed enough to get us on the podium. Every point matters.

You can do this.

The cars will kick ass. The drivers will kick ass.

Empress will make podium, and the douche bag media and Felix can eat crow after we do.

I can do this.

My pep talk gives me a false sense of security, but I'm holding on with both hands because it's showtime.

***

Second place and a DNF.

Not what we really needed, but at least we have one on the podium. Amaro Racing managed first, and Legacy rounded out in third.

It still feels like a failure, though.

I'm speed walking my way back to the garage after talking with the FIA about some bullshit penalty they gave Alejandro even after he DNFed. It seems more and more like a useless endeavor to try and explain things to them, but one has to try. It was about the wing adjustments, so it needs to be addressed one way or another.

"Woah, where's the fire?" Felix's voice draws my attention.

"With the stewards, apparently," I grumble, still annoyed that Alejandro is going to have a grid penalty for the next race because of their nonsense.

Felix gently pulls at my elbow, leading me behind the offices and mostly out of sight.

"Let me go, Felix." I yank at my arm, but his grip is stronger than I realized.

"Come talk and cool down."

"With you? Absolutely not. I'm good." I'm not good; I'm fuming. Am I taking out my frustration on Felix? Yes, but I can't find it in myself to care.

His grip barely loosens, but it's enough for me to rip my arm out and continue on my way.

"I have an open ear if you do want to talk," he calls out after me.

Hand above my head in a half-assed wave, I book it back to the Empress garage like my ass is on fire.

There, I proceed to run straight into Beckett's body because I'm so distracted.

"Shit. I'm sorry. I was distracted." I step back.

"No harm done. You okay?"

"Yep, just irritated with the FIA's decision."

He stares a little too hard at me, and I'm worried he can see everything I'm not saying. How the pressure is starting to take its toll. How a certain silver fox is starting to distract me. How I'm not sure I can pull off this job right now.

"Are you sticking around for a couple of days?" he asks.

"Umm, yeah, maybe. I haven't really gotten to explore Monaco. I just have to be back to Austin by Friday."

"I'll let Sydney know, but take your time. I'm sure we can fill in if you want to stay longer."

I nod in thanks before moving around him to head to my office. Once there, I drop my forehead to my desk.

Some time in Monaco, alone, will probably do me some good.

***

A knock at my hotel door makes me hesitate.

No one is still here. Everyone has already left to go back to where they call home until the Canadian Grand Prix in two weeks.

Maybe Beckett and Sydney ordered me room service? Usually, she'd tell me ahead of time so I'm prepared.

Peeking through the peephole, I jolt back at what I see.

What the hell is Felix doing at my door?

"Please open the door, Antoinette." His strong voice sounds through the door.

Slowly, I crack the door just a sliver.

"Why are you here?"

His smirk disarms me. "A little birdie told me you were still in town, so I wanted to invite you to dinner."

"Why?" *Fucking Sydney. I know this was her doing.*

"Because we both need a break, and I'm paying."

I eye him for longer than I should because my mind is working overtime trying to figure out if going is a good idea or not.

His smirk grows to a genuine smile. I'm not sure I've ever seen him genuinely smile in person, and it's . . . disarming. *Dammit*, I cave. Self-control is nowhere to be seen when you combine his glasses with those straight white teeth.

"Give me ten minutes." I open the door wider, wordlessly inviting him in, as I turn to go to my bedroom. I hear the door shut, assuming he followed me in but needing a minute to figure out my approach for tonight.

The closet has a total of three outfits in it. A dress, my blazer and nice slacks, and my work polo. All staples I carry to every race, even if I live in the polo and comfortable work pants.

So, it's between the little black dress and the blazer/slacks combination.

If I go with the dress, it says I'm open for certain things. I'm not sure I'm really ready for something like that. If I do the blazer, it screams business dinner, which I also don't feel like this is.

I suck at this shit. I can't imagine how I'd be if this was actually something exciting like a date.

I finally settle on the dress but pair it with the blazer. Dressed up but doesn't scream date. *Because that's not what this is.* If I have to remind myself every five minutes, so be it.

I throw my hair up in a low bun so I don't have to think about it; hair is poking out at every angle because of the length, but it'll do.

"Okay, where are we going?" I ask as I emerge from my room.

I didn't even get a chance to look at him entirely when we talked through the door, too blinded by that damn smile of his. But now? I'm at a loss for words. Dark jeans that I bet fit his ass like a glove meet a short-sleeved button-up shirt. The casual look that I was pondering not all that long ago is far better than I could have ever imagined. He even has different glasses on. These ones are tortoise shell, betraying his sophistication for a quirkier look, but nonetheless attractive.

Shit, I'm in trouble.

"Antoinette?" He ducks down to catch my eye.

My face heats at the realization that I just got caught checking him out. "Yep?"

"I said we're going to the seafood place that overlooks the ocean. Are you good with seafood?" His brow furrows as if thinking he screwed up the choice of food.

"Love it. Let's go." Picking up my purse, I open the door but he's right behind me, taking over and ushering me out.

Flashes of how Brad used to take control of every single situation trigger a response I'm unprepared for.

"I can get the door," I snap at him, speed walking to the elevator to get some space between us.

There is no logic, but this gut reaction to even a minor similarity between Felix and Brad has my hackles raised.

It's better this way, though. There is nothing between us, and there never will be. One drunken kiss, and an unhealthy infatuation with the man, doesn't fix all my deep-seated issues. If anything, it makes them worse.

The elevator doors open while I'm very distracted in my head. Felix's hand briefly touches my back to lead me in, and I tense. He drops his hand in an instant. When I turn around, his eyes swirl with confusion, but there's no way I can explain the mess of thoughts that are in my head right now.

In truth, I should probably opt out of dinner, but it feels like a waste of effort, honestly, and fresh fish sounds so fucking good right now.

Felix doesn't push, though, doesn't ask the questions I know he's dying to ask. He lets us ride down to the lobby in silence while I harden my exterior and put on my bravado. No need for this man to see more of my mushy, barely functional center.

I walk out the front doors and stop, realizing I have no clue where we're going.

"The car. It's for us," Felix answers my unasked question before walking ahead of me and opening the door.

The drive is a quiet affair. I'm attempting to get my bearings and my resolve all in one go. He seems content to let me have my internal freakout.

It's actually very kind of him, not that I'll tell him.

We get seated with our drink orders given before I chance conversation.

"So, what are you still doing in Monaco?"

"Truth?" he asks.

"I would prefer the truth, always."

He nods, intertwining his hands on top of the table. "Sydney called me and was worried about you. She asked me if I would take you out for a meal to see if I could help your stress levels—her words, not mine." He smiles.

"Ah. Gotcha." I deflate. He's not here willingly, just for a favor.

"But if I knew you were staying in town, I would have done the same. It's not a pity dinner, Antoinette." The soft tone of his voice softens the blow a little.

Our drinks get delivered, and I gulp half of my gin fizz in an attempt to loosen up. It's going to be a long night if I can't.

"I'm sorry. I'm super stressed out and high-strung. It makes for terrible company," I offer as a sort of truce.

"Nothing to apologize for. What's stressing you out? Just the pressure of the job?" he asks with full interest.

"Mostly. Those boundaries you were talking about a few weeks ago are really hard to set." I smirk.

"That they are. Want to talk about it?"

"I suspect Sydney already told you a good chunk of it. I'm not really doing a good job of taking care of myself. Working too many hours, forgetting to eat, all things that aren't very sustainable."

He nods. "Been there. I think it took me three years to actually let go of the reins. Don't wait that long. I almost had a heart attack."

"What?" I gasp at his nonchalance.

"My ex-wife—wife at the time—took me in when I was complaining about my heart racing and being dizzy. Actually, she lost her damn mind and yelled at me for five minutes before she took me in." He smiles fondly, and jealousy bleeds into my veins.

He said ex-wife. You knew this about him.

"But you were okay?"

"Mostly. Had heart palpitations and was told to slow down. Which was complicated and difficult when I was still fairly new in this position. I had a lot to prove, and it felt like a huge roadblock."

"What helped you take the steps you needed to have balance?" I ask with genuine curiosity.

"My kids." His smile is bright with a touch of sadness. "I remember my youngest, Emilie, asking me if she could come on one of my trips so she could spend time with me. She said work was the only thing I cared about, so if she could come, maybe I'd care about her too. She was young, didn't really understand what those words meant, but they were what I needed to realize I wasn't being a good father to her and her brother." He pauses. "Still aren't, really."

"I'm sure that's not true," I offer, even though I really have no clue what their dynamic is.

His snort of laughter is anything but funny. "It's a work in progress. I'll leave it at that. What about you? How'd you get into this job?"

The server interrupts our conversation to take our food order, and I'm grateful for the time to decide how much to really get into.

"I'm an engineer by trade. Got into the racing side of things randomly and worked my way up the ranks in Formula 2. I'm honestly not sure how my name came up in conversation with Sydney and Daisy, but I had an interview with Daisy and Beck, and the rest is history."

"Must have been some interview."

"Ha! I couldn't tell you what I said. It was so surreal. Like one of those out-of-body experiences. But this opportunity . . . After the last few years, I don't want to waste it." The seriousness of my words isn't missed by Felix.

He doesn't pry, though. He waits me out to see if I'm willing to open up like he just did.

"I was dating a guy for a few years. I had been unhappy for a while, but it felt impossible to leave. He was . . . controlling. Everything came to a head when I signed my contract in Miami last year. He was with me and came to dinner with Beck, Sydney, Daisy, and Luka. It was a complete shitshow. I was so embarrassed, but I didn't know how to just leave him."

My heart pounds in my chest as I relive those days.

"He wouldn't just let me leave," I whisper.

"Is he still bothering you?" Felix's voice is unlike anything I've heard from him before. His jaw is clenched so tight I'm afraid he'll crack a tooth.

"Occasionally. I have it handled, though." *Kind of.*

He looks too hard, seeing too much in my eyes.

"The pressure to succeed on my own is what drives me. I'll admit I don't have a healthy balance, but I'm attempting to work on it."

Our food gets delivered, but Felix doesn't say anything else. It's unnerving. I want his approval, in some ways. Because of the position he holds, his reputation, but it's more than that. I *like* him. Even if we can't be together, I want him to think I'm doing a good job. That I'm capable.

That damn need for approval conflicts with my need to be self-sufficient.

The next words out of his mouth have my drink halting halfway to my gaping mouth frozen by shock.

Chapter 11

Felix

"I could mentor you."

What the fuck am I saying right now?

"What?" Her furrowed brow probably matches mine.

"Maybe mentor is the wrong word choice. I could help you, essentially, figure out how to delegate and work through the kinks to get you in a better place."

I'm not sure *that* word choice was any better, to be honest.

Antoinette is still looking at me like I've lost it, and maybe I have.

"Did Sydney or Beck ask you to do this?"

"What? No!" Outrage is my first reaction until I remember that Sydney did ask me to take Antoinette out to dinner to force her to take a break. "So, dinner tonight, Sydney did ask me to do. But this would be something else entirely."

Jesus, forty-eight years old, and I'm tongue tied.

"Break this down for me." Her hands intertwine in front of her.

"I don't really have a plan," I concede, but ideas come to me on the fly anyway. "Maybe we have a standing date after each race where we go to dinner and debrief. Or in between practices. Whenever, really. We could try different things to see if it helps you disconnect from the job," I ramble.

"Standing dates?" She smirks.

Of course that's the part she hyper-focuses on. Though, I'm no better because the idea of dating Antoinette is far too appealing.

But she's off limits. This is just a work thing. To help her not burn out within a year.

Keep telling yourself that.

"Meetings. Get-togethers. Take your pick." I fake exasperation at her nitpicking.

"We'd have to be discreet. God forbid someone get pictures of us and throw wild accusations around."

I nod, but I fucking hate that she's already this jaded. It's smart, but it shouldn't be this way.

"We could . . . create dummy emails and put all communication through there. It's an extra level of caution but would protect us both." My mind flashes to the messages that were sent to my entire team by the woman I don't talk about anymore. There's no chance that Antoinette screws me over. Not with how badly she wants to keep a good reputation, but there are snakes in the water everywhere. It's wise to be smart about this.

"Feels extreme but necessary," she muses.

Our food gets dropped off, interrupting our conversation. We both dive in, eating in silence until most of our plates are cleared.

"Why do you want to help me?" Her voice is so small I want to punch the asshole who ever made her feel like she needed to be anything other than her bright, intelligent, powerhouse self.

"Because Formula 1 needs you. You represent so much more than Empress and racing in general. I have a daughter, and although I'm not always in great standing with her, she needs women like you to look up to. To show there are no limitations. You're the first woman team principal in a sport that's notorious for nepotism. You've had to work for every inch, and I think that's worth preserving."

"Well shit, how do I say no to that?" She brushes a finger under her eye subtly, trying not to let her emotions get the best of her. "I think I'd be an idiot to not take the great Felix Karlsson up on some help." She chuckles before turning serious again. "And thank you for saying that, about being a role model to young girls."

My head dips in acknowledgement, but words won't come. The entire conversation is too much, too overwhelming, and yet I want so much more. Good thing I just gave myself the perfect groundwork to learn more about this dynamo.

Talk turns to logistics within the schedule and how to maneuver time to her benefit, and before I know it, the servers are cleaning up around us. Our server stands off to the side when I look over to him with a nod.

"Looks like we shut down the place. You ready to go? We can keep chatting elsewhere." I stand up, having already paid a while back.

I hold my hand out to help her, but she drops it as soon as she stands. The loss and my reaction to it shock me more than this entire night. It brings me right back to her straddling my lap and kissing me.

I want more of that.

But I can't have it. Especially if we're going to work together in any capacity.

In the car, she turns to face me. "Okay, I like the email idea, so we should set those up." She snags her phone and pulls something up before looking to the ceiling in thought. I mimic her motions, bringing up the general website to create an email. It takes me less than two seconds to think of something that'll work.

"You think of something?" I smirk.

"I think so. Here, type yours into a new email." She shoves her phone into my hand. It doesn't have her address visible, but I'll see it soon enough. Typing it into the address book, I add my initials instead of my name. Never hurts to be extra cautious.

When I hand it back to her, our fingers touch. I catch her eyes and hold her stare. This, what we're doing, is dangerous. It's stupid and foolish, and the chance of someone seeing us together multiple times is high. This isn't like two team principals having lunch periodically. No, because she's a woman, rumors will fly no matter what we say.

Not to mention being close to her in any capacity tests my willpower to the maximum.

The car comes to a stop, jolting us out of our reverie.

"Shall we?" I gesture to the hotel in front of us. We're both lost in our own heads, processing what we just agreed to. I don't even realize we're staying on the same floor until the elevator stops and she walks out.

"Is there a scheduling person who likes to put us close together?" I chuckle as

I follow her to her door. When she stops in front of it and looks up at me with a grin, I laugh more. "Seriously, I'm next door again."

"Seems like something is at play, for sure. Thanks for tonight, Felix. I appreciate it more than I can tell you." She rocks up on her toes and presses a kiss to my bearded cheek. Before I can register what just happened, she's disappeared behind the door.

I lean against her door, my head falling back against it with a sigh, not ready for the evening to be over.

This entire situation screams problematic, but I can't find it in myself to care. If anything, I'm chomping at the bit to get more time around Antoinette.

Shifting my weight off the door, I turn left to the next hotel door a little farther down. Once I'm inside, I strip out of my clothes and toss my glasses onto the nightstand with my other two pairs. As I pull on a pair of sleep pants, I debate spending a few minutes out on the patio but decide against it, just in case Antoinette is out there. I don't want her to think I'm stalking her or forcing myself into her quiet space.

My phone dings with a message of sorts. I sigh, hoping it's not a driver with a crisis. I don't want something like that to ruin the high that this night has been. I pick up my phone and see a notification for the new email address I created. The smile that spreads across my face is unstoppable. Maybe we're both excited to see where this thing takes us.

From: AB (wannabebosslady@genericmail.com)

To: FK (Swedish_Boss48@genericmail.com)

Subject: Testing 123

Hi.

Is this thing on?

Just wanted to say thank you for tonight. It was . . . really nice to take my mind off of the job for a little while. I also wanted to say, as a general rule, if you ever want to discontinue this thing we're doing, just say the word. No hard feelings, no harm done. That offer is open indefinitely.

The next race is the Canadian GP, obviously. Can we grab dinner or lunch after? I promise not to bug you incessantly. Lord knows neither of us have the time to be emailing each other non-stop.

Okay, I think that's all I had.

Thanks again,

-T

My smile only grows. I can feel her nervousness through the email, and it makes me want to knock on her door and reassure her that I wouldn't have offered it if I wasn't serious. It's also a side of her that I haven't really seen. Sure, I've seen her hesitations and struggles with the job, but she's never *unsure*. Unlike her made-up email address, she already is a strong leader. She just hasn't seen it yet.

From: FK (Swedish_Boss48@genericmail.com)

To: AB (wannabebosslady@genericmail.com)

Subject: RE: Testing 123

Hello again,

Yes, I believe this thing is on. I appreciate the "out", even though I see no reason for it. I'll extend the same offer, though. There is no pressure here. Whatever you need to talk about, want to talk about, or just want to complain about—all that this job entails—I'm here for all of it.

Dinner after the Canadian GP sounds wonderful. I know a great little place downtown that's discreet and delicious. Hope you like Italian food.

Get some sleep, darling. We've got a busy couple of weeks ahead of us. My email is always open. Any time, day or night.

Good night,

-F

I hit send before I second-guess it. Rereading it only after it's too late. In an effort to not outright write her name, I used the moniker that's been slipping out, and now I can't brush it off as anything other than what it is—a term of endearment. Something I've never called a woman before, not even Steph.

I stare at my phone for a couple of minutes, willing her to write back, but she doesn't. It's been a long day, and the usual race day fatigue is hitting me hard. The second my head hits the pillow, I'm asleep. Thoughts of Antoinette scatter through my dreams, and for the first time in far too long, I wake up well rested.

And horny as hell.

Not the best combination when you have a plane to catch. But I won't take matters into my own hand. That's a line I can't cross—yet. Not while it puts her job on the line. If I have it my very delusional way, the first time I come to thoughts of Antoinette will be in her presence. Not down the shower drains like a college kid.

I have willpower and the obscure hope that maybe, just maybe, these debriefs could lead to something in the long term, when our jobs are no longer a factor. Crazier things have happened.

Chapter 12
(Transcript)

Interviewer: Quite the drama for a Canadian Grand Prix. Are you happy with the results, Toni?

Toni Bailey: For the most part. Sawyer had a great race and good pace. Unfortunately, it wasn't enough to overcome his penalty from qualifiers, but we'll take a podium regardless.

Interviewer: And what about Suarez?

Toni Bailey: We're working to find a solution for Suarez. He's been struggling for most of the year, so our goal is to get him and the car up to pace with Sawyer, and I'm hopeful we can accomplish that soon.

Interviewer: Are you saying that Suarez isn't falling in line with this new direction you've taken the team?

Toni Bailey: Now, now, let's not put words in people's mouths. Just because alterations to one car are working, it doesn't mean that translates to a completely different driver. It's a learning experience for everyone. Alejandro is committed to working with his team to get himself and the car into the best position they can. That's really all we can ask for.

Interviewer: Hmm. Rocco at Guardian seems to have other ideas.

Toni Bailey: Oh?

Interviewer: He made a statement that you're favoring Sawyer and throwing Alejandro to the side. Your goal is Drivers' Championship or nothing, and you're putting all your eggs into one basket.

Toni Bailey: Maybe Rocco should be worrying about the state of his own team before throwing stones. I seem to remember a few DNFs in the past three races for them.

Interviewer: We'll be looking forward to seeing the changes for Suarez in Spain, then.

Chapter 13
Toni

White-hot rage runs through my veins.

Media conferences are by far the worst part of this job. They're all assholes, and no one is out for the truth anymore. All they want are controversial sound bites so they can write bullshit articles for clickbait.

The fact that Rocco decided to be a total asshole when they aren't even in the points ninety percent of the time is icing on top of the cake. I'm not sure what I did to warrant his attention, but I need to find a way to not internalize it because I'm about to crawl out of my skin.

Locking the door behind me once I'm in my office, I slump down into my chair and try to breathe through my anger.

My shoulders have just started loosening up when there's a ding from my phone.

From: FK (Swedish_Boss48@genericmail.com)

To: AB (wannabebosslady@genericmail.com)

Subject: What a twat

You okay? I heard Rocco's comments during his media conference, so I know they grilled you hard. Don't worry about that prick. He can't even keep an assistant because he borderline sexually harasses them all. (That's a whole other issue.) You're a threat, and that's why they are all taking shit out on you.

Do you still want to do dinner tonight?

-F

My gut twists at the email. First, because of course someone like Rocco is that much of a dick that he can get away with what he is, but also because I'm now a target. I might have been since the first race, but now it's not just the media. It's other teams, and I'm sure it'll only get worse.

I make a mental note to look into Rocco's shit and see if I can anonymously whistle blow his ass. If I know he's mistreating his staff, I'm not going to sit back and let it happen.

My heart is also rapidly beating at the fact that Felix is checking up on me. He's taking an extra step by keeping track of what everyone is saying about me. It's more than any man has ever done for me before.

From: AB (wannabebosslady@genericmail.com)
To: FK (Swedish_Boss48@genericmail.com)
Subject: RE: What a twat
Yeah, that sucked, not going to lie. I would still like to go out to dinner if that works for you.
-T

If I write more, I'll say too much, open myself up too much, and I'm feeling a little too frayed at the moment for that. His reply is quick.

From: FK (Swedish_Boss48@genericmail.com)
To: AB (wannabebosslady@genericmail.com)
Subject: Re: Re: What a twat
Meet me at Alice's on Fifth in twenty minutes.
And wear something that will stand up to this wind; I'd like to take a walk after. While you look stunning today, I don't want you to get cold.
-F

Felix is a conundrum. Every time I think he's pulled back, that he doesn't want anything past this . . . mentoring thing we're doing, he says something like that to throw me for a loop. Or he calls me darling. I like the endearment a little more than I should, if I'm honest. Not writing him back feels safe, so

I give myself five minutes to sit in my office and do nothing before snagging my overcoat and calling for a ride. It takes just over ten minutes to get to the restaurant. When I pull up, Felix is standing with his hands in his pockets and collar up to shield from the wind. Our eyes meet, and I know in this second that I'm in trouble with this man.

I'll try to hold back, try to shove all this attraction so far down deep it'll never see the light of day. But damn, there's something about him that's so different from who I usually gravitate toward. He's *nice* even if he doesn't want people to see it. He has this reputation on the grid that's so different from what he's been showing me, and it makes my curiosity about what else I can coax out of him stronger than ever.

Too bad we have too much at stake. Giving in isn't worth the heartache or the potential fallout with our jobs.

As long as I remind myself of that constantly, I'll be fine.

Right? God, I hope so.

Digging through my purse, I snag some money before I hear the driver's window roll down.

"Thank you. Have a good night." Felix's voice sounds, drawing my head up. He's handing the driver money before shifting back to my door and opening it.

"I could have gotten that," I mumble, unsure of what to say. I know with him money isn't an issue, but it still makes me feel uncomfortable. I've always paid my way, or hell, with Brad I paid for everything. This shift is hard to accept without making a fuss. Felix wouldn't let it fly, though; I know that much.

He doesn't give me a reply, instead bends his elbow for me to take and arches his eyebrow in a way that tells me I don't want to challenge him right now.

Walking into the small eatery, I barely register the homey Italian vibe with the feel of Felix so close to me. He's barely guiding me, and yet it feels like the softest blanket wrapped around me in comfort on the coldest of nights.

The stress of the day, of the entire race weekend, melts down my shoulders in his presence.

My natural comfort level around this man is concerning, but it's also such a relief that I don't want to give it up.

When we arrive at the table, he unhooks his arm from mine, pulls out my chair, and waits for me to sit so he can push me into the table. Tingles run through my body at the gentlemanly gesture. *So, chivalry is not dead.*

"I didn't know you had it in you," I say under my breath just low enough that he shouldn't hear me, but I want him to. I need some back and forth with him, some normalcy to round out this shit day.

"I think you'll be surprised to find what I'm capable of, Miss Bailey." He smirks. It's something I haven't seen on him before, not like this. This smirk is playful, *sinful*, and just what I need.

"Oh, do tell." I tilt my head as he takes his seat opposite me.

"What would be the fun in that? I'm really more of an action man, after all." He says it so carefree as he focuses all his attention on his menu. It throws me for a loop, how he stays so unaffected by this string pulling us together.

"Hmm, I hear a lot of words from you but haven't seen much action." The words pop out of my mouth without thought. I slap my hand over my mouth, my eyes wide when I realize what I just said.

Felix drops the menu down just enough for me to see his arched eyebrow.

I'm wildly unprepared for whatever game I just stepped into, but I also can't come to my senses enough to pull away.

He holds my stare before clearing his throat. "So, how do you feel after the race?"

Felix's abrupt topic change forces me to take a minute for my head to catch up.

"Uh, it was mostly okay, given the circumstances. Sawyer did well to recover some points. Alejandro is still struggling, though." I sigh, rubbing my temples.

He opens his mouth to talk but is interrupted by the server. I pick the first thing I see on the menu before turning my focus back to Felix.

"How do I stop myself from working every waking second? Like, right now, all I want to do is pull out my phone and see if the engineers have come up with anything to help Alejandro, but the whole point of this is to stop the burnout."

"You realize that you are one person. Even if you bug the engineers right now, what does that accomplish? It takes time out of your evening and theirs in order to answer you. It means you don't get a break, and they have to stop what they are doing to make sure their boss is taken care of. If you let go, they will contact you when they have something. That's their job. Same with any of your employees. Trusting your employees is the only way you get a break. That also means if they aren't trustworthy, you need to get rid of them." He sips his drink.

"Cutthroat," I mumble, picking up my drink as well.

"That's the world you signed into."

"But does it have to be this way? Can't we build a better way?" I know it's pointless to dream. Hell, we're dealing with seventy-five years of tradition. One little woman isn't changing shit in this business.

"Antoinette . . ."

"I know. It was a stupid thought."

"It wasn't stupid; it's just not how our business works. Every team wants the best of the best. Those who are nicer, who give more leeway to their employees, are the ones at the back of the grid. The more you win, the more money you make. Money equals power, as it does in many industries, but this one happens to be extremely high stakes." He lets my head ruminate over his words.

I know he's right. I know he's trying to get me to step back and realize I can't change everything, but after so many years being stuck in shitty relationships and shitty jobs, I can't accept the status quo anymore.

"Maybe I'm not cut out for this." I let my head fall back, hoping to avoid his disappointment at my words, and take a deep breath.

"Absolutely none of that. Formula 1 needs women like you, like Sydney. It's going to be a big challenge, though, if you keep trying to do everything yourself. We have the triple weekend coming up, and you'll be dead on your feet if you don't find a way to take care of yourself." He's not scolding me; he's caring for me in his own way. Or maybe I'm creating something out of nothing because I'm so drawn to him.

"So how do I take care of myself?" I smirk, wanting to get away from the self-doubt. It's not who I am anymore.

And yet you regress back to it every time things get difficult.

Felix stares at me a little too hard until I start to squirm.

"Do you trust me?" he asks.

"Uh, sure."

"I need a yes or no. Do you trust me?"

Do I trust him? I barely know him. How can I trust him when every man I've gotten close to has shown me they can't be reliable?

"Yes," I say instead of the resounding no I should have.

"Eat your dinner, then. I have an idea."

Chapter 14
Felix

I must be losing my damn mind. That's the only explanation.

Doing what I'm about to do is going to cross boundaries even more so than we already have, but I can't stand to see her so down about herself, to doubt herself.

So, I'm being reckless.

We're driving back to our hotel, but I ask the driver to stop off at some generic pharmacy.

"What do you have planned, Mr. Karlsson?" Antoinette says in a sly tone.

It makes my dick twitch. The steadying breath I take does nothing to quell my attraction to her. I attempt to focus on my task as the driver pulls to a stop.

"It's called pampering," I tell her before I jump out of the car. A hand on the door, I lean back in through the opening so we're eye to eye. "Stay here. I'll only be a minute."

With a flick of my wrist, I shut the car door before she can protest. I don't even acknowledge the store clerk as I hustle to where the facemasks and other things are.

It takes me all of five seconds to realize I don't give a shit which ones I get, so I grab them all. Could I just send Antoinette to the spa? Sure, but that won't be until tomorrow at the earliest, and she's likely leaving. It has to be tonight, and this is the first thing that popped into my head. I usually do a facemask or spa after race day as a way to disconnect from everything. Tonight, I transfer that knowledge to the woman who is throwing me for a loop at every turn.

I grab everything from bath bombs and bubble bath, to lotions and hair masks. It doesn't matter if we use them all; I want options.

Five minutes later, I'm walking out with two full bags. Antoinette eyes me from her seat as I attempt to keep the contents hidden for a while longer. I don't want to give her the opportunity to completely shut down the idea.

We're back at the hotel before she has a chance to grill me. I try my best to keep the bags behind my back as I extend a hand to help Antoinette out of the back seat.

"You're being awfully cryptic over there, Felix." She smiles.

"My room or yours?" I ask, dodging her statement. If I look too hard at my actions, I'll see that this isn't about helping her relax at all.

"Umm, mine is fine."

We make small talk about some of the FIA drama to ward off the awkward silence in the elevator. She pauses at her door, her shoulders rigid with the tension we're both feeling. Her body visibly deflates with a sigh as she swipes her key card, the soft beep and mechanical whir of the lock announcing her resignation to the uncertainty of what's about to happen.

That just won't do.

"When's the last time you had a spa day?" I ask as I gently close the door behind me.

"Uh . . . maybe last season?" Her head tilts as she tries to figure out the last time she was pampered. A damn shame if you ask me.

"That changes today. It's too late for the actual spa, so I'm bringing it to you. Go get changed into something comfortable, and I'll get everything ready."

She stares at me unmoving, and I resist the urge to squirm under her gaze. *It doesn't mean anything. I'm just helping her not focus on the job for a couple of hours.*

Antoinette nods before spinning around and heading toward the bedroom. I pick up the phone in her room, dialing room service and ordering some snacks and wine before organizing all the self-care items on the table.

There's enough here to do twenty spa days. A little overboard? Perhaps.

Maybe we can make this our standing date.

The voice inside of my head has some pretty grandiose ideas about a woman I'm desperately trying not to get more involved with, contrary to my actions today.

"Okay, now what?" Antoinette walks out in a silk sleep set. Shorts that are loose but cut short and a short-sleeve shirt that reveals more of her body than her professional attire ever would. Her figure is that of a woman, not a supermodel who has no shape, no curves. The shorts hug her ass, short enough to glimpse the crease between the back of her thighs and those round globes that bounce when she walks. My hands itch to trace the curve of her waist.

And let's not discuss her tantalizing breasts. There'll be no containing my erection if I allow myself to think about them.

I clear my throat and shake my head to refocus on my object here tonight. "Now, we set up in the bedroom, if that's okay."

"You're doing it with me?" Her eyes light up as they look back and forth between me and the things I've laid out on the table.

"If that's amenable to you." I bow my head.

Before she gets a chance to answer, we're interrupted by a knock at the door. I grab everything I ordered, handing the man a generous tip before turning around and wheeling it to the bedroom.

I don't look at Antoinette for fear that she'll kick me out because I've overstepped. I want to stay. I want to show her that she's worthy of being spoiled, worthy of being treated like a woman, not just a team principal.

I know we had a plan with this mentorship, but I'm going off the rails and not apologizing.

A muffled shuffling follows me, but I don't look at her yet. Instead, I set up our snacks that are already on the tray I requested, on the bed, and pour a couple glasses of wine. Then, and only then, do I finally look up at Antoinette.

My heart drops. Are those tears in her eyes? *Oh shit, I fucked up.*

"I'm sorry, I can leave—"

She stops me by holding her hand up.

"This is . . . No one has ever done something like this for me. I'm sorry. I'm just a little caught off guard."

"I overstepped," I concede, ready to leave her with all the food and facemasks, and call it a night.

"No! No, you didn't, I promise. I just never expected you, of all people, to do something like this." I arch an eyebrow at her words. "That's not what I meant. I mean, you're known for being the asshole on the grid. No one would expect you to go all out like this. Or for you to want to stick around for it too. Fuck, that came out wrong." She hangs her head, but it only makes me smile.

I walk up to her and take her hand in mine. "Antoinette, I think you'll find I'm a very surprising man when you really get to know me."

"I think I'm learning that," she whispers.

"I'd like to stay and join you in this impromptu spa day, but I understand if you'd like privacy instead." Now that I know she's not upset at my actions, just shocked, I want to show her a new side of me. One only Steph is privy to.

You're in too deep already.

My subconscious may be correct, but I can't find it in myself to care.

"I would really like that. Thank you . . . for all of this."

"Don't worry your pretty little head about it." I squeeze her hand before letting it go and heading out to the living area. "Do you want to the works or just start with a face mask?" I call out.

"The works, obviously!" she yells back with a giggle.

I pick up enough stuff to make sure she's pampered head to toe, as well as a few things for me. I see my outfit in my peripheral and realize I can't exactly relax in my usual uniform of slacks and a button-up.

"Is it okay if I run to my room and change really quickly?" I ask as I deliver the items to the bed.

"Oh, of course!" She's already sipping the wine, humming, with her eyes closed at the taste.

"Perfect. Why don't you get this on your hair while I do that, and when I get back, we can do everything else."

Her smile is blinding. I don't think I've ever seen her so excited or carefree as she is in this moment, and I realize with startling clarity that I want to be the man who makes her look like that every single day.

Careers be damned.

But I can't. Because she deserves a chance to do big and wonderful things in this sport. It doesn't mean I won't try to skirt the edge of decency to make her smile, though. Push just enough to see this smile but not enough to call it a relationship.

Completely doable.

I change and am back within five minutes. I find her with her wet hair up in a mess of a bun, lying on the bed with her feet propped up on a pillow, sipping wine and snacking on some crackers.

"Don't start all the relaxing without me." My voice is lower than normal. The wide expanse of her thigh is sending my thoughts to a space they can't be right now, especially while wearing joggers.

There she goes again with that smile. "I already feel ten pounds lighter."

"Good. Let's try for twenty," I say with a business-like tone. "May I?" I gesture to the bed next to her, and that's when she finally opens her eyes to look at me. Her gaze travels the length of me, tattooing every centimeter of my skin.

"You changed your glasses," she murmurs.

My hand automatically goes to the glasses resting on the bridge of my nose. My black pair because they're my most comfortable.

"How many do you have?" she asks.

"Three. Depends on my mood, and I like to make sure they go with my outfits."

"You are very high maintenance, Mr. Karlsson." She smirks at me. "Please join me." She nods to the space next to her.

"I like to think of it as sophisticated."

"Whatever helps you sleep at night."

"Relaxing helps me sleep at night," I say pointedly as I lie down on top of the comforter.

"Touché. Okay, what's first?" she asks, bouncing up onto her knees to look at the selection, careful not to spill her wine. The childlike movement captivates me, makes me crave more. But I reel in my libido, starving as it is, and focus on the task at hand.

"Facemasks, then maybe talk or watch something while that sits. Or you could take a bath." Lord help me if she picks that. Knowing she's naked behind a thin little door might just set me off.

"Talking sounds lovely. I feel like it'll give me a chance to talk about something other than work for a change, even if I don't really have a life outside of my job." She chuckles.

I grab the nicest facemask I was able to get, tear it open, then carefully unfold it. "May I?" I ask, even though I know it's a terrible idea.

"Oh! Umm, sure." She leans forward just enough so I'm able to apply the mask.

The first touch of her skin sends heat radiating all over me. It's like the heater has suddenly turned on. I can almost feel little droplets of sweat forming on my brow. It takes me longer than I care to admit to smooth out the mask, making sure it's folded perfectly to cover her entire face while not getting in her hair. Once it's in place, I take my index fingers and smooth it over her gorgeous fucking skin. It's mesmerizing, being able to touch her like this. To trace the lines of her face and imagine it in a different scenario, where it's just her and me, no faux spa day, and I'm drawing lines along every curve of her body, not just her cheek, with my fingertips.

A breathy little sigh comes from Antoinette, and I damn near lose it. I have to close my eyes and take a deep breath to focus all my energy on not popping a boner right now.

"All done," I quietly murmur, not wanting to break the spell. Her eyes flutter open. That heat I was feeling when we started this? It's reflected in her eyes.

"My turn." Her grin is dangerous. Aphrodite herself looking at me.

I lean back against the headboard, hoping this small distance will help my restraint.

She picks up one of the packs, ripping it open before settling against my side. Thank God she doesn't straddle me again.

One hand comes up and carefully grabs my glasses, sliding them off before setting them to the side.

Her chest is rising faster, her lips parted, and I can do nothing except sit here and struggle with myself to not fucking touch her. If I touch her, it's over. This won't be a spa day. It won't just be friends meeting and venting about their jobs.

No.

It'll be the touch that breaks me.

Her touch is soft and careful. Like she's afraid to mess it up. But she continues her motions until my face is covered by the cold sheet, barely heated by her fingers.

Then she mimics what I did to her, trailing her fingers across my face to smooth the mask out.

My teeth are gritted, and my fists are clenched tight. It's all I can do to keep my hands to myself.

That's not what tonight is about.

I absolutely cannot touch this woman any more than I have.

Chapter 15

Toni

Fuck it.

That's what runs through my head as I smooth the facemask on this dichotomy of a man. As I watch him struggle to stay still, his focus is on me with so much unspoken emotion.

Fuck it.

Cupping his jaw with one hand, I swing my leg over his hip. I stay high on my knees, not sitting on him because I'm still not sure if he's going to run out the room yelling.

"Is this okay?" I whisper, scared to break whatever connection we have.

"No." He groans, tilting his head back before dropping it back down and meeting my gaze. "Yes, but it shouldn't be okay. Dammit, Antionette." He still hasn't touched me, but I see the barely held restraint in his eyes, and it gives me a sense of courage, a burst of confidence that takes over my actions.

I shift closer to him, my hand still on his jaw, both of us still with our face masks on. It should be comical, ridiculous even, but it's not. It's sexy as fuck.

My body is now a couple of inches from his. I'm not quite flush with his lap or his chest, but I'm close enough to feel his breathing, how he pants with need.

"I'm okay with this," I tell him softly. If I could tell him I'm more than okay with it and will die of horniness if we don't do *something* tonight, I would. But he's caught up in what happens outside of these doors, and I'm honestly thankful one of us is still semi level-headed.

He holds my gaze then moves his hands to my hips, slowly pulling me down on his lap. The instant I feel his erection, I moan. I can't help it. Knowing he's hard for me is one of the biggest turn-ons. This man holds so much power, yet

I'm reducing him to nothing more than a wanton man.

It's powerful as hell.

I don't realize my eyes have closed and my head has tipped back until I hear his words.

"Look at me, darling. I need your eyes."

My head jolts up and meets his blazing eyes. His hands skim up my hips, catching on the fabric of my shorts, before they slide under my shirt. He doesn't move any higher, content to keep his hands on my waist. My hips shift, attempting to get some friction.

"Need something?" His dangerous smirk only eggs me on.

"I'd like to have an orgasm at some point." I arch an eyebrow at him and bite my bottom lip, trying not to smirk.

"Brats don't get to come. You should learn that now."

"I think you underestimate my willingness to wait for you to be ready."

"Bold statement when I hold all the control."

"Do you?" I tilt my head in question as I grind my hips down against him.

"Yes, I fucking do." He abruptly lets go of me; our only point of contact is my very needy pussy and his dick covered by his pants. "Do you have a vibrator in your suitcase?"

"What?" I lean back, trying to figure out why he would need a vibrator.

"Yes or no, Antoinette."

"Y-y-yes."

He lifts me with ease, placing me next to him. He gets up with zero struggle, no signs that he's barely hanging on, and I'm not sure what to do with it all.

I'm horny, willing to break all my rules because this man is being kind, and sexy, and so fucking sweet to me.

He walks to my suitcase, digging around before pulling out the little vibrator not much larger than a bullet.

"This will do," he murmurs before turning back to me.

"I'm confused."

"Sit forward, and I'll explain."

I follow his direction, scooting forward as he slides onto the bed behind me.

The vibrator drops to the bed next to us as his hands take on a life of their own. They slide up my legs that are currently sandwiched by his, to my hips and across my stomach before they reverse their path.

"I'm going to give you that orgasm. And when you use this little vibrator during race weekends, you'll think of me every single time," he whispers in my ear before lifting me a little and sliding my shorts down my legs just under my knees.

My head tips back against his shoulder at his words. I'm ready to be consumed by this man no matter the cost.

His hands move to the inside of my thighs, gently pushing them out and over his surprisingly muscled legs. My back arches at the movement, pushing my ass back enough to feel his hardness, but I don't get the chance to focus on that. Felix moves his fingers up and down the inside of my thigh, working me up even though it's not needed. All he needs to do is go a little higher, and he'll see just how wet I am.

"You like the idea of that, huh? Thinking about me and the pleasure I can give you when you try to get yourself off. I wonder if it'll be as good. Or if you'll be calling me when it isn't." His fingers graze the edge of my pussy, not quite hitting my clit, making me whimper. "God, that sound makes me want to see how many times I can get you off. I want to hear it as you beg me to stop because you don't think you can take anymore."

"Felix." I moan out his name as his palm finally cups my needy cunt.

"That's right. Say my name, darling." His hot breath hits my neck before he presses a kiss there.

My hips are attempting to grind against his hand, but his other halts my hips. I let out a frustrated groan, and I feel him smile against my neck.

"You are so fucking sexy," he murmurs.

"And you are a fucking tease," I growl.

"You love it."

"I actually hate it."

"You're dripping down my hand, so I'd say you don't."

"I'm just horny."

"Do you get this wet when you're alone?"

I don't answer him. I can't because he's right. It's not just because I'm horny, but I want to hold onto some of my control. Fighting him on it helps me do that.

"That's what I thought." He kisses my neck once more before moving to my shoulder, his hand never moving. Then I feel his teeth against my shoulder at the same time his fingertips swirl around my clit. He bites down hard enough to hurt, and all my breath leaves me.

It's too much stimulation at once. My hips try to push against him to put more pressure on my clit because despite what I'm telling him, I'm really fucking close. I'm never this wet or turned-on alone. It's a means to an end when I'm alone.

This is the opposite of that.

This is desperation.

Need.

I need this orgasm like I need air.

He licks the flesh he just abused before nuzzling it. "You're so close. I can feel it. Feel your little clit pulsing against my finger."

"Felix, please," I beg.

"You're gorgeous when you beg."

I whimper, and he rewards me with more pressure. It takes an embarrassingly short amount of time before my orgasm slams into me. I'm flying high and gasping, pleasure rolling throughout my entire body, before I even grasp what's happening.

As I come back to myself, I hear Felix murmuring in my ear.

"That's right, darling, come all over my hand. This is just the start. Breathe through it. That's it. Good."

I'm not coherent enough to form words. I wouldn't even know what to say in response because the way he's talking me through it is so damn sexy I can barely function.

He cups me again, pressing against my overstimulated nerves, and I relax back into him.

Then I hear the unmistakable sound of my vibrator.

"I can't," I whine.

"Oh, you absolutely can and will." There's no softness or mercy in his tone.

I jolt when I feel the vibrations against my thigh.

"Easy, darling. I'm giving you a moment to catch your breath."

It's like a silent command goes through my body, and I heave in a deep breath. I go lax at the support he gives from behind, even with the vibrator tracing a pattern on the tops of my legs. He shifts his legs, opening me up more for him as he drags the vibrator to my stomach, inching it lower as I melt into him. His other arm wraps around me, just under my breasts, to hold me where he wants to be as the other dips the vibrator lower, right over the nicely trimmed hair I have leading to my overstimulated pussy.

"You are so beautiful like this."

"Pliable?" I ask, attempting to be snarky.

"Mine." He accompanies the word by putting the vibrator directly on my clit, making me scream out.

My hands clutch to his, wanting to keep him holding me while also taking the vibrations away.

"You're not in control here, Antoinette." He tsks before dragging the vibrator down through my wetness and pushing it inside of me. I gasp at the different feeling. "I'm going to pull all I can from you, and you will sit here and take it. You will crave it every time you even look at your fucking vibrator."

"Felix." My hips grind against his hand, forcing the vibrator deep, and the movement puts my ass in a position to drag along his cock. A quiet moan sounds in my ear, and it fuels me. I'm not sure what comes next, but I'm now determined to pleasure him as much as he is me.

"Fuck." He bites out as he picks up the pace.

I feel another orgasm building, but I'm not there yet. I'm not sure I'll get there; I've never come twice so close together.

And then the arm around my torso slides down, and his fingers tap my clit. *Shit, maybe I can come again.*

We're moving together now. Humping while he's working me over, splayed for his enjoyment.

The beginnings of the pull, deep in my pelvis, start. I clench around the vibrator, desperately wishing it was his dick.

"Holy shit I'm close," I breathe out.

A grunt is his only response as he doubles down on his ministrations.

He increases the vibrations, and I'm gone. Floating above us somewhere, watching as I writhe against him, silently screaming.

"Fuck," he grits out as the hand that was on my clit shoves my hips back against his and holds me there.

Did he just come?

Subdued moans fill my ears, and I'm giddy at the prospect that I just made this pillar of a man come in his pants.

My smile is bigger than it's ever been as I collapse against his body.

"You're a fucking enchantress. Bewitching me and pulling me under with you," he pants.

I feel like a goddess. Powerful and strong.

Felix made me feel this way. The only man to ever put me first. The only man to take control over both my body and mind. He helped me to stop thinking, to take a true break. The best fucking orgasms I've ever had in my life were a bonus.

It's then that I realize we both still have our face masks on, mine a little skewed from the vigorous movement. A giggle bursts from my chest.

"I'm glad orgasms make you laugh," he grunts.

"No—" I gasp, trying to stop laughing. "We both still have our masks on." I still have shit in my hair too that's probably all over his shirt now.

"Mmm, so we do." Deft fingers pluck at the one covering my face then his before he tosses them on the floor. He grabs a package from the pile of things he brought in—wet wipes—and wipes his hands off thoroughly before tossing that as well.

"What—" I'm cut off when his fingers smooth over my face, rubbing in the extra serum and gently massaging my face.

"This is what relaxing feels like," he says.

"Does your kind of relaxing always involve orgasms?"

"Never, usually." His tone says he's just as confused as me with what just happened. I can't say I'm upset with it, but it does change everything.

Once he's done with my face, he picks up my legs and puts them together inside his once more—a tender move that catches me off guard.

"I need to get cleaned up," he says before pressing a kiss to my neck.

The reminder that cleaning up means changing because he came in his pants makes me giggle again.

"You should be proud of yourself. I feel like a teenager again." He lifts me up and sets me back on my side before standing up. The wet spot is beyond obvious and has me biting my lip. "Don't look at me like that. I'm trying to be a gentleman."

My eyes shift up to his. "I kind of like the ungentlemanly side of you."

"You might kill me." He sighs, pinching the bridge of his nose before snagging his glasses from the side table and putting them on.

Yeah, I think everything has changed.

Chapter 16
Felix

It's been a week and a half since I crossed every single boundary I had set for myself with Antoinette. And I can't bring myself to feel bad about it. We've emailed a little bit, flirted a lot within them, but neither of us has been willing to discuss the bigger ramifications.

That night in Canada has been on my mind every single minute of the day. How the hell am I supposed to focus on anything other than how the woman made me feel? How she got me so worked up, how she was so fucking sexy I creamed my pants like a teenager.

I'm on the Legacy plane, flying to Spain for the first race of the triple weekend. No days off for almost the next month. It's the hardest part of the season, and to say I'm a little worried is an understatement. Between our cars not performing and my head all fucked up over Miss Bailey, I'm not looking forward to any of it.

My phone lights up with a message. I debate not opening it, but it could be my kids. Instead, I find a message from Steph.

My heart clenches hard that she could ever think showing up for a race with our kids could be a distraction. Sure, it'll take some scheduling, but it's never a distraction.

I sigh, putting my phone face down and contemplating a way to distract Steph from Antoinette. The last thing I need right now are my two worlds colliding. I keep things separate for a reason.

My phone dings again, and I growl in exasperation. That is until I find an email sitting in my inbox from the woman taking up all my brain space.

From: AB (wannabebosslady@genericmail.com)

To: FK (Swedish_Boss48@genericmail.com)

Subject: Stress Management

So . . . how am I supposed to not be panicking at the prospect of having three straight weeks of stress? Any chance we could get a repeat of Canada?

Hopeful and slightly addicted to your orgasms,

-T

My bark of laughter interrupts the silence in the place.

To: FK (Swedish_Boss48@genericmail.com)

From: AB (wannabebosslady@genericmail.com)

Subject: RE: Stress Management

Well now, with a closer like that, I find it hard to say no. But you knew that. I think we should plan on dinner, and depending on how the races go, there's potential for more. Maybe.

I can't do anything after Austria, though, not even dinner.

Trying to be good and not cave to your demands, but also desperate for a round two,

-F

I know I'm fucking things up. Instead of pulling back, I'm diving in full force. She emails back immediately.

From: AB (wannabebosslady@genericmail.com)

To: FK (Swedish_Boss48@genericmail.com)

Subject: RE: RE: Stress Management

Copy that for Austria. Do I get to be privy as to why? Totally okay if not.

I think all of your talk about staying professional is your way to stay safe, but then you throw things in our emails, like your closing, that throw me for a loop. It's . . . confusing.

Probably using your office to get away this weekend,

-T

I sigh. Getting into this over email isn't something I want to do. This is a conversation for in person, and one we need to have sooner rather than later.

To: FK (Swedish_Boss48@genericmail.com)

From: AB (wannabebosslady@genericmail.com)

Subject: RE: RE: RE: Stress Management

Meet me at my room when you get into town. I'll email you the room number.

Apologetically making things complicated,

-F

Now I need to think about how I want things to go with us. I need to pull back, to draw a firm line in the sand. I just hope I'm able to actually do that once I see her in person. She's addicting in the best way, and it's hard to not fall into her instead of pulling back.

As if my next three weeks weren't complicated enough, now I need to have a conversation I don't want to have and deal with my family. Oh, and that's on top of my already stressful job where, hopefully, our cars decide to fucking perform.

I'm not hopeful I'll survive.

***

A knock at my door sends my heart rate flying.

A very dressed-down Antoinette with no make-up, messy hair, and sweats on the other side damn near makes me do something stupid. Like kiss her in the hallway in full view of drivers and employees.

I clear my throat. "Come in."

She follows me inside, shutting the door behind her.

"So, I—"

"Umm—" We start talking at the same time as I turn to face her. I nod and hold out my hand in a gesture for her to continue. She takes a deep breath.

"I feel like this is all about to end." Her sad smile ends all thoughts I had about pulling away.

There's something about her that makes me want to see where this goes, even if it's not in a serious capacity.

"Honestly, that was sort of my plan, but I changed my mind." Her head tilts in question. "This"—I gesture between us—"is so damn complicated. And it's a terrible idea, really, but I can't seem to stop wanting you."

Her smile is blinding. "That's an interesting way to win a girl over."

Laughter chokes out my words. "I, ah, yeah, apparently I'm not great at this." I run my hand behind my neck. "I would like to keep things how they've been. We need to also be extremely discreet."

"Agreed. So let me clarify. You want to keep doing dinners, flirting through email, and occasionally giving each other orgasms of epic proportions after an at home spa night?" Her smirk says so much more than her smart-ass words do.

"Keep it up, darling."

"No orgasms, then? Just dinner dates and fun emails?"

I crowd her back against the door, so close she has to tilt her head back to look up at me. "This is why I can't give you up. You make me feel twenty-five again. You force me to have fun."

"Sounds terrible."

"It's dreadful. People might start thinking I'm nice." My fingers lightly trace down her arm before lacing with hers.

"That would be a tragedy."

"Catastrophic," I murmur as my lips graze her cheek.

"Can't have your reputation damaged by little ol' me."

"You're more dangerous than you let on."

"You just said I was fun." She pops out her bottom lip in a playful pout.

"Fun is dangerous to my wellbeing."

Her cheek moves with her smile. I brush my nose back and forth against it, breathing her in and getting more and more lost in her words.

"I kind of like seeing this side of you," she whispers.

"You're the only one who does see it."

Before the conversation gets more serious than it already is, I finally press a kiss to the lips I can't stop thinking about. She has my head a fucking mess, and kissing her means my head gets a break from her too-close-to-home words.

I finally drag myself away from her, pulling back just enough to see her eyebrow soft and unfurrowed, her long lashes fluttering across her pink-tinged cheeks, her plump lips slightly parted, a hint of a smile at the corners. She looks peaceful. Happy.

Yeah, I'm in big trouble with this one.

"I have to head down for the media conference," I mutter, not wanting to break the moment.

"Lucky me, Sydney got me out of it today." Her eyes finally open. Her blue are irises nearly engulfed by her pupils, betraying her need.

"Lucky you, indeed. I'll see you at practice?"

"I'll be there," she whispers.

We stand there a minute longer. No kissing, no talking, just taking each other in before she clears her throat.

"I'm on the door. I can't leave."

"Oh, of course." I step back, letting her have enough space to open the door.

"Oh, and Felix?" She turns around before she pulls it open. "Good chat." She smirks as she walks out as if she didn't just derail everything I had intended for this conversation.

The door clicks shut, and I lean back against it, sighing happily.

Antoinette Bailey is going to be a problem in my life.

***

Practice Two is upon us after an abysmal Practice One. I barely had time to sleep with all the adjustments we needed to figure out before today.

I'm so fucking tired, and yet my eyes keep getting pulled down the pitlane to a certain bothersome woman. I swear she got dressed today just to fuck with me.

Her pencil skirt isn't practical in this environment, and her shirt has one button too many unbuttoned. It's a good thing she's two garages down from me because if she were any closer, I'd be struggling to contain my erection right now.

And possibly groping her for all to see.

Jesus. I scrub my hand down my face after taking my glasses off. She just might be the death of me.

Even with Steph it was never this way. We had a practical relationship. Sure, we had a good time when we were younger, but it was never this all-consuming feeling that Antoinette is forcibly giving me.

"Johnny's car still looks like shit, but at least Pavel's seems to be better balanced," Rick, the lead engineer for Johnny, says. It pulls my thoughts from Antoinette just enough to focus on my damn job.

"What the fuck is happening with the fucking balance of these cars? It should not be this difficult to figure out." My sharp tone tells everyone on comms that I'm pissed. "We need to hold an all-engineers meeting after this shitshow."

"Yes, sir. I'll send an invite," Rick says, and not two minutes later, my phone pings with the new meeting invite.

I'm sick of us looking like amateurs, and I'm about to get down to the bottom of this.

We hold the meeting immediately after things die down after Practice Two. At least Johnny was able to salvage things and give us hope for qualifiers tomorrow.

I wait for everyone to sit in the conference room before starting.

"I refuse for this season to go down as my worst ever. We're better than that, and it's time we figure this bullshit out. We're not leaving here until we find some improvements or a solution to this fucking balance problem."

Groans sound from the table.

"Am I keeping you from something? Is it not your job to make sure these cars run well enough to win a goddamned championship? Take some pride in your work." I scoff at the lack of zeal in the room right now.

A throat clears as a hand raises, and I can't contain the eyeroll.

"We're not in fucking primary school. What?" I bark.

"I tried to discuss this with you at the beginning of the season, but—"

"And what did I tell you to do?" I remember him attempting to bypass his bosses.

"To talk to my supervisor."

Said supervisor is red faced and looks like he's about knock him upside the head. That tells me he didn't actually talk to his boss about anything.

"I see. It looks like you failed to do that. Remind me of your name?" I pace the front of the room.

"Newman, sir."

Newman. I was way off.

"What was this grand idea you had?" His boss, David, is shaking his head next to him. A subtle sign for him to shut the fuck up, but Newman apparently doesn't see it.

"I have a new design for the front wings."

"And the front wings are the thing causing our balance issues?"

"Umm, well, no, not exactly."

"So why would we change the front wing?"

"Because I think it's affecting our aerodynamics." Newman's voice gets more and more unsure as he speaks.

I turn to David. "Are our front wings a problem?"

"No, sir. Our aerodynamics look good, and we're not seeing any unnecessary drag from them."

"I see." I stare at Newman, begging him to cower since he decided this was the time to bring up such a ridiculous change.

"Why did you think today of all days was the right time to bring this up?" I ask, instead of berating him like I really want to.

"I just— Uh, I had been thinking on it for a while, and with everyone here, it seemed like . . ." He trails off when he sees the thundercloud on my face.

"Sit down, Newman," I command before turning to the rest of the group. "Does anyone have any ideas as to why we have a *balance* problem?" I ask, looking hard at Newman when I specify.

"I think we need to go back to the drawing board with the anti-roll bar geometry," Rick says, scrubbing his face.

"What's the timetable on something like that?"

"I mean, we can change the angles pretty quickly; the problem is testing it. We're already at qualifiers, which means we don't have a practice to see if what we did changed anything for the better."

"So, on back-to-back-to-back races, it would be a bad idea to adjust that and pray for the best, is what you're saying." I roll my neck, trying to release all the built-up tension.

"It's doable, but it could also mean that the problem gets worse. Giving ourselves time to test it would be better."

I think about it as I pace. All the engineers are fidgeting, nervous about my decision. Newman looks equal parts scared shitless and pissed off as hell. *Good. That'll teach him to overstep again.*

"I want it done before the next race. Start doing simulations of the adjustments, and after the race here, we should have a general direction to implement. We'll test it in Austria, see how it goes, and adjust before Silverstone if we need to."

"Yes, sir," sounds from around the table.

"Dismissed," I tell the crew, and they all file out of the room.

Plopping down into one of the vacated chairs, I pull off my glasses and rub the bridge of my nose.

The ping of my phone pisses me off almost as much as that meeting did. It's only when I see who the message is from that my shoulders relax and a barely there smile touches my face.

From: AB (wannabebosslady@genericmail.com)

To: FK (Swedish_Boss48@genericmail.com)

Subject: Sustenance in the morning?

Now, this might be crossing into territory you'd rather not, but hear me out. Can I stop by your room with some coffee (or tea) tomorrow before we need to be at the paddock?

You seemed a little . . . tense during practice today. I'd like to help start your day off right.

Not using double meaning at all in this message,

-T

And just like that, the shit day disappears.

Chapter 17
(Transcript)

Interviewer: Still having problems with the cars, eh, Felix?

Felix Karlsson: Was that supposed to be a question?

Interviewer: Fine. What solutions do you have to save your season?

Felix Karlsson: We have lots of solutions. Why would I tell a media pundit specific solutions for all to hear? You know how it is in Formula 1.

Interviewer: You can't blame a guy for trying.

Felix Karlsson: I actually can. Do we have any other . . . engrossing questions?

Rocco Bianchi: Be nice, Felix.

Felix Karlsson: Any questions about anything of importance?

Interviewer: Well, how do you feel about Empress leading the charge and making it very difficult for anyone to catch up with currently?

Felix Karlsson: It's all part of the sport.

Rocco Bianchi: No one is immune to problems. It's just a matter of time before something happens and the rest of the grid is able to catch Empress.

Felix Karlsson: Or we could give credit where credit is due.

Rocco Bianchi: Or you could focus on your own problems and fix your fucking car. Then we wouldn't need to hear you bitch every day.

Felix Karlsson: Testy there, Rocco. Got some problems yourself, I think. Maybe you should do some internal reflection since you seem so keen to project.

Interviewer: All right, I think that's it for today.

Chapter 18

Toni

After a first and sixth place finish in Spain, there's been zero break or down time. I was able to sneak some kisses when I dropped off coffee—tea for Felix—before qualifiers but the rest of the time has been quick glances and emails.

We didn't have time to do dinner since he had to immediately leave for Austria to deal with the car issues.

And now, I'm exhausted and stressed.

We just finished qualifiers, where we hold pole position and seventh, but somehow that prick over at Guardian keeps trash-talking us. The FIA launched a bullshit investigation into how many engine units we've used. Like we would try to cheat the fucking system. The politics in this business are just ridiculous.

Luckily, the FIA concluded that we were fine, no harm done. But the harm to my nervous system is far reaching.

I don't think about what I'm doing; I just act. Walking over to Legacy's hospitality area, I beeline it for his office, nodding to the receptionist as she eyes me.

I push open his door without knocking.

"Oh my fucking God am I over today. This is—" I jolt at the sight in front of me.

Felix is at his desk, and there's a gorgeous woman closer to his age bent over it, looking at something he's showing her.

"I am so sorry. I should have knocked," I apologize. Yes, I'd love to be nosy, but it's not my place. We're not officially together; we aren't partners. We're just two adults having fun.

And I hate it a little bit. I wish there was even a hint at exclusivity, but I don't want to push him either.

"No trouble at all. I'm actually very excited to meet you," the woman says, straightening up and walking to me with her hand out. "I'm Steph, Stephanie Karlsson."

Holy shit, it's his ex-wife.

I'm sure I look comical, my eyes wide and mouth gaping like a fish out of water, but outside of shaking her hand I have no words.

Am I supposed to act like busting into a rival team's office is normal? Am I supposed to act like we've hooked up?

My eyes shift to Felix's. His smirk doesn't put me at ease.

"Steph, don't scare her. Antoinette, this is Steph, my ex-wife. She won't bite, I promise."

"I am so sorry for just barging in here," I say, still shaking the poor woman's hand. I finally drop it and turn to leave. "I'll just stop by later."

"No! Please stay. I promise we were just going over the kids' schedules, and that's doesn't need to get done immediately," Steph says, looking back at Felix.

There's a silent exchange between them. Using only their eyes and head tilts, they come to some sort of an understanding as Steph nods.

"I would love to do lunch with you, possibly bring the kids. Our daughter is your biggest fan and would love to meet you. I understand if that's too . . . much at the moment, but we'd love to pick your brain." Her smile is warm, friendly.

"Oh! Umm, sure! I could probably do something later today if that works." My attention is snagged by Felix who is smiling. *Smiling? A genuine smile at work? What alternate universe is this?*

"That would be amazing. Felix has my number, so just text me a time and place, and we'll be there."

She's gone just as fast as I came in here.

"So, that's my ex-wife," Felix says as soon as the door to his office shuts.

"Umm, yep, sure seems like it." I laugh awkwardly, unsure of how to handle all of this.

"I forgot to let you know they were all in town for the race this weekend. It's close to home, and the kids like the action occasionally. I'm . . . working on our relationship."

The hesitation and slight sadness in his tone makes me desperate to dig deeper, but again, that's not my place.

"No, that's wonderful! I'm sure they're happy to spend some time with you. I just needed an escape, but I can head back to the hotel." I turn to leave, but a hand on my arm stops me.

Well, he's spry when he wants to be.

"What happened?" The furrow of his eyebrows displays his concern.

"Just the usual bullshit. Rocco's being a dick."

"Sit." He pulls me to the little seating area in his office, and I plop down, sighing.

"I'm sure you saw the FIA investigation."

"I did, but I was sure you were clean, so I didn't think much of it."

"We were, obviously, but it still has me on edge. What did I do to piss off Rocco?"

"Likely nothing. He has small dick syndrome, I'm afraid." His aristocratic tone marrying his choice of words has me snorting out a laugh.

"Oh my God, I wish I had that recorded."

"That would be blackmail."

"It'd be for my own personal enjoyment."

"What else would be for your own personal enjoyment, Miss Bailey?"

"Well, I was coming here to see if we were on for dinner at some point since we couldn't make last week happen, but with your family in town, I'll just do room service."

I refuse to meet his eye. If I do, I know he'll see the disappointment. He shouldn't even factor me in when his family is here, and I don't want to put him in a position where he has to.

"Hey." His finger lifts my chin, forcing me to look at him. "I've been with them most of the week. What I haven't had most of the week is you. I'd really like to do dinner tomorrow night, but I'd also really like it to be room service."

I shiver at the heat in his eyes.

"Okay," I whisper.

"And you can cancel on Steph. She's nosy but well-meaning. That doesn't mean you have to have lunch with my ex and my kids. If it's awkward for you, I can make your excuses."

"Absolutely not! I said I would go, and I'm true to my word. I mean, sure, it might be a little awkward given the fact that it seems like she knows something is going on with us, but the kids will be there, right? It's not like she'll give me the third degree over our relationship . . . right?" I cringe at even using the word relationship around this man. And let's not discuss my rambling.

"You're sure? She won't say anything in front of the kids, but they're adults, so if she happens to get you away from them, there's no telling where she'll take the conversation. And for the record, I haven't explicitly told her about our arrangement. She made an assumption, and I . . . well, I didn't correct her."

Now this is interesting.

"So, what do I tell her if that conversation happens?" I arch an eyebrow, feeling less insecure.

"You tell her whatever you want to tell her. We're not playing games here, Antoinette. She knows me, and you know me. I'm sure you'll both bitch about me. I won't be upset by anything you say."

I smile at his attempt to put me at ease.

"Are you sure you're okay with me going out to eat with them? Your kids won't freak out?"

"Oh, my kids will freak out but only because they'll be meeting the great and amazing Toni Bailey. Emilie, I swear, is your biggest fan, and Henrik . . . Well, Henrik is a twenty-year-old male." His cringe face makes me laugh.

"Are you saying your son has a crush on me?" I goad him.

"Can we not talk about Hen like this? Please. I already had to listen to him talk about you while acting like I didn't want to bend you over my desk at every turn." He sighs.

"Poor thing. How can I make it better?" I smirk.

"You're trouble." He shakes his head, picking up my hand and lacing our fingers together. "You sure you're okay? Don't let Rocco get to you. He's trying to buy his way to a better team, but he's going about it the wrong way."

"I know. Doesn't make it any less stressful." I scoot closer to him and lean my head on his shoulder.

"How are you feeling in the stress department otherwise?"

"Honestly? Better. I'm mostly trusting my engineers to fill me in with problems and any solutions they come up with. It's cleared up a lot of time, although I still worry."

"The worrying doesn't stop, I'm afraid."

"Nature of the beast," I murmur.

His thumb moves back and forth over the top of my thigh as we sit there taking a break from the mayhem. I lean into him, breathing in the scent that's uniquely him. My mind wanders to how much I want this man. How much I wish we could date like a normal couple and not be relegated to the shadows. But I also know I'm just damn happy to be close enough to him to see who he really is. Not the pretentious asshole he is on the paddock. Not the tough-as-nails boss who expects the best.

No.

Around me, he's fun and flirty and so fucking sexy it makes me ache all over. He makes me feel worthy. Like I'm more than just a piece of meat, there only to satisfy his every whim.

Brad really did a number on me.

"I'm looking forward to tomorrow evening." His voice rumbles against the crown of my head.

"Me too," I whisper.

No matter how dangerous it is to my heart in the long run. No matter if I'm not able to hold on to him for good, I'm taking whatever he wants to give me right now.

***

My hands are sweaty.

I got Steph's number before I left Felix's office and set up a late lunch. Now, I'm second-guessing the entire decision to go through with this.

"Toni! Thank you so much for agreeing to lunch. These are the kids. Well, adults now." She winces at the reminder. "Emilie and Henrik." She gestures to the kids behind her.

Henrik is a damn twin to Felix, and it's jarring to see. Emilie is a combination of Steph and Felix, and she's gorgeous.

"It's so nice to meet you both."

Henrik shakes my outstretched hand with a grin. Emilie surprises me with a hug before I realize what's happening. My hand is pinned between us, and I laugh at the action.

"Em, really, give her some space," Steph scolds.

"She's fine, I promise." Emilie pulls back with a look of pure admiration on her face, and I almost tear up.

"I'm sorry, I'm just really excited to meet you."

"Well, that's super flattering, thank you. Shall we sit?" I gesture to the table.

Drinks are ordered, and conversation really starts flowing.

"So, are you both in school?"

"I'm wrapping up my architectural degree this next year," Henrik says.

"Oh, that's exciting. What made you choose that?"

"I'm fond of numbers, and I like the idea of building things that will stand the test of time." He smiles with pride.

Just like his father, this one.

"And what about you?" I ask Emilie, who still seems a little starstruck.

"I'm going to San Francisco in the fall. Starting to study fashion." She's shy when she answers, and I want to draw her out of her shell a little.

"That's amazing! I know literally nothing about clothes and fashion, as I'm sure you can tell," I joke.

"You're fine!" she says with false confidence, causing me to laugh harder.

"Seriously, I'm terrible. I had to have my boss set me up with a personal shopper before I started the job because all I owned was black work pants and polos."

Emilie cringes at that, making the whole table laugh.

"This world forces you out of your comfort zone if you aren't born into it,"

Steph says after we settle down.

"Isn't that the truth. I feel like, sometimes, I'm the only person not born into it. But I have my whole team of ownership. None of them were in the business until recently, but I think we're doing okay," I tell her.

"Okay? You're doing more than okay. You're giving the whole grid a run for their money. And my dad aside, I'd love nothing more than to see all those teams pissed the hell off that you're kicking their asses," Henrik says with the first real show of emotion from him.

"I appreciate that, but we're just trying to do our best." The diplomatic answer feels wrong with these three. If anyone knows the bullshit politics, it's them. Maybe not the kids, but Steph surely knows how messed up things can get.

When I look over at her, I know I'm right based on the grimace her face is sporting.

Sighing, I decide a little honesty could go a long way. I'm not sure why I feel the need to have these three people on my side, but the very distant hope that Felix and I could turn into more has delusional thoughts in my head.

"It's . . . hard. The backstabbing amongst other team principals. The constant changes to the cars. It's a lot to keep up with. Your father has actually been really insightful on how to avoid burnout."

The three of them look at each other with a knowing look, and I know I just showed my hand. However unintentionally, all of them know now there's more to the story between Felix and me.

"I'm actually thinking about picking up something on the side as a sort of hobby. Something like self-defense or martial arts," I throw out there in an attempt to get them to stop thinking about Felix and me together. After all the shit with Brad, though, this has been on my mind to start.

"Oh! Yes! I've done some self-defense classes in the past. I'll send you the information," Steph says, and just like that, the talk of our potential relationship is put aside for now.

Food gets ordered and delivered, with conversation staying on more neutral topics. I find out just how much of a fan Henrik is of the sport and how much

Emilie looks up to a woman in a male-dominated field. It's a much-needed boost for me. The knowledge that I'm inspiring even one girl is enough to push through all the nonsense.

"I'm going to run to the restroom and then check out that water fountain," Herik announces as he sends Emilie a look.

"Oh, I'll meet you over there." She stands up, making it very obvious they plan to give Steph and me some alone time.

"Subtle." I laugh as they walk away.

"They haven't quite learned the way to not make things so obvious. Something they could learn a lot about from their father, honestly."

"He is quite discreet." As soon as the word is out of my mouth, I slump back into my chair. Steph's triumphant smile tells me how this conversation is about to go.

"I'm going to cut the bullshit. Felix and I have a wonderful relationship now. Our marriage was a good one, but it was clear after we had Emilie that we work better as close friends. We'll always love each other, but the divorce was mutual."

"You don't need to—"

"I do, I think. Because if I know Felix, and I'd like to think I know him well, you scare him. He dealt with . . . a sort of scandal while we were separated. Although it's beyond yesterday's news, he never forgave himself. It's why he punishes himself by staying away from the kids for as long as he has. They didn't fully understand what was happening at the time, and as kids, the divorce was hard on them. That was almost eight years ago now, and he's never pulled himself out of his pity party."

"They were young; it's hard to explain the intricacies of a relationship to children," I offer.

"It is. But they're grown now, forgiven both of us, but he doesn't quite understand that. Since the season started, though? He's different. He's making more of an effort with the kids, helping Henrik with internship applications. Talking about helping move Emilie to San Francisco. The kids are . . . thrilled to have their father back." Her eyes glisten with unshed tears. "You did that," she whispers, shocking the hell out of me.

"I-I really didn't." I hold my hands up.

"I'm telling you all of this because whatever you are to him is big. Both of you may not realize it yet, but his outlook on a lot of things has changed since he met you. I won't pretend to know your story, but everything you've told us today tells me he's been good for you too. Don't let this world of high society influence your relationship. Don't let it derail you because you think you have to keep things hidden. He's been burned by this before, and I know how difficult it will be to pull him out of that thinking. Just . . . don't give up on him. He's a wonderful man."

I'm speechless. Of all the things she could have talked to me about, encouraging Felix's and my relationship was not one of them. I thought she'd warn me off, at the very least.

"I, umm, don't know what to say." I wring my hands together in my lap, lost for words.

"There's nothing to say. I just needed to let you know, from someone who knows exactly how Felix is, to stick it out if you feel anything for him. He'll come around, even if it takes him a while."

I just nod, shell-shocked by the whole interaction. The kids eventually wander back, and we finish a wonderful lunch before parting company. Emilie makes a promise to send me outfit ideas, and Henrik says he's rooting for Empress tomorrow. The easy conversation helps me breathe easier since my talk with Steph.

Chapter 19

Toni

I'm nervous.

For the first time since Felix and I started this—whatever we're doing—I'm nervous to see him. Who knows what Steph told him, and considering Legacy didn't get any points in this race, I'm not so sure what kind of mood he'll be in.

The knock I've been waiting for still startles me. I count to three to make it seem like I wasn't just standing here waiting for him.

The door swings open, and I lean against the doorframe.

"Hi."

"Hi." He's dressed down tonight. Joggers and a T-shirt paired with the tortoise shell glasses that really do things for me.

Our perusal of each other is quick. He brushes past me, and I shut the door behind him. Steph's words about not hiding ourselves flicker through my thoughts, but I push it away.

"You look beautiful, darling." He steps closer to me, wrapping an arm around my waist to pull me closer, and I melt into him. All thoughts of Steph's and my lunch discussion are gone.

"I'm in grubby sweats and an oversized tank top," I deadpan.

"And you're beautiful."

I lose myself in his gaze, in the conviction of voice.

Clearing my throat, I pull free from the hold his presence has on me. "So, dinner..." I grab the room service menu I had put on the entryway table.

"Just get two of whatever you're having." His gaze is locked on me, more intense than usual, and it's unnerving.

"Umm, okay, yep, I can do that." I fumble around, trying to get my phone out of my pocket. The effect he has on me is so distracting I have to turn around to dial room service. I pick the first thing that looks halfway decent. Felix's stare sears my back the entire time, and I suddenly feel like a teenager with her first crush, except her crush is a famous movie star who is wildly out of her league.

I hang up the phone but don't turn to face him. The heat of his body hits my back as his arm snakes around my middle. I suck in a breath, and it gets caught in my chest.

"Breathe. What's got you so worked up? The race went well. You're wiping the floor with Rocco. What's going on?"

"I—" *Can I just tell him truthfully how I'm feeling? He's always honest with me.* "I'm worried about what Steph told you."

I feel his chest bounce before the sound of his laughter escapes him. Spinning around, I smack his chest.

"I was really stressed! Don't laugh at me."

"I can tell." His laughter mellows, and in its place is his genuine smile. "Why are you worried about that?"

"Because she's important to you and you have kids together. She's not going anywhere."

"And you plan to stick around a while, do you?" His smile drops, and his serious eyes burn a hole through me.

"I mean— I'm not assuming. I just—"

"Hey." He stops me from sputtering, with his hands on my shoulders, ducking down to make sure I hold his gaze. "Steph, and the kids for that matter, loved you. As a person, as someone who I may or may not want to spend more time with. They had nothing bad to say. Steph actually had bad things to say about me, but I digress. I told Steph you would think she was interrogating you." That grin I love slides back on his face.

"I don't know how to do any of this," I confess.

"Do what, darling?"

"Deal with bigger things than dinner, orgasms, and flirty emails." I let a shy smile appear.

"You are pretty damn good at those. And you don't need to worry about anything else. Just be you. After all, everything that makes you who you are is why I enjoy spending time with you."

"You're being quite the flatterer, Mr. Karlsson. Is that because you would like to partake in some of those orgasms we were discussing?" I arch an eyebrow at him, more comfortable with the direction this conversation has taken.

I'm not ready to dissect things between us, and it appears he isn't either.

"If I recall, it's your flirty little emails that get us both worked up, not the other way around."

"I really don't see you complaining."

"Oh, I'm not." He starts pulling me closer to him when a knock sounds at the door. He leans down and presses a quick kiss to my lips before answering the door.

With our food here, all thoughts of getting physically acquainted again vanish.

But that's okay. We have time.

***

"You should have seen his face. I swear he looked like he was about to cower in a ball if I moved even an inch closer to him."

"I watched the video!" I laugh. "Rocco talks a very big game, but standing up to you in an interview was not his wisest decision."

"He's really itching to be the center of all my angry attention."

"I think I would pay to see that." I smirk at Felix, who's reclining on the bed, talking more animatedly than I've ever seen him.

"You know what I'd like to see?" he asks.

"What?"

"You. Naked. At my mercy."

"Hmm, I don't know. Feels like an awkward segway. Feels like maybe you need to work harder for that one." I try so very hard to keep a straight face, but his crestfallen look makes me crack. "I'm joking." I chuckle before I grip the edge of my shirt and pull it up over my head.

"Work harder? Is this not hard enough?" He snags my hand, placing it on top of the tent in his pants.

"I mean, *that* is hard, yes, but it still feels like you're getting off a little easy." I can't help but laugh at my own double entendre.

"If I get off any easier with you, you'll leave me for someone who can last more than two minutes." He grumbles, dragging my hand up his torso to his mouth, before he kisses my palm.

The action is so tender in comparison to the conversation we're having that my mind stutters to keep the banter going.

"I don't know. I kind of like you. I'm not sure I want to get rid of you." I try to inject my words with playfulness, but when his eyes meet mine, I know I've failed. I let him see just a little too much of the truth.

His gaze shifts between my eyes like he's making a decision about how to move forward after such an admission.

"Then show me how much you like me." The tension in my shoulders melts away at the smirk he gives me.

Playful, I can do. Serious and thinking about the future? I can't handle that right now. Felix seems to know that, thank God.

"Show you?" I slide my sweatpants down my legs and kick them off to the floor. "It seems I'm showing you a lot while you're lying there fully clothed."

"What are you going to do about it, darling?" That wicked gleam in his eye sends arousal coursing through my veins. This is such a contrast to the last time we did anything of this nature. With Felix, I never really know what to expect, but that's half the fun. He keeps me on my toes, keeps me guessing, and my control freak ways *love* it.

I stare at him, taking in every inch of his body, trying to decide what to do. There are so many things that I want to do to him that my head can't narrow down to one.

That is until I notice the wet spot on his joggers.

My fingernails scrape up to the top of his thigh, not touching his dick yet but close enough to let him know where I'm headed. I switch legs, his taunt muscle twitching under the sensation. It's only then that I move my hand, dragging one finger up the length of his erection. The sound of his heavy exhale fuels my confidence.

Hooking my fingers into his waistband, I wait for him to lift his hips so I can pull his pants and boxer briefs down. The fabric brushes along his legs, but I make sure to stop it around his knees. I want him a little trapped, a little restrained in a way.

He's large, and by large, I mean huge. Way bigger than anything I've been around. I'm nervous yet intrigued and wholly turned on.

Still off to his right side, I lean over to kiss his exposed leg. My hand gently grips his cock, sliding up as my kisses move higher up his leg.

Felix's moan makes me double down on my direction. I pump him a couple more times before I kiss up his length, then finally his tip that's weeping pre-cum.

"Jesus," he breathes out, thumping his head against the headboard.

I trace my tongue up the length of him, wrapping my lips around his tip, finally getting to taste him. And fuck does he taste good.

Perfectly Felix. Clean, slightly salty, with an edge of sweetness.

I stop thinking altogether. I want to show him as much pleasure as he showed me. The challenge is too good to pass up, so I shut my mind off and just feel.

Sliding down slowly, I ease into it. The goal is to take him as deep as I can, so I need to work up to it, especially given his size. His hands fist at his side like he's trying to not take control, and it just makes me grin. Well, as much as I can with his dick in my mouth.

"Your mouth is fucking divine."

The praise motivates me to test my boundaries. When I hit my gag reflex, I force myself not to pull back. My tongue shifts against him, sending his hand into my hair. He fists the strands hard, not yanking it, but definitely letting me know I'm not as in control as I'd like.

"Keep that up, and we'll just prove how easily I come with you." He gasps, arching his hips as I pull back, following my mouth.

"I feel like that's more of a compliment to me," I say before going right back to it.

After a couple more pumps, his other hand cups my cheek.

"God, you are gorgeous like this. Mouth full of me, ass popped out like an invitation. It's taking everything in me to let you have your fun." His words are almost a growl.

That arousal that's been steady since I took my shirt off? Off the charts now with his dirty talk. Who knew this sophisticated, mostly uptight man had it in him.

But you get to see a different side of him.

I do, but I'm desperately trying not to look into it further.

I pop off of him with a smile. "My fun? It might be a little more serious than fun, Felix. If it's just fun, maybe I shouldn't let you come." I arch an eyebrow at him.

"That mouth of yours is going to get you in trouble, darling."

"Bring it on." I don't give him a chance for rebuttal; I go back to the blow job that I'm absolutely still in control of if his moans are anything to go by.

I set a steady rhythm, repeating actions that make him moan, and before too long, he's gasping for breath.

"Toni, I'm going to come." He sucks in a breath, but I can't get over the fact that he just called me Toni.

His fingers tighten in my hair as his hips jerk one last time, his cock pulsing as his release hits the back of my throat. I moan around him and drop my hips to the bed, grinding against nothing in an attempt to get some relief.

Felix barely finishes before he hauls me off of him and scoots down the bed. He manhandles me by my waist, picking me up and placing me above his head to straddle him.

"Oh shit." I gasp at the first touch of his tongue.

"Sit on my face, darling. You had your fun. Now, it's my turn."

"There's that word again—" I can't finish my sentence; his tongue circles my clit, and his arm wraps around my thigh so he can press a finger into me.

He hums against my overly sensitive skin, making my back arch as I drop down more onto him. I have no control over my hips as they start to shift in the same rhythm his fingers set.

I'm lost in the motion, lost to anything else happening in the world.

"I could have you sit here like the queen you are every single day and be so fucking happy."

My heartbeat stutters at his words. Before I can grasp onto his meaning, my body takes over, euphoria blooming from where his mouth is devouring me, and I come so hard I have to grip the headboard to stay upright.

"Good. That's so good, darling. I really want one more," he murmurs from underneath me.

"I can't," I whine.

"Let's try for me. You're doing so well. I just want to make sure you know that even though I come quickly with you, I'm not completely useless."

A laugh bursts from my chest as he presses a kiss to my inner thigh before moving back to my sensitive clit.

It takes me an embarrassingly short amount of time until I'm coming again, helpless against this man and the way he commands my body.

Chapter 20
Felix

Nothing brings down the high of being with Antoinette faster than a phone call from one of my engineers.

I've been riding high for two days now, and the bubble I've been living in has just burst.

"What do you mean you still don't have answers?" I rub my temple in an attempt to lessen the headache that's brewing.

"I mean, we're still having issues, and we can't pinpoint where it's coming from. It should have at least gotten better but, as you've seen, it hasn't."

"I want a meeting with all the engineers and directors immediately. Call me when you've set it up." I hang up, not wanting to talk more, afraid I'll blow a fucking gasket.

It's not his job to organize meetings, but everyone is feeling the effects of the terrible season, and I think everyone wants to get this shit figured out.

Five minutes later, my phone rings.

"Meeting is set for 12:30. Everyone has confirmed."

"Thank you. I'll see you in a little bit." I sigh as I end the call.

What a clusterfuck.

My phone dings, and my instinct is to just throw it at the fucking wall. But that would be irresponsible, so I take a deep breath before looking at what is undoubtedly something that will piss me off.

Instead, I get a pleasant surprise.

From: AB (wannabebosslady@genericmail.com)
To: FK (Swedish_Boss48@genericmail.com)

Subject: Needy girl

Hi. I know it's only been two days, but I'm not going to lie . . . I want to increase our . . . dinners.

Email me back if that's agreeable. Forget you ever saw this if it's not.

Slightly scared I just ruined some great orgasms for myself,

-T

Little does she know it would take a lot more than asking for me to ever be put off by her.

From: FK (Swedish_Boss48@genericmail.com)

To: AB (wannabebosslady@genericmail.com)

Subject: RE: Needy girl

Funny you should ask, as I was thinking the same thing. Can you get to Silverstone early?

And darling, don't be afraid to ask for what you want. There's a good chance I'll find a way to make it happen.

Just you wait to see what I can do to your body,

-F

The tension my last phone call ran through my body dissipates with one email. I'm not entirely sure what I'm doing with Antoinette, but I am sure I don't want it to stop.

She brings a levity to my life. I've never been anything other than serious, and she dismantles that in a split second. My phone notifies me of a new message, and I fumble to open it.

From: AB (wannabebosslady@genericmail.com)

To: FK (Swedish_Boss48@genericmail.com)

Subject: RE: RE: Needy girl

I can absolutely manage that. I'll send you the info when I have it.

I've never . . . I've never had a man care about what I want, so this is new.

Sounds like a challenge if ever I've heard one. What about what I can do to your body, F?

Game on,

-T

A minx is what she is. No, a siren. I'm weak against her charm and conversation.

I'm screwed if she ever realizes that I could see more with her. She'll drop me faster than a pitstop. What future does she have with an almost fifty-year-old with grown children? What can I really bring to her life that she can't manage on her own?

A crisis for another day because I already have one to take care of today.

***

"Summarize," I bark to start the meeting.

I'm done being patient. I've asked for more from them, and we've made zero progress.

Men take their turn telling me what they know as of today. Things they've tried as well as the piss-poor results that followed.

"Sir, we've had an engineer quit yesterday. Newman Fillom put in his immediate notice in order to take a job with Guardian," Rick tells me when it's his turn.

Newman . . . Newman. It sounds familiar. I give him a blank stare in response.

"He, umm, he's the one who talked about the front wing with you." Rick clears his throat.

Suddenly, things click into place.

"So, you're telling me I shut him down, and then a couple of weeks later, he magically has a job at Guardian and is leaving with no notice?" I ask pointedly.

"In a sense. He doesn't have a non-compete in his contract, but he did sign an NDA, so I wouldn't worry about him." His confidence does not leave me hopeful.

Every ounce of happiness that Antoinette injected into my veins with those emails is long gone. In its place are dread and irritation at my current situation.

"You had better hope he gives a shit about that NDA. It'll be your ass if I find out he's selling secrets. I'll take the legal fees out of your salary." I move on to the next person, barely hearing his update, but I act engaged nonetheless.

My phone dings, so I pull it out, hoping by some miracle it's the solution to all my problems.

It's not, but it's pretty damn close.

From: AB (wannabebosslady@genericmail.com)

To: FK (Swedish_Boss48@genericmail.com)

Subject: Rainy week

Just saw the forecast, and it's going to be rainy as fuck, so I rented a little place close-ish to the track. You and me, and not a hotel room we have to sneak into? Sounds like a recipe for multiple orgasms.

Can't want to show you my skills,

-T

The smile on my face has a mind of its own. It doesn't realize I'm in a meeting where serious shit is happening. No, it's reveling in this feeling that Antoinette gives me.

"Sir?" A throat clears, snapping my head up.

"I apologize. Repeat that."

Ignoring the looks of interest on everyone's faces, I push thoughts of Antoinette from my mind until I can be alone.

"I was just saying we saw minor improvement last race, so adjusting the anti-roll bar more in that direction should see us with more improvement."

"And any idea why this wasn't caught in development? This should have been an easy spot and adjustment. Why is it taking a whole fucking season to figure this out?" I ask.

"We're going back to check plans from the very beginning to see if we can pinpoint where things went astray…"

My phone alerts me once more as the man carries on. I don't even pretend that I'm not checking it.

From: AB (wannabebosslady@genericmail.com)
To: FK (Swedish_Boss48@genericmail.com)
Subject: RE: Second Thoughts
You know what? The rental was too much. I can cancel it. No worries. I should have checked with you first.
Still expecting multiple orgasms,
-T

Whoever made her feel like she didn't have control within her own relationship needs to have a date with my fits. And maybe my knees too. I can't leave her thinking I don't love the idea of seclusion with her.

From: FK (Swedish_Boss48@genericmail.com)
To: AB (wannabebosslady@genericmail.com)
Subject: RE: RE: Second Thoughts
I apologize; I'm in a meeting. Please don't cancel. The idea that I can make you scream my name without fear of being overheard is too damn good to pass up. Send me the bill please, and I'll meet you there tomorrow.
Think of a number, then double it—that's my orgasm goal for you,
-F

"Felix? Is it okay if we start working on this?" Rick says with an arched eyebrow. His eyes shoot to my phone in question, but I owe him no answers.

"Yes. Send me updates every four hours with progress please." I turn to leave and feel every single eye on me.

I never check my phone if I'm in an important meeting. I'll glance at it to make sure it isn't Steph or the kids, but I never openly ignore a meeting in order to read something else I just received.

But it's Antoinette.

I have zero common sense when it comes to that woman, and I know it's only a matter of time before it truly gets me into trouble.

From: AB (wannabebosslady@genericmail.com)
To: FK (Swedish_Boss48@genericmail.com)
Subject: RE: RE: RE: Second Thoughts
I will not be sending you the bill, but here's the address.
Seven,
-T

Antoinette Bailey is going to get me into more than trouble.
She's going to make me fall for her.

Chapter 21

Toni

Felix and I should rent a place at every race.

I'm curled up under the covers, with my eyes closed and a smile no one could take off my face. It's barely been twenty-four hours, and yet that orgasm count that Felix said he would be keeping track of is dangerously close to double digits. I feel wrung out in the best possible way, yet I still want more. Because we haven't actually had sex yet. Just mind-blowing foreplay and oral.

I'm starting to think there's a conscious reason behind that. I'm not complaining because the man gets it done, but in the back of my head, I wonder if it's something about me. Maybe he's holding me at arm's length still.

I crack my eyes as I hear him enter the bedroom. Mused hair, glasses askew, just joggers on, and he's never looked so sexy.

"You look happy," he says as he sets down the tea he made next to me.

"I am very happy. And relaxed," I tell him as I slowly sit up. The sheet drops to my waist as Felix freezes beside me.

"I swear this will be the only fucking time I ask, but can I get you a shirt? If I have to stare at those gorgeous breasts of yours, we will not be taking the break I so desperately need. I'm almost fifty; I don't have the stamina I used to." He blows out a steady stream of air, eyes still firmly on my exposed chest.

"Hmmm, I don't know. Your stamina seems pretty fine to me. What are you up to now? Nine?"

His smirk is devious. "Ten. You may have blacked out during that one with the vibrator."

God damn him and his sexual prowess. It's criminal how fucking good he is. And that's without any penetration from him!

"You're a fucking beast," I mutter as I reach down to the floor and pick up his T-shirt. It's tight around said breast, but it'll get the job done.

"I'm honestly not sure that helped my case." His eyes are still zero in on my nipples making themselves known through his Legacy T-shirt.

I smirk, grabbing my tea and taking a sip.

"So, how's work? Do you feel like you're able to delegate more?" He changes the subject, walking around to sit on his side of the bed.

"Mostly. I trust the engineers, and they've been good about communicating with me. Admin is . . . a mess." I sigh. "There are still a fair number of people who have a grievance with Sydney taking over things, so they like to take it out on me by ignoring requests or being petty about them."

"Does Sydney know?"

"No, and I'm not telling her. She has enough going on. I can handle it; I'm just tallying up the offenses so I can fire them."

"Viscous. Maybe you do fit into this world better than you think." He smiles over at me.

"It's just annoying. We're adults, and yet they act like teenagers throwing a tantrum for not getting their way. I mean, they all got raises this year. I'm not sure why they're pissed off."

"You gave them all raises, even though you didn't get money from the Constructors' Championship last season?" He arches an eyebrow.

"Yes. Unlike you, I reward hard work regardless of outcome," I snark before toning it down. "I just thought it would help with retention, and Sydney agreed."

"I get it. How's Alejandro doing?"

"Better, for the most part. He's been spending time with Nate—Nathan Murphy, Beck's old trainer—and Cruz—thanks for him, by the way—to work on things like reaction time and fitness. Nate's a godsend with the mental stuff too, so I think that's helping more than they're telling me."

"Maybe I need to poach him," Felix muses.

"Don't you dare! I will withhold orgasms from you!" I say.

"I don't need an orgasm to be happy, darling."

"I was talking about mine." My saccharine sweet smile makes him chuckle.

"You know me too well already." His words jolt both of us out of our playfulness, and I'm desperate to not dig deeper into that statement.

"How about you? How are Johnny and Pavel?"

"Annoyed, frustrated, pissed—take your pick. I do think we figured out what needed to be fixed, though."

"That's good," I murmur, taking another sip of tea.

"It's good and bad. It really shouldn't have been an issue from the beginning, so I'm not sure why it became an issue. They're adjusting the anti-roll bar's angle, and it seems to be helping. Now it's just narrowing down the angle, and we should be fine."

"Why wasn't that caught from day one? That's a very simple thing to look at, especially when dealing with balance problems. Your engineers should have picked up on it right away." I look up at him and see the barely concealed anger. "Sorry." I cringe.

"Nothing to be sorry about because you're right. I'm still trying to piece together why something so obvious was missed. Johnny's been telling them to check it for weeks."

"Hmm, any new engineers on the team? Maybe new graduates who don't know what they're looking for?"

"That would mean my team is completely inept at training someone new, as well as double-checking their work."

"It would," I concede. It's probably not that, but I can't imagine how frustrating it is to find such a simple solution to something that's derailed your entire season.

"We had an engineer up and quit two days ago. No notice, took a job at Guardian."

That makes me sit up.

"With Rocco?"

Felix nods like he knows where my train of thought is going.

"You think he's suspicious."

"I think he wanted more attention and more praise, which he wasn't going to get from me. Maybe he messed with things as a 'fuck you' before he left. Most engineers at least give the courtesy of notice and make sure the rest of the team is up to speed with what they are working on. This, plus the timing feels . . . odd."

"Does the rest of your team agree?"

"Haven't mentioned it."

"Why not?" I would have been knocking down doors, interviewing everyone about what they knew.

"Because if I'm wrong, I lose the trust of my entire engineering department. You motivate with money. I motivate with trust."

My inexperience feels like a monumental chasm talking to him about this. His approach and mine are complete opposites, yet I feel like I'm getting a master class from him on how to sustain this job.

"So, what's your plan?"

"Do nothing."

"Do nothing?" I can hear the outrage in my voice.

"What can I do, Antoinette? He's not my employee anymore. The team is tracing back to when the problem started, and if they find he's attached to it at all, they'll be more than happy to let Rocco know. If it comes from me, it looks petty. Like our little spats lately have been affecting me."

"What's the deal with you two anyways? I feel like there's more to the story."

"Very astute of you, Miss Bailey." He smiles over at me before sliding down the bed and pulling me to him. I curl up against his chest after I put my tea down as he continues. "We were both up for the Legacy job. We ran in the same circles, but I would never have called us friends. Friendly, maybe. He bombed his interview, and instead of owning up to that, he blames me for the fact that he didn't get the job."

"What an asshole."

"The biggest. He went downhill from there. Has hopped around the bottom-tier teams, but he's been with Guardian for a few years now."

His fingertips trace patterns on my back, lulling me into a daze.

"Tell me why you second-guess so many things between us," he says softly.

My body stiffens at the command. "I don't—"

"You do, and that's okay. I'm just trying to understand what led to that. If it was me, or your past, I just want to make you comfortable with . . . me." He sounds conflicted, like he was going to say something else.

I take a deep breath, willing my muscles to cooperate, and decide to lay it all out there. We've been doing this thing for a few months now; he should know about my past relationships.

"I was with my ex, Brad, for a long time. Six years. Before that, I had a string of very short-term boyfriends who never did anything for me, so they didn't go anywhere. Brad wiggled his way in. I saw his need for control as freedom at first. I didn't have to make decisions. I didn't have to think past my job, which was extremely taxing on me at the time. It felt like a relief." His whole hand now runs down my back. "I told you I had started to see things clearly before I got this job, but it was more than that. I was secluded. He was a classic narcissist with a mean streak a mile wide. Knew how to guilt trip me with the best of them, and I fell for it every time. He moved us away from everyone I knew, all my friends, and a job that I was doing well in. But he was the love of my life; he was supposed to know what was best for us and our future." Even as I say it, I can't keep the bitterness from my words.

"When did you realize?" Felix's voice is hoarse with restraint.

"About six months before Sydney offered me the interview. He had gotten worse. Wouldn't let me do anything without running it by him. He would demean me whenever I had something positive to say. The interview at Empress went well, and all he said was that there was no way I would get hired because I looked like a slob. I think his exact words were: 'You wouldn't fit into that high society world looking the way you do. You'd need to lose a bunch of weight and actually do your hair.' So yeah, that was . . . hard." I have to blink several times in rapid succession to stop the tears from falling.

"You said he was still bothering you," he grunts, gripping me tighter.

"I can't believe you remember that." My laughter is anything but happy.

"I remember everything about you, darling," he says softly, and I wish I could read into that statement more, but I know I can't. This is just for us to let loose—nothing more, nothing less.

"He finds excuses to stop by the house. I've had to change the locks a couple of times."

"What the fuck? Call the cops!"

"I have." I sigh, not really wanting to get into it but also needing to calm Felix down. "They say because there isn't proof of a physical threat that there's nothing they can do. I also can't nail down a restraining order for the same reason."

"This is how people get murdered. They aren't taken seriously when they have stalkers," he growls. I'd almost find it sexy if I didn't hear his words.

"He's not a murderer," I whisper, not sure I actually believe that. Brad may not kill, but I know he'd do bodily harm if pushed far enough.

"How do you know?" he explodes. "How do you know for sure? You don't. You need to get out of that house. Move, relocate, whatever."

"I don't need to do shit, and I won't have you telling me otherwise." I sit up, outraged.

"Shit, Toni, I'm sorry." He scrubs his face. It's his use of my nickname that really stops me in my tracks. "I just . . . How the fuck am I supposed to react to hearing you have a stalker?"

"I don't know, just listen? I'm barely home anymore as it is."

"That doesn't make it okay. There has to be a way to get him to leave you alone."

"I've looked into it all. Had my lawyer do the same." I collapse against the bed, exhausted at this turn of conversation.

"Hey," he murmurs, lying down beside me and cupping my cheek. "I'm sorry. I'm just worried about you. I can't— I don't want anything to happen to you."

"I know," I whisper. And I do, but things with Brad aren't something I want to dwell on anymore.

"Would it help if I told you about my relationship fuckups?"

"Maybe," I draw out.

"You already know that Steph and I separating was mutual, but we didn't tell anyone for a while. I honestly can't remember why, but it probably had to do with the media and the kids. Well, we weren't legally divorced yet but had been separated for quite a few months at that point, when I started seeing the communications director at Legacy."

"Oh shit."

"Oh shit is correct. Steph didn't care, obviously, but it also wasn't something we wanted to get out before we officially announced our divorce, especially for Emilie and Henrick. To no one's shock, it got leaked. I had to do major damage control at Legacy to keep my job as well as dealing with my kids now hating me because they thought I was cheating on their mom. Steph was the best through it all, but I still felt like a failure at all facets of my life."

So many things make sense now. Why he was so adamant we don't get close. His relationship with his kids, and how they seem completely fine with him, but he still struggles with them. Steph subtly hinted that there was a history that affected him deeply to this day.

"Who did it? I mean, did you ever find who leaked it to the press?"

"I did."

I have a bad feeling.

"She did—the woman I was dating. She didn't want to be in the shadows anymore. She got vindictive and wanted to hurt me when I tried to end it with her."

"Oh my God, I can't believe she did that," I gasp.

"So, this . . . chemistry between the two of us scared me. Still does, honestly. I won't survive a repeat. It's why I was hesitant to start anything in the first place."

"I feel like such an asshole for pushing you." If I had known, I would have stepped back. I wouldn't have pushed or caved—I can't remember who made the first move—no matter how strong the attraction to him was.

"No, that's not why . . ." He sighs. "That's not why I was telling you. I made a conscious decision to pursue you. I knew the stakes."

He presses his forehead to mine as I try to reconcile this new information.

"Nothing could have stopped me from coming for you. You have this hold, this power over me that defies any logic. I like you, Antoinette."

"I like you too." My eyes close, soaking in his words. "We still need to be cautious, though. If we decide to make things more . . . serious, then we can figure out all the HR bullshit. While we're still figuring things out, we need to keep things under wraps. I never want to put you in that position again."

"And that's why I jumped in with you. You are the kind of person who doesn't have a malicious bone in your body. You could never intentionally hurt anyone, let alone someone you care about. And Steph never liked Cierra. She made it very known that she didn't trust her. Steph has nothing but wonderful things to say about you. She actually asks me about you more than she asks about me."

"Your whole family is just so good," I murmur.

His lips press against mine. The kiss deepens for a minute before he pulls back.

"I want you to think about what I'm about to ask before you answer me." I nod before he continues. "I want to . . . I want to make a real attempt at a relationship here. With you. Not just getting together after races. Not just having dinner and orgasms. Not just emailing each other, although that's still probably the best way to keep things under wraps until we decide we're ready. I want to spend off-weeks with you and bring you coffee after late nights working. I want to rent little houses for every race so I can hear you scream my name without worry. What I'm asking is this: Antoinette Bailey, can we take this to the next level and label this thing between us? Can I call you my girlfriend?" He grimaces a little at the label, and I roll my lips to stop from laughing.

"You are very cute when you're flustered."

"Well, I wasn't exactly planning on this today," he mumbles. "And I'm forty-eight years old. Girlfriend just feels wrong."

"I'm thirty-five and, not going to lie, the title still makes me a little giddy."

"Then girlfriend you are. If you say yes," he quickly adds.

"I say yes." I smile.

"Then what do you say to spending summer break somewhere? Just the two of us, for two and half weeks." His eyes glitter with promise, and who I am to say no? It's only a few weeks away. Maybe then I can convince him to finally have sex with me. If he won't when we're officially together, then I really need to broach the subject.

"Sounds heavenly." I kiss him once more, knowing our time is coming to an end before work calls.

"If you have anywhere you'd really enjoy going, let me know. I'll plan everything."

He kisses me once more before looking at the time and sighing with realization.

"Duty calls," he says.

"It does, but I'm glad we did this."

"Me too, darling. Me too."

Chapter 22
(Transcript)

Interviewer: We've got a full house today. Thank you all for joining us. I wanted to start with some information that broke within the last few hours. Rocco, you hired on one of Legacy's former engineers, is that correct?

Rocco Bianchi: It is. Newman Fillom is the new race engineer for Malcolm Acheson.

Interviewer: So an ex-Legacy driver is getting an ex-Legacy engineer midway through the season. That's interesting.

Rocco Bianchi: Was there a question in there?

Interviewer: Just curious as to why Newman didn't come over with Malcolm. It's not a secret that Malcolm has been struggling; it would have been smart to help him keep consistency.

Rocco Bianchi: Why don't you ask Felix that question?

Interviewer: All right, Felix, anything to add?

Felix Karlsson: I never knew there was interest in Newman. If I had, I would have told him to go where he wanted to go.

Rocco Bianchi: That's a lie, and you know it.

Felix Karlsson: How is that a lie? Did I stop him from going over there now?

Rocco Bianchi: I know exactly what you would have done.

Felix Karlsson: Sounds like you're using a personal bias against me to cloud your professional one.

Rocco Bianchi: You're the one with car problems, not me.

Felix Karlsson: If I remember correctly, you've had four crashes in the last six races, no? I would be sure to focus on your own issues at the moment. What did you tell me last time? Oh, that's right. 'Focus on your own problems and fix your fucking car. Then we wouldn't need to hear you bitch every day.' It was quite a lovely sentiment, actually.

Rocco Bianchi: You slimy—

Toni Bailey: Boys, now, now, we're trying to have a nice conference here.

Interviewer: Yes, moving on to you, Toni, how are you feeling about the season? Seems like you're pretty unstoppable this year.

Toni Bailey: As I always say, the drivers are the reason we're doing so well; they should take all the praise. I'm just a talking head.

Rocco Bianchi: Yeah, we know that's all you're good for. Talking and what's between your legs.

Felix Karlsson: That is enough.

Interviewer: Rocco, that's inappropriate. We're done here. Toni, we apologize.

Toni Bailey: No harm done. Women in this industry and many others are used to the implication.

Felix Karlsson: Apologize. Right now. That's not how we speak to women.

Rocco Bianchi: Luckily, you aren't my daddy, Felix. I do apologize for getting off topic. I'll be sure to have Newman stop by and say hello.

Interviewer: Well, good luck to both you and Toni this weekend. We're looking forward to seeing Legacy and Empress battle.

Chapter 23
Toni

Rocco Bianchi is a grade A asshole who needs to be taught a lesson.

I don't care if he says that shit behind my back. I don't care if he says it to my face, honestly. What I do care about is saying it to a journalist who will have the soundbite and quote on every major website within minutes.

Where the fuck is his head at? To be that unprofessional in that setting is unforgivable. I swear Felix was about to knock him out.

A flicker of a conversation Felix and I had not too long ago, about Rocco having accusations thrown his way, rises to the surface. I don't think Felix told me anything in great detail, but it's enough of a hint that I should dig deeper.

Deep enough to bury Rocco.

If he thinks I'm going to take his words lying down, he has got it all wrong.

I only submit to one man, and he's earned the fucking right.

My phone goes off multiple times as I pace my office. I debate ignoring it, but it's probably Sydney.

Sydney:

Holy fucking shit I can't believe he said that.

Daisy:

What an absolute asshole. You okay, Toni?

A group chat, even better. At least I don't have to have the same conversation twice.

Me:

> Totally fine. Just shocked, honestly. What did he hope to gain from that?

Sydney:

> I don't know. You have time for appetizers and drinks? It's been a while since we've gotten to sit down and just talk.

Daisy:

> Oh! Luka and I found this cool little place down the street from the Vanstone that's perfect.

Me:

> Sounds great. Let me know what time, and I'll be there.

Thirty minutes later, I'm sitting at a table, waiting for Sydney and Daisy. Sydney was right; it's been a long while since we just got together and chatted. Usually, quick calls about work or emails take over our life, but these two are the closest things I have to friends currently.

"So, interesting thing just happened." Daisy sits down, Sydney right behind her.

"What?" I ask.

"Ran into one Felix Karlsson at the Vanstone, which I thought was odd because isn't he staying where everyone else is? Empress employees are the only ones at the Vanstone. But then he asked us if we'd seen you." Her smirk does nothing to hide her intentions with this line of conversation.

"Oh, well, I told him that's where I was headed because he wanted to check on me after that abysmal interview." I attempt to brush it off, but Sydney and Daisy eye each other.

"But you aren't staying at the Vanstone." Sydney arches an eyebrow. "And I heard through the grapevine that Felix wasn't staying with Legacy either."

Jesus, just call these two Mulder and Scully. I almost snort at my comparison but reel it in just in time.

"And, dear detectives, does he always stay with Legacy?" I smile back.

"Unless we're in Belgium, yes," Sydney says immediately. I forgot the two of them are actually friends.

"Well, that's some interesting information you have there."

"Come onnnnnnnnn," Daisy whines. "I watched the interview; it was so obvious."

"What was obvious?" I look between the two of them.

"That you two are together in some capacity. You should have seen the look on Felix's face when Rocco went off. I swear I've never seen the man show so much emotion. The second Rocco walked off, he turned to look at you with so much worry on his face. There's something there." Daisy points her finger at me.

I look to Sydney for help, but her smile is even bigger than Daisy's.

My mouth opens once, twice, then slams shut when I realize I can't tell them anything. We agreed to keep things between us until we were ready to tell people, if we actually stay together. Daisy and Sydney count as telling people.

Sydney seems to pick up on my dilemma. She reaches out for my hand, squeezing it. "Hey, you don't need to tell us anything. I'm sorry we pushed. Just know that neither of us will say anything to anyone . . . other than Beckett and Luka."

I do laugh at that one. At least they're honest.

"I appreciate that." I chose not to say anything else. I won't betray Felix's trust after what he's told me about his ex.

"Now, about the asshole," Daisy says after we order drinks.

Now this, I want to talk about. "I want to dig into him."

"Dig into Rocco? About what? Not that I'm not game," Sydney says, holding her hands up in front of her.

"F— Someone told me"—they smirk at my almost slip-up—"that he has a history of abusing his power, specifically with women."

Their smiles drop in a second. The server delivers our drinks, and Sydney orders the entire appetizers menu before we're alone again.

"How do we help?" Sydney asks.

"I, uh, honestly have no clue. I hadn't gotten that far. When he said that during the interview earlier, I remember . . . a person . . . talking about some allegations, and I just knew I couldn't let it go. His temper is getting the best of him, and he doesn't like seeing a woman at the top of the grid, beating not only him but every other team."

"So, do we wait him out and let him hang himself? Or are we being proactive?" Daisy bounces in her chair. It's so fucking good to see her back to this wild, unrestrained version of herself. Luka and she had a terrible time last year, but it seems like things have worked out. It helps that pregnancy looks phenomenal on her.

"Proactive," Sydney and I say at the same time.

"I'm not letting him hurt or target someone else if I can help it," I say.

"Agreed." Sydney nods.

"Okay. I can look into his job history and see if anything gets pulled up." Daisy taps her chin in thought.

"I can ask Pierce if he knows someone who can do some digging," Sydney says, speaking of her old boss and owner of Vanstone Properties.

"Oh my God, no. Pierce will think I'm on a wild goose chase instead of doing my job."

"Are you kidding me? I bet he jumps in full force because he's been bored lately. Both kids are in school now." Sydney smirks.

"Retirement not as fun as he thought it would be?" I ask.

"Oh, Jane's keeping him busy, I'm sure."

"Okay, we don't need to talk about Pierce's sex life," Daisy says with a disgusted look on her face.

"I'll discreetly ask around the garage and see if anyone knows anything," I tell the girls, redirecting our conversation back on topic.

"I'll do a social media sweep. He seems like a guy who would be stupid enough not to cover his tracks."

We all laugh in agreement at that.

Our food gets delivered, and the three of us dive in like we've been starved for days.

We're finishing up filling each other in on other life things, actively avoiding any work talk, when Sydney gets a serious expression on her face.

"I just want to say that we're so impressed and happy that you're on our team. You've stepped up to the plate more than I ever thought possible. You work more than I ever did, if that's even conceivable, and we've got your back no matter what. And if, say, you were to be interested in one silver fox, we would be thrilled for you. We'd also say if he hurts you, we'll break his leg."

I choke on my drink. "Jesus, why are you two so extreme?"

"Because people are highly put off by it and it's fun." Daisy shrugs.

I'm damn glad I'm on their good side.

"Seriously, though, you deserve some happiness after all the shit Douchebag put you through," Sydney says. "And the man we are definitely not talking about is a good man."

My throat closes at her words and support.

I clear it. "Well, on that note, I need to check in on things before heading back and trying to get some sleep."

"Sleep, sure!" Daisy calls out as I walk out of the restaurant.

It takes me one rideshare and fifteen minutes to get back to the little rental Felix and I have. I find him in the kitchen, squeezing some fresh orange juice.

"Well, aren't you fancy?" I say, kicking off my shoes.

"Hi." The smile he gives me could make me melt right through the floor. It's somehow so much *more*. Like he's not just happy to see me, but he's more at ease now that I'm back.

I've never had anyone look at me like that.

"Hi."

"Is it cheesy to say I missed you?"

"Absolutely cheesy, but I like it." I grin.

"Well, that's good. I assume you got some food with the lovely ladies of Empress?"

"I sure did. I got a sweet interrogation from them too." I walk up to him and wrap my arms around his middle.

"Yeah, didn't expect to run into them." He grimaces.

"It's all good. I neither confirmed nor denied anything, but they definitely know something's up."

"You can tell them. They're your friends," he says, looking down at me.

"I— We didn't walk about it, and I didn't want to overstep without talking about it with you first. Especially with your history."

He searches my eyes for a moment longer before he leans down and kisses me with everything he has.

"Thank you. That means . . . everything," he says once he's pulled away.

"I hate to be the Debbie downer, but I have to be up obscenely early tomorrow for practice, as I'm sure you do too, so I'm heading to bed early," I tell him.

"That's why I was making orange juice. I know we have catering, but coffee and orange juice, depending on my mood, is usually my go-to first thing in the morning as I get ready." He looks almost shy at his explanation.

"Well, thank you. I need coffee to barely be functional." We've never had a morning that wasn't filled with orgasms, so it'll be a first if we manage to actually have coffee before heading out to the track.

"Noted. You ready to crash?" he asks as I barely hold in a yawn.

"Very ready."

We spend the night wrapped in each other's arms, sleeping better than I have in years.

Chapter 24
Felix

This race is like night and day.

We altered the anti-roll bar again based on what we learned in practice and qualifiers, and it went well. We, at least, weren't back of the grid.

Then race day came.

Our turns look sharper. Our straightaways are immensely better.

We're halfway through the race, and both our drivers have gained places and are in the points. For the first time all year, we may actually be making progress.

But I'm also worried it's just an anomaly. All the cynicism really is doing wonders for me right now.

Rick talks to Johnny on the team radio, discussing our pitstop plan again, as my mind wanders to Antoinette.

Things feel . . . easy. Almost too easy if I'm being honest. This morning, we woke up, drank our coffee together as we got ready, stealing little touches and kisses. Then we left separately so as not to arise suspicion, and I fucking hated it. Hated that I couldn't hold her hand as we walked to the paddock together. Hated that we had to hide as if she's anything like Cierra, who was just looking for clout.

That's the thing about Antoinette: she doesn't need me.

It's more apparent by the day. She may have some baggage—hell, we all do—but she's capable, strong, and incredible as a team principal. She doesn't even see it.

"Felix?" My headset sounds, pulling me out of my head.

"Yeah?" I grunt.

"Safety car. We're pulling them both in for fresh soft tires then telling them both to go full out." Rick eyes me. He knows my head isn't completely here, and that's unacceptable.

"Perfect. No battling each other. No crashes," I state the obvious.

"Of course." He nods but doesn't turn away from me. "You okay?"

"Perfect. Just hoping the race stays the way it's going. We could use the metaphorical and literal win."

My gaze moves from the monitors to the pit wall two stalls down from us.

God, she looks gorgeous.

Her hair is up in some gorgeous updo that took her two minutes to do. Her royal purple button-up only highlights her skin tone.

The sounds of a successful pitstop fill my headphones, so I pull my attention away from Antoinette and look behind me at the crew. My eye catches on Rocco as I do.

His slimy smile penetrates my distracted haze enough to see Newman Fillom next to him, rubbing his hands together.

Rolling my eyes, I turn my attention back to my crew. Their dramatic villain act is exhausting and frankly, immature. Whatever Rocco did to lure Newman away, good for him. I don't want people like that on my team,

Ten laps to go.

I force myself to refocus. This is turning into an important race. A turning point, if you will. And thank fuck for that.

Ten laps go quickly. Sawyer and Empress are in the lead, but Johnny is sitting comfortably in second. Guardian somehow has the third spot, and my mind catches on that.

Sure, it's not unheard of for a bottom dweller to podium once in a while, but this seems . . . convenient. Guardian has consistently been struggling, and I can't see them magically picking up the pace in one race enough to podium. Get in the points? Sure, but not top three.

Cheers erupt around me, making me realize I've been trying to connect the dots for longer than necessary.

Final lap around brings Sawyer the win, Johnny second, and Matthew Guthrie from Guardian rounds out the top three. Pavel does well for us too, landing in seventh and getting points. It's a far cry from the last couple of months, and I couldn't be more relieved.

I just hope it keeps going.

The trophy ceremony is quick, as per usual, and I'm walking back to my office before the last spray of champagne flies.

"Fancy seeing you here," Sydney's voice calls out a couple of feet away from me.

"Hey there, stranger. How are you feeling?" I ask, knowing her rheumatoid arthritis has been acting up lately.

"Better. Adjusted my meds, and it's miles better than a month ago, thank God." She falls into line next to me as we walk.

"That's great to hear."

"Thanks. So, listen, I'm glad I caught you and was wondering if you had time to grab a bite to eat once you finish up for the day."

"I have a lot of work to catch up on," I mumble. It's not that I don't want to have dinner with my friend; it's that I'd rather take advantage of the last night Antoinette and I have together for a while.

"Oh, I'm sure you do." She smirks.

Well shit, I forgot about her and Daisy grilling Antoinette about us.

"I promise to make it quick. You can always play catch-up on the plane or during the week."

"I can't say no to my favorite protégé."

Her snort of laughter makes me smile.

"Give me ten minutes, and I'll be ready."

"I'll text you the place."

Twenty minutes later, I'm pulling up to a little hole-in-the-wall tapas place. I left an email for my assistant and a note for Antoinette on the kitchen counter of the rental.

"Tell me how things are going," I say as soon as I sit down.

"So good. Honestly, Toni's been incredible, and the team has really rallied behind her approach. Beckett and I have been able to actually relax and spend time recreationally traveling."

"That's wonderful, really. I'm happy you both are able to enjoy some free time."

"And what about you? Any fun things happening in your free time?" An arched eyebrow tells me everything I need to know.

"What free time?" I deadpan.

"It's what you should have, considering the career you've made for yourself. It seems like you're working harder than ever this year." She decides to bypass anything regarding Antoinette and me, but it's at the expense of something else I'm not sure I want to talk about. "It's been a hard year. Things haven't been going our way." The food she ordered before I arrived shows up, and we start picking at it.

"Today went well, though."

"It did." I sigh. "Finally."

"What changed?" She's the only person who could ask me car specific questions like this and I wouldn't immediately think she's up to something nefarious. Well, she and Antoinette.

"No clue. Our balance has been shit. The anti-roll bar has been getting tweaked for a few weeks now, and this is the first time it has worked. Which doesn't make sense, considering it *should* be an easy adjustment."

"Suspicious of anyone?"

Somehow, this woman who didn't grow up in this sport, who had a team fall into her lap, knows more than most in the field. She picks up on the littlest things and hits the nail on the head.

"Sort of, although I'm not entirely sure how he would have accomplished the sabotage."

"Want to talk it out?"

I look at her; she's completely open to listening and being a friend, not a colleague.

"What the hell," I concede. "We had an engineer quit with no notice and immediately take a job at Guardian."

"Not uncommon in this sport."

"No, but giving no notice, combined with him attempting to get us to change our front wing even though we've had no problems with it, has my hackles raised."

"And then Guardian podiumed," she muses.

"Exactly."

We sit in silence, the only sound our forks clinking on the plates as we scoop food into our mouths, while she mulls over the information I just gave her.

"I mean, it would be stupid as shit for him to leave, join another team, help the other team by sharing all from things he's learned-slash-stolen from Legacy." I nod as she works through it. "But it's not impossible."

"But what does he have to gain from it?" I ask.

"A promotion is most likely. Was it Newman Fillom?"

"I swear you are scary sometimes. How do you figure this shit out?"

"Well, the process of elimination is pretty easy to work through. He's the only one hired at Guardian recently, and he kept staring daggers at you on the pit wall. Seemed like a good guess."

"Doing something like that, though, his reputation and hope for a long career in Formula 1 would be shot. I just don't see someone attempting to sabotage at this level." I've seen a lot in this sport, but never someone actively stealing and sabotaging a team.

"Doesn't mean it can't happen. Desperate people do desperate things."

Her words frighten me more than anything. Up until this point, I thought it was maybe incompetence. Maybe a fuck-up on someone's part. Hell, I was hoping it was, but now? I have to look at it from all angles, and right now, it sure as hell seems like Newman had a hand in this clusterfuck.

"Speaking of desperate people, how are things with Toni?"

"How is that a segway? Who's desperate?" I chuckle.

"Well, judging by the looks you both give each other, I'd say the two of you are. Now, Toni didn't tell me or Daisy anything, so I don't expect you to because despite your asshole exterior, you are a gentleman through and through."

"Thanks, I suppose."

"But I do want to say, don't fuck around with her if you don't see it going anywhere. She's been through too much to go through that."

"Is this a big sister warning?" I smirk, not only giving away that there's something going on between the two of us but also hinting at the seriousness.

"This is a friendly warning. For both of you, honestly. You both have been through enough shit with romantic partners. If you add in the complication of your jobs, this isn't the easiest road to take with a relationship. I just want to make sure *both* of my friends don't get hurt."

I stare at her for a beat before doing something reckless.

"It's serious. For me, it's serious." The words are barely over a whisper. Confiding in someone other than Steph feels like progress, though. Navigating this thing between Antoinette and me, when we have the jobs we have, is hard enough. Maybe bringing someone into the fray as a person to bounce things off of isn't such a bad idea.

"I can tell." Sydney smiles over at me. "They showed you on the broadcast today randomly, and your attention wasn't on your team. No one would have put two and two together because you couldn't see Toni, but I knew."

"I don't want to mess this up, but the last relationship I had wasn't ideal. I mean, private things getting leaked to the press and a backstabbing girlfriend isn't ideal, not to mention the isolation from my kids." I try to make light of it, but it's a real fear for me.

"Toni isn't like that, and you know that, otherwise you wouldn't have risked anything for her."

"I know."

"Have you told Steph?"

"She figured things out, much like you have."

"And that's why I love her." She smiles wistfully.

"And why the two of you are never in the same room with me. I can't handle the two of you," I gripe.

"Well, I know you want to get back to a certain someone, but I just wanted to talk to you about it. It's been a while since we just sat down over some food."

"It has. We shouldn't let it go this long again." Despite my outward annoyance, Sydney is one of my best friends. She stood up to me for Beckett, and I knew she was one of the few people who would see through the dickhead layer.

"We shouldn't. I'll let you know which races I plan on coming to, and we can do lunch between practices." She smiles as she stands up. "Bill's paid. Enjoy the rest of your weekend."

"Next one's on me!" I call as she leaves, waving a hand over her shoulder so I know she heard me.

Well, two things I didn't expect to happen today: Thinking there's someone sabotaging my team and telling one of my closest friend about a relationship Antoinette and I just agreed to.

But the time for overanalyzing both situations is over. Now, it's time to head back to my woman before we have to endure at least a week without each other.

Chapter 25

Toni

Belgium is one of my favorite races. It's not overly hyped up, the crowd is always a good time, and it feels like a low-pressure race.

As I look out the floor-to-ceiling window in my hotel room, I pull out my phone and open up a new email.

From: AB (wannabebosslady@genericmail.com)
To: FK (Swedish_Boss48@genericmail.com)
Subject: Bored
I think I liked our arrangements last race over this one. After that cute little rental, this hotel room just feels . . . stifling and sterile.
Do you have media today?
Maybe our race weekends should look a bit different,
-T

Only one more race after this until summer break and extended time with the man I'm rapidly falling for. I just need more *time*. With our schedule and responsibilities, it's hard for us to get a lot of time together. I can't let go of everything holding me back until we have more time together. But man, no matter how idiotic it is, I *want* to fall for him.

From: FK (Swedish_Boss48@genericmail.com)
To: AB (wannabebosslady@genericmail.com)
Subject: RE: Bored

Maybe we should look into making it a thing. And yes, unfortunately, they have me scheduled with R and someone from Amaro—they haven't confirmed who yet. So, if you get a message after about how I want to wring his neck, I apologize now.

Sign me up,

-F

From: AB (wannabebosslady@genericmail.com)

   To: FK (Swedish_Boss48@genericmail.com)

   Subject: RE: RE: Bored

   Glad I won't be there. Shall I look for a place in Hungary?

   I swear if he pulls what he did in the last media conference, the owners of Guardian are going to fire him. There's no way they want that kind of publicity surrounding them.

   Miss you,

   -T

Everything feels too good to be true right now. Between holding the lead for not only the Drivers' Championship but the Constructors' as well, and this relationship with Felix, life seems too positive. That may just be me and my trauma, but I know life doesn't stay like this. There's no way one person can have all that good in their life.

Sydney does. Daisy too.

But they deserve it. They both went through so much to get where they are that they merit all the happiness they sacrificed for.

I don't think I am that lucky. But I'm going to hold on with both hands for as long as possible.

   From: FK (Swedish_Boss48@genericmail.com)

   To: AB (wannabebosslady@genericmail.com)

   Subject: RE: RE: RE: Bored

I can't in Hungary. The owners will be in town, and I have to wine and dine them. I apologize, but Zandvoort for sure. Any thoughts as to where you want to go for summer break?

I think I miss you more,

-F

That little bit of self-doubt rears its ugly head again.

What if this is his way of slowly distancing himself? What if he doesn't really want a girlfriend and that's why he doesn't want to stay together in Hungary?

Nope. I'm not doing this. I'm not going to analyze everything to death when he gave me a perfectly good explanation.

I think some people call this growth.

It sucks, and I hate it.

Another message pings, interrupting my tumultuous thoughts.

From: FK (Swedish_Boss48@genericmail.com)

To: AB (wannabebosslady@genericmail.com)

Subject: RE: RE: RE: RE: Bored

No, I know I miss you more. I'm sorry I've been so busy the last week and will continue to be until the owners get their fill of my time. We can do a house; I'm just not sure how much time I'll actually get there. I wish I could just come back to a little house after this media conference and kiss you. Show you how much I love those little freckles on your nose and cheeks. I also had a thought about summer break. I know Sydney can get us a room as long as it's a Vanstone, so what do you think about somewhere different, like Croatia?

The man who wishes he could call out and show you how much he misses you,

-F

My heart skips a beat. It's like he subconsciously knew I was second-guessing everything. The need to be discreet is like being in a long-distance relationship but the other person is only feet away from you most of the time. It's strange and hard to navigate.

From: AB (wannabebosslady@genericmail.com)
To: FK (Swedish_Boss48@genericmail.com)
Subject: Thank you
Croatia sounds amazing. I've never been. The only places I've travelled to have been for work, so a true vacation will be wonderful.
Thank you.
You somehow know when I'm too in my head. You know exactly when to reassure me and how to cast my doubts aside. I don't know how you do it.
I'll handle Hungary if you handle Croatia.
Beyond smitten and grateful,
-T

From: FK (Swedish_Boss48@genericmail.com)
To: AB (wannabebosslady@genericmail.com)
Subject: RE: Thank you
You're my girlfriend, so no thanks needed.
I'll see you soon,
-F

***

The hustle and bustle before qualifiers are always stressful. It's not like we're able to change huge things between practice and now, but everything feels like it's dire straits.

I haven't seen Felix except from the paddock and pit wall, so that's making me edgy as well.

Sawyer's chief engineer, Mason, sidles up next to me as I walk to the pit wall.

"Everything's looking good. Sawyer's happy with the new additions, so we'll see how it performs."

"Good. Alejandro?"

"I was told he's much happier in the car with the last two major changes. He's actually excited for qualifiers."

Well, thank fuck for that. It's not that he's been doing terrible. It's just that the discrepancy between Sawyer and Alejandro is large, and he's getting a ton of flack about it.

"Good. Let's hope we can kick some ass and shut some people up today."

He smirks at me as I take my seat. I'm zeroed in and ready to shove a pole position in Rocco's face since he yet again brought me up in his interview pre-practice. I'm not sure what I did to piss him off, but if he wants something to be pissed at me for, I'll give it to him.

Pole position, shutting him out of the points, and crushing Guardian in the Constructors' feels pretty apt.

Like clockwork this season, qualifiers go great. Sawyer gets pole position, and Alejandro even manages third. I don't take for granted how well Sawyer's doing, but it is nice to needle Rocco every time he does well.

I'm walking back behind the paddock to the offices of Empress when a body slams into mine.

"Hi! Sorry, I didn't mean to run into you that hard." I look down at Emilie's eager yet apologetic face.

"No harm done. How are you?" I ask with genuine curiosity. She's emailed me a couple of times with "must have pieces" for my wardrobe, so of course I bought them immediately.

"Good! Move is getting closer, but I'm excited."

"Emilie, my God, girlie, give the woman a break." Steph breaks through the crowd, huffing for breath.

"She's fine." I smile at Steph.

"I apologized!" Emilie huffs in annoyance as she turns to her mother.

"All right, drama, calm it down." Steph leans in to give me a hug. "How are you?"

"Good! Busy, the usual, you know."

"Still on for lunch?" She tilts her head in question.

"Of course!" I gasp, trying to act like I didn't completely forget even though it's on my calendar.

"You forgot, didn't you?" Steph says with no malice.

"I may have slightly forgotten, but it's on my calendar so no one scheduled anything." I cringe.

Steph laughs. "No worries. Felix gets the same way. You guys have too much on your plates, I swear."

"Possibly. Let me just stop by the office, and I can meet you by the exit?"

"Sounds good. I have to find Henrik anyway."

I grab my purse from my office and make sure things are cleared with my assistant before heading back out to find the Karlssons. As I approach them, I recognize a familiar figure added to the bunch.

"Toni! We rounded up Felix too. Hope that's okay," Steph says when I walk up.

"Totally." How awkward can it be? The man I'm dating and haven't seen in a week and a half, with his ex-wife and adult kids at lunch.

Yep, not awkward at all.

Felix looks down at me with a fond smile on his face, but there's anxiety there too. I know he struggles with his kids, but maybe my presence will help to ease the tension.

Emilie talks a mile a minute, and Henrik struggles to get in even a word when he can the whole way to the restaurant.

It would be comical if the big warning in my head wasn't saying this is too much, too fast.

It's been, what? Five months? Not even a full five months because we didn't start the . . . flirting until after the season had started.

It's too soon to be having lunch with my new boyfriend's ex-wife and kids.

We order in between Steph updating Felix on things while I sit here feeling like a third wheel.

Until Emilie starts talking to me.

"Be honest, did you like the stuff I sent you?" she asks in earnest. It's hard to remember she's only eighteen most of the time. She's so confident and aware of herself. She knows exactly who she is and what she wants to do with her life, and it's jarring for someone like me who, a year and a half ago, completely started her life over at the ripe old age of thirty-three.

"I absolutely loved it! Bought them all immediately. If I had remembered we had lunch scheduled, I would have surprised you with them."

"Oh my gosh, I'm so glad. I have about a million more, but Mom said I needed to pace myself and not overwhelm you."

"I appreciate her insight." I laugh. "But you can send me as many as you want. I can't promise I'll get to them all in a timely manner, but I will look at them all," I promise her.

If the hearts in her eyes are anything to go by, that was the right response.

"So, Henrik, you graduated, yes?" I ask, trying to remember his timeline.

"I did, a few weeks ago. Into the rat race I go." He chuckles, so like his father it's almost eerie.

"I wish I could say it'll be great, but sometimes companies aren't all you hoped they'd be. But you've got a good head on your shoulders and will navigate it all well."

He doesn't say anything, but the sudden silence around the table makes me look around.

Steph is staring at me like I'm a rock star making her presence known to her fans. Felix looks at me like I hung the damn moon, and the kids look like they've orchestrated the whole thing.

"I, umm . . ." I trail off, unsure of how to react to the attention.

"So, what are your plans for summer break?" Steph asks me. I'm not sure that's a better direction for conversation, honestly.

"Umm." Perpetually being unsure of myself is an old habit I fall back to when I'm uncomfortable. I don't know how much Felix has told Steph. I don't know if he's even told his kids about us, and I'm sure as hell not going to be the one to break that news to anyone.

"Antoinette told me she's actually taking a vacation this year." Felix smiles at me, his words a lifeline.

"Yep, vacation." I clear my throat. "Sydney has the Vanstone hook-up, so she's forcing me to take a vacation. Something about an Empress tradition, but I have no clue what she's talking about." That much is true at least. She said forced vacations are an ongoing joke within their circle of friends.

"Oh, that'll be nice. I swear I try to get this one to take an actual vacation during break, but the most I can get out of him is being in one place for two weeks." Steph points her thumb at her ex-husband.

"When we were little, Mom used to plan huge trips for us. We'd get time off of school, and Dad would come . . ." Henrik trails off.

"I remember when we went to Disney World in Japan," Emilie chimes in.

I look over at Felix with a small smile on my face. A glimpse into the life he used to have and that he's actively working on is something I didn't know I needed.

"I've seen pictures of that one. It looks amazing," I tell Emilie.

"It was! Probably my favorite trip ever."

"And my least favorite," Henrik grumbles. Felix grins at his mini-me.

"Maybe we should think about doing another trip. For old times' sake," Steph says with a smile, but her face falls and her eyes widen in horror like she realizes she messed up.

Not that I think she's messed up. They're technically a family, always will be. If Felix wants to ditch our agreed-upon vacation to spend more quality time with his kids, then who am I to stop him? I'll never be the woman who gives him a hard time about that.

Working on his relationship with Emilie and Henrik is important to him.

"You should go this year. Make it a last hurrah before Emilie moves and Henrik starts working his life away."

The second I suggest it, I know it was the wrong move.

"Absolutely not," Felix says with authority.

Emilie looks crushed, and Henrik just looks disappointed. Steph cringes, and I wince at creating this huge wedge between them.

"Forget I even—"

"Kids, I have something I want to talk to you about. I was going to wait, but I think this might be the best time," Felix cuts me off. I suddenly feel like I should be anywhere but encroaching on their family discussion.

Steph stops me from standing up with a hand on my arm. She shoots a wink my way, a smile on her face, and I'm not sure why she's feeling good about any of this.

"It's fine if you don't want to do anything," Emilie snips.

"Emilie Maddox Karlsson, give your father a minute to actually talk to you," Steph chides her daughter.

"What I'm trying to say is that I can't go on a summer trip with you guys because I'm already going with someone else."

I gasp at the turn in conversation. I didn't realize he'd be telling them so soon *and* with me present.

"Who?" Herik asks with a smirk before his eyes dart to me.

Well, at least one kid isn't oblivious to everything. He'll do great in the corporate world.

"Antoinette," Felix simply says.

Emilie's gasp forces my eyes away from Felix. She's staring at me with such hope, such excitement, that I know I'm seeing things.

"About time," Henrik mumbles with a smile.

"Don't act like you had a clue." Felix scoffs at his son.

"Oh please. Any time any of us bring her up, you look like a lovesick puppy."

Steph's laughter fills the entire dining room. Luckily, it's mostly empty thanks to race weekend.

"I feel like I shouldn't be here for this," I whisper.

Emilie gets out of her chair, walks over to me, and wraps me in a hug. "I'm super excited about this. Are you actually dating? Or is this super new and we just blew your cover?"

"Both, actually," I squeak out as she tightens her hold.

"Em, ease up," Felix says as he takes his glasses off and rubs the bridge of his nose.

"Oh no. Dad's annoyed."

"Just because I take my glasses off does not mean I'm annoyed," Felix grumbles. Everyone at the table, except me, laughs like he told the funniest joke ever.

"Okay, now that cat's out of the bag, what about a compromise?" I deflect. "What if you guys take a week to go on a trip, and then the second week, Felix and I can do what we had planned?" I offer. I really do think a family trip like old times will make old hurts disappear. They already act like it's water under the bridge, but maybe Felix needs this to see that his kids don't hate him. That they are actually really supportive of him.

"We had plans . . ." Felix murmurs to me.

"I know we did. And we can still have them, but next year you won't get this time. They will both be too busy."

I feel Steph's hand intertwine with mine, making me look over at her. Her eyes are filled with tears as she mouths, *Thank you*, to me.

I don't feel like I've done anything. Just suggested to a family, who needs time together more than most, the gift of actual time together.

"So, we're doing this?" Emilie asks with excitement.

"I guess we are. Where to?" Felix asks.

His smile is blinding, brighter than I've ever seen it, his eyes a little misty, but he quickly blinks it away.

I couldn't stop my heart from falling now, even if I wanted to.

Chapter 26

Felix

As I board the private plane to Isola d'Elba, I can't help but feel like there's someone missing.

Steph and I decided something relatively close would allow for the best use of time, so we settled on a little island off the coast of Italy.

But I wish Antoinette was here.

I didn't expect to tell my kids about us at that lunch a couple of weeks ago, but I didn't stop to think before I opened my mouth. I'm not upset at the turn of events, though.

If anything, I'm more grateful than ever.

It allowed me to see just how fucking amazing my woman is. She not only got along with my family but immediately suggested cutting our time in half.

Steph and I talked after. Antoinette was right. We're losing time with our kids, and this could be the last time we go on a family vacation like this. The one thing that Steph said that's been on my mind on repeat? Don't fuck it up with Toni.

Not because she fits in well. Not because Steph or the kids like her. No, because she put my relationship with my kids before anything else. Even more so than I did.

I owe her a lot.

An epiphany it's taken me almost eight years to have.

Stubbornness is a Karlsson trait after all.

"You're daydreaming again," Steph says as I take my seat next to her.

"I do no such thing," I quip back.

"It's cute, almost like you're a teenager again." She smiles over at me with a sparkle in her eye.

"You always were a romantic." It was part of the reason we couldn't stay together. She wanted hearts and flowers, and I just didn't have that in me.

"You like to say you aren't, but I'm calling it right now: Toni will dig in deep, and before you know it, you'll be buying her flowers and little gifts just because. Making time for her in your busy schedule because you just have to see her."

She smiles at me, but there's a pang in my heart at her words.

"I'm sorry I couldn't—didn't—do any of that for you."

"None of that." She waves her hand at me. "I didn't say that to make you feel guilty over our relationship. I said that because I always knew that, one day, a woman would come around and knock you on your ass. Change everything you knew about yourself and turn you into a lovesick sap."

"And you believe Antoinette is that woman?" I try to inflict boredom in my tone, but the grin on Steph's face means I failed.

"If the shoe fits."

"All right, enough talk about your love lives. We're going to Italy!" Emilie says with a squeal as she settles in on the other side of the table. Henrik joins but doesn't say anything.

"Just your father's love life." Steph winks.

"Well then, we should even it up and talk about yours," Henrik adds with a mischievous grin.

"Nope. This is a family trip, and we're keeping it to just that. No more talk of other partners for the time being." Steph immediately shifts the direction of conversation.

Well, that is interesting. Maybe things are more serious with her mystery man.

The short, roughly three-hour flight is occupied by card games and reminiscing about other trips we've made as a family.

There's no animosity, no talk about what happened seven years ago when we divorced, just enjoying each other's company.

It's freeing in a way. Cathartic to my insecurities and healing a part of myself I thought was a lost cause.

By the time we land, laughter is the only sound on the plane.

A little under an hour later, we're touring the house we rented that overlooks the water.

"Oh my God!" Emilie squeals like only a teenage girl can. "Hen, take a picture for my socials." She slams her phone into his chest as he rolls his eyes at her. But like the dutiful brother that he is, he takes multiple shots and angles.

"This is gorgeous, Fee," Steph says as we stand on the patio.

"Thank you."

"For what?"

"For agreeing to do this one last time. For making sure the kids didn't hate me while I figured my shit out, even though they should hate me."

"Felix, they never hated you. They were just trying to understand things as children. No child expects their parents to split, especially on great terms like we did. Hell, even adults don't understand us, so it's understandable it took Hen and Em a minute to comprehend."

"But I stayed away. Barely came back to Belgium to be in their lives."

"But you still did. You called them all the time, no matter how awkward. You supported them behind the scenes and always will. Don't discount what you did do just because you're hung up on what you didn't do."

"Is this you psychoanalyzing me?" I smirk at her.

"Hell no. I don't want inside that head any more than you do." She snorts.

"So, tell me more about this relationship of yours." I attempt to catch her off guard.

"Good try, Fee, but not happening." She walks off, leaving me shaking my head.

***

Two more days on this gorgeous island.

Two more days until I get to fly to Croatia to be with Antoinette.

I'm both ecstatic and melancholic.

This week with Stephanie and the kids has fueled me in a way I wasn't expecting. We've been sightseeing, we've relaxed on the beach, and we've talked.

There's been so much talking I thought the kids would get sick of it, but they've been open and receptive to it all.

It's like I get a second go in life, not stuck thinking my kids hate me and that I'm failing at my career.

My outlook on *everything* has changed.

Steph and I are currently sitting under a huge umbrella while the kids swim in the ocean.

"His name's Kade. He owns a restaurant a few blocks from the house."

Startled, I turn to look at her.

"I turned him down ten times before I finally agreed to a date."

"Why?" My eyes bug out at the shock of her saying no ten times.

"Because I wasn't sure how the kids would react. I wasn't sure if I even wanted to go through that again." She pauses. "Because I was scared."

"But you said yes to a date?"

"I said yes to sitting in his restaurant while he worked and stopped by to talk to me when he could."

A bark of laughter comes from me. "You're cruel."

She smirks, but it's softer than usual. "He closed the restaurant down."

"Good man."

"One of the best. He continually forces me out of my comfort zone. Pushes me to not stay safe in my own little world." Her words pierce my brain.

"That's what Antoinette does for me. She doesn't even realize she does it, though."

"I think we've been hung up in this fallacy that just because you and I didn't work out another relationship won't. I mean, for God's sake, we're not that old!" she says in outrage, but not to me—to herself. She's probably told herself many times that she's too old to find love, which is ridiculous.

"You've got an incredible career that you've worked your ass off for, great kids, and a mostly non-shitty ex-husband. You're a catch, Steph; he'd be stupid to not see it."

"You aren't shitty at all, just wildly stubborn. And yeah, Kade made me see that more. He never pushes me more than I can handle, but he also doesn't let me get away with pulling away from the hard stuff."

"I think I told Antoinette about Cierra within a month of our 'arrangement'."

"Woah, she might be better than Kade at that, then." She smiles at me. "I'm so damn happy you found her. I don't know the circumstances that put you in the position to date a colleague, but whatever it was, I'm glad."

"But what if the same thing happens? What if it all falls apart simply because of our jobs and how high profile it all is?" I ask her.

"Can I ask you a question?"

"Always."

"Can you see your life without her in it? If you look toward the future, what do you see?"

"Antoinette. Every single time. I see us sneaking off during race weekends. I see us renting places for every race weekend so we can still have what precious little time we get together. I see us vacationing on summer break every year. But I'm also scared I'm holding her back."

"How so?"

"She's just starting in her career. Hell, I could leave tomorrow and feel like I've done a lifetime of work."

"But you won't because you won't go out the way the team is right now."

"I won't, but the idea is still there. She has years in this career ahead of her; I'm coming to the end of mine. Where does that leave us?"

"With you having lots of time on your hands to follow her around like a puppy dog."

"Be serious." I scoff.

"I am serious! I mean, money isn't an issue for you. If you want something to do, help her be the best fucking team principal out there. She's the first woman in the job, but she won't be the last. Make it so others coming up can aspire to dethrone the normal hierarchy in Formula 1 because she showed them they can. The sport will be all the better for it. She's the perfect person to throw weight behind too because she doesn't want it. She doesn't want the recognition, doesn't want the clout. She just wants to do a good job. Her ego doesn't get in the way of the right move, just like yours not so long ago. You're the best for a reason, so why not pass the torch to someone you actually give a shit about?"

"That's how this whole thing started. I told her I would mentor her because she couldn't stop working, couldn't figure out how to have a life and the job at the same time," I mumble, not wanting to give Steph the satisfaction of yet again picking up on things only she can.

"God, I love it when I'm on the right track." She sighs happily and leans back. "When I saw Emilie's reaction to her, and then when she actually got to talk to Toni? I knew that Toni had the power to impact things in Formula 1 on a much larger scale. She's such a damn good person too."

"She is." This vacation with my family is showing me exactly how good she is. The kids have brought her up more than once; Emilie practically drools over her as a role model.

All roads lead to Antoinette, and now it seems I have bigger decisions to make.

"Kade and I are getting serious. We've discussed marriage and if that's something either of us would ever like to do again, but also know that I plan to be with him forever, even if we don't get that piece of paper. I think it's time for both of us to find our happiness."

"I think you may be right."

My mind is going a mile a minute with ideas and plans. I've held back with Antoinette, not just mentally but physically as well, and I think the Croatia trip is the perfect time to let it all go and fully choose her. I didn't even realize I was doing it, to be honest, but this trip has opened my eyes.

She's more than worth the risk, and if worse comes to worst, retirement doesn't sound all that awful.

Chapter 27
Toni

Am I having a panic attack? Maybe.

I do know I can barely catch my breath when I look up at the place Felix found to rent on this gorgeous oasis in Croatia.

We're spending a week here, less than we ultimately planned for, but the only time we're taking off falls under the mandatory two weeks where all of F1 can't work. We could spend a couple more days here, but there's always work to be done, and we can't play hooky even if we wanted to. Too many people rely on us.

"Felix . . ." I trail off as I spin around to face him.

He's got a shit-eating grin on his face because being humble is not in his nature. "It's terrible, isn't it?"

"The worst. I don't know how you found a place so crappy," I deadpan right back to him. "Seriously, this is too much." I switch back to how I'm really feeling.

"You said you haven't travelled much outside of work. I wanted to do it right."

"Right you did, indeed. This is like a mansion. We won't even be able to spend time in all of the rooms."

"We will if I have a say in things." His dangerous smirk kicks up my heart rate.

We still haven't had sex. And while I don't hate everything else he does to earn those orgasms, I'm starting to feel like there's something wrong with me, with us. I know I just need to talk to him about this week and see where things stand, but I'm a chickenshit and I'm not sure I'm ready to hear the truth.

"Mm-hmm, I'll believe it when I see it."

His smile drops as he takes two steps toward me and cups my cheek. "There are . . . reasons I've held that part back with us." *Guess we're doing this now since he's a mind reader.* "They have nothing to do with you. I want you so fucking bad I can barely stand it."

"Then why?" I whisper.

"Because I don't just have sex, darling. It means something to me. I haven't had sex in seven years. Oral? Sure. Other forms of foreplay? Absolutely. But it's been a long time since I've done anything more. I equate sex to how far I've fallen, if I can see a future together. I hold that part of me back as a failsafe. If I'm able to protect myself in some small way, maybe I can make it out intact."

"That's . . . depressing." Mostly because he doesn't see a future with me yet; meanwhile I'm hook, line, and sinker for this man.

"In all honesty, it is. But I also haven't been seriously looking for someone to share my life with, so it's never been an issue."

"Do I make it an issue?" My voice is so small; I'm scared to hear the answer.

"You make it a big fucking issue. I don't want you to think it's because of you. It's never been because of you. It's because I am honestly not sure how to do relationships anymore. It's been a long time for me, and I never intended for us to turn into anything."

I wince at his words.

"Hey, I know that sounds awful but hear me out. I couldn't stay away from you, couldn't step back and just be a friend. I was doomed from the start. You had your hooks in me, and I was helpless to resist them. You make me want to be reckless, and that's not who I am."

"So, am I making you regret things?" I ask, my mind running a million miles at his words.

"No! God no, I'm fucking this all up. Come here." His hand grabs mine, and he pulls me down the long hall to the main suite.

He sits on the edge of the bed and drags me onto his lap so I'm straddling him.

"You, Antoinette Bailey, came out of nowhere. I wasn't prepared for you. I still don't think I am. But I'm just a simple man with you, born to serve your every whim and take you places you've never been before. This is a lot in a short amount of time, but I need you to know that I not only see a future with you, but I see *everything* with you."

Well shit, how am I supposed to respond to that declaration?

"What happened in Italy?" I blurt out because my mind can't catch up to his words. Sure, we've said we're in this, but this feels bigger—life-changing huge, honestly.

He chuckles, gripping my jaw. "I saw things clearly for the first time."

I search his eyes for any clue to what he's getting at; everything he's said since we arrived is swirling in my mind.

I open and close my mouth a few times, unsure of what to say. Does this mean all the walls are completely down between us? Does this mean we're having sex in every room of this house? I have no clue.

"Darling, you're it for me. I can't pretend to know the future, but I want you in it. I want you with me through Emilie moving to the States and causing me to have a heart attack. Through Hen starting a full career and struggling through the dynamics of that. Through them both finding their partners in life. To supporting Steph in her relationship." My eyebrows shoot up, and I smile at that one. "I want to see you wipe the floor with the asshole team principals who doubt you. I want to watch you inspire countless women to do whatever they want to in life. I want to watch you thrive and be the lucky asshole you get to come home to when you're taking over the world."

My eyes well up. "Jesus. For a man who doesn't usually say a lot, that was wildly impressive and overwhelming."

He doesn't say more. It's like he knows I need time to process everything he's said. Instead, he presses a kiss to my lips.

"Darling, you're it for me."

"...be the lucky asshole you get to come home to."

They aren't just words. They're a vow, a promise to support me and our relationship no matter the cost. The risk has always been great. There's potential for a huge fallout if someone decides to cause a fuss, but he's telling me he's all in.

"What if the FIA won't allow us to be together? What if people start accusing us of trading secrets or something when this gets out?" I can't help but ask as I pull away.

"Fuck the FIA and anyone who thinks they can tell us how to live our lives," he says with passion.

"But that's not really how things work," I gently remind him. "If rumors start, they'll be believed. It doesn't matter if it's true or not. I know Sydney won't care, but what about the owners of Legacy? Could you lose your job?"

"Hey," he says softly, kissing me once more. "I'll handle the fallout if it comes to that. I'm an old bird; what can they really do to me?" He smiles.

"Don't say that! They can do a lot." I smack his chest without any real harm.

"Antoinette, darling, we can worry about that if it comes to it. But right now?" He pauses, and I nod for him to continue. "I'd really like to fuck you and make you truly mine."

Unrestrained heat floods my veins.

"We haven't even toured the whole house yet," I murmur, trying to hide my grin. Testing him might be one of my favorite things.

"I'll tour the whole fucking house with my cock inside of you if you don't strip and lie down," he growls, lifting me effortlessly onto the bed as he stands up.

I'm powerless to do anything but stare as he unbuttons his shirt, revealing the expanse of his chest. The hair on his chest trails down his stomach that isn't perfectly muscled or flat, even though he's in good shape. I watch as his hands deftly undo his belt, ripping it out of their loops before holding it up.

"Do I need to tie you up and rip your clothes off?" He arches an eyebrow.

I squeak as I scramble to slide off my loose linen pants. The tight tank top I'm wearing gets thrown to the floor shortly after, leaving me in just my bra and panties.

"Those too." He nods to my lingerie as he tosses his belt to the ground.

I can't take my eyes off of him as he unbuttons his pants at the same time I unhook my bra. We move in tandem, sliding clothes down limbs and unabashedly getting naked in the middle of the day.

"You are the most gorgeous thing I've ever had the privilege to see," he whispers.

"Even more gorgeous than the L20?" I ask, referring to the car that won him not only the Drivers' Championship but the Constructors' too, as well as holding a bunch of speed records that no one can touch.

"A hundred times more gorgeous than the L20." His hand skates up my leg as he kneels on the bed. "You have no idea how much you make me *feel.*"

His hand continues on the outside of my thigh as his other slides up my side, up to my neck, and into my hair, a trail of goosebumps rising in its wake.

"You've changed everything for me, and you don't even realize it." He rubs his nose along my cheek.

I love you is on the tip of my tongue, but I know it would just be a reaction to his words. It's not that I don't care deeply for him—I do, enough to risk my entire budding career to be with him—but I'm not sure it's love yet.

We've only had what feels like stolen moments together over the past few months. Is that enough time to know if this is love?

My hips jolt as his fingertips trail over the bend in my hip, inching ever closer to where I really want his fingers.

"Easy, darling. We're going to take our time. Warm you up. Get you nice and wet for me so I can do everything I've been hungry for," he says against my cheek.

His dirty talk could get me to orgasm; I fully believe that.

A whimper sounds in my ears. *Was that me? Do I sound like that?*

We've been circling this for months, and I'm no longer in control of my body now that I actually get to have sex with this man.

"Breathe through it. I know you're worked up, but slow it down." His large hand splays against my lower belly and pelvis, his fingertips almost touching my clit. With a mind of their own, my hips are rocking, trying to move his fingers lower.

"I can't," I pant, unable to draw myself out of the frenzy of being so turned on by this man.

"You can. Breathe with me. In," he says as his hand slides lower, covering my pussy. "And out." He moves it up, removing all pressure from my clit.

"Felix," I growl in frustration.

"In." He repeats his movements, making me go crazy. "And out."

"I fucking can't." I fist the sheets, trying desperately to keep control over myself, but between knowing what's about to happen and Felix's words still flying through my mind, I feel lost in the abyss.

"Hey, look at me." He pulls back a little, shifting my face so I'm forced to look at him. "I'll get you there. I'll help you through it all, but I've felt you, darling, and I don't want to hurt you. Let me get you soft enough to take me. Besides, the second I'm inside of your perfect little cunt, I know I'll blow my load, so I'm just making sure you're blissed out and sated before I do so."

That makes me chuckle and pulls me out of my lustful haze just enough to calm down.

"Good. That's so good." The swirl of his fingertips against my clit makes me gasp. "My God, you're going to come so fast for me, aren't you? You missed me this last week, didn't you, darling?"

"So much." I moan as a finger slides inside of me without ceremony.

"We're both a little overenthusiastic." He grinds against my thigh, leaving a trail of pre-cum as he does.

"Then put me out of my misery!" I gasp when he twists his finger.

Be careful what you ask for. That's the lesson I learn right this second.

His teeth clamp down on my shoulder as his palm hits my clit. His fingers pump inside of me with no mercy, and I come almost immediately.

"Good, darling. God yes, squeeze my fingers just like that." He moans before sitting up on his knees.

His dick is practically dripping pre-cum, and it's the most attractive thing I've ever seen on a man before.

I did that.

"Your little wanton body is making my plans go out the window," he pants as he stares between my legs.

"Is that a bad thing?"

"Absolutely not," he says as he slips his finger inside of me again before pulling it out and pushing two in. The stretch makes my back arch off the bed.

"Take one more, darling, then I'll give you what you truly want," he murmurs.

My only response is a whimper. Words won't be coming for a while now. True to his word, the next time he pulls his fingers out, he adds one more, gently pushing three inside of me. The stretch doesn't hurt, but it does feel like I'm almost at my limit. It's so full that my legs start to close. *I just need a minute.*

"Legs open." His sharp command, followed by the sting of a smack to my inner thigh, has my pussy clenching around his fingers. A wicked smile on his face tells me I'm in trouble. "You liked that. We'll have to experiment with that one later because I might die if I don't get inside of you immediately." I'm suddenly very glad we did the whole "are you clean and covered" talk a while ago.

He removes his fingers, grabbing my ankle and pulling it up to his mouth as he uses the hand that was just pleasuring me to fist his cock. Kissing his way up my leg, he bypasses anything that would give me true pleasure, and moves to my stomach and chest before leaning over me once more.

"Slow, okay?" he asks.

I nod and hold my breath. It almost feels like my first time. It's too intense, too all-feeling, and I just have to endure it while my emotions are going haywire.

I feel him notch against me as he kisses me once more.

"Breathe. I promise I won't hurt you. In fact, I think you'll be begging me for my cock daily after this," he murmurs with a grin as he slides the head in.

I choke out a laugh, which makes me clench around him before he slides in more.

"Fuck, no laughing. I'm not even halfway, and I could come so hard right now." He groans.

"I like the sound of that," I tell him honestly. It's good to see he's as overwhelmingly affected by this as I am.

"I like the sound of you orgasming." He grunts as he slides in deeper, making me gasp.

He presses his forehead to mine, eyes wide open and looking at me like I'm the savior of his entire world. I couldn't look away if I tried.

"You're mine, Antoinette, just as I'm yours. I'm irrevocably remade into a man worthy of you." Then he thrusts the rest of the way in.

I'm surrounded by stimulation, physically and mentally. It's consuming in the best way. My mouth opens on a silent scream as Felix grips my ass hard in one hand, grinding me against him without pulling out.

"I'm going to apologize right now." He sounds pained as he clenches his eyes. "I promise to make it up to you."

"Make what up to me?" Confusion hazes my brain even more than pleasure, and I can't piece together what he's saying.

"The shear rate at which you're about to make me come. It's shameful, really."

I giggle at the absurdity of his words. "Feel free to make it up to me any time you wish." I barely get the words out before he pulls back until his head is the only part still in me and then slams into me to the hilt.

"You won't be able to walk out of here in a week." He punctuates his sentiment with another hard thrust, making my back arch as I moan.

"Challenge accepted."

"Don't." *Thrust.* "Tempt." *Thrust.* "Me." *Thrust.* "You." *Thrust.* "Little." *Thrust.* "Minx."

He barely gets the last word out before he moans into my neck. His grip on my ass is so hard I know it's going to bruise, but I revel in the reminder that I made him lose control.

I feel his cock twitch as he empties himself inside of me. With a heavy sigh, he lets his body sag against mine, all of his energy spent.

"Jesus, I lose my head when I'm with you," he pants out.

"The feeling's mutual."

We stay like that for mere seconds before he's hauling himself up to his knees, still firmly planted inside me.

"What are you doing?"

"Making you come on my cock. The first time I'm inside of you, you will have an orgasm surrounding my dick. There is no world in which I don't feel you clench against me the first time we have sex."

His words alone have my pussy gripping harder around his still hard dick.

"Just like that, darling." He smirks before moving his hand to my pelvis. He presses down a little as his thumb moves to hit my clit. The added pressure with him still inside of me hits a spot I've only been able to accomplish with extreme concentration.

"Holy shit," I breathe out.

Then he starts to gently thrust. That, combined with the clit stimulation, has me screaming his name in mere moments as I squeeze him hard enough to make him groan.

"You look positively ravished, darling."

"And you look far too cocky." I try to catch my breath.

"Is it cocky if I made you come harder than you ever have before?" He holds his hand against my lower belly, content to not move while I come down from the high.

"How would you know?"

"Because if I kept going, I'd have made you squirt, and I would bet my yearly salary you've never done that before."

My arms fling over my face in embarrassment. "Date an older man, they say. He has experience, they say."

"Who the fuck is they?" he growls.

"It's fictitious."

"Are you embarrassed about how close you came to doing that?" he asks, gently pulling my arms away from my beet-red face.

"I'm embarrassed that you knew that when I didn't! And how the fuck are you still hard?" I ask, shifting my hips.

"It's a blessing." He grins. "And just because I could tell what was happening with you doesn't mean I've done things with lots of women. I promise you I haven't. I'm just attentive and know what I'm doing."

"And arrogant."

"Well-versed."

"Smug."

"Eager to please."

His expression drops before he leans down and kisses me again.

"Next time, I'm kissing you more. I missed this," he murmurs against my lips.

I have no more playful words or thoughts, only emotions and a relaxed body as he finally pulls out of me, making me wince.

I'll definitely be a little sore later.

Felix heads to the bathroom quickly, coming back with a damp cloth as he moves back between my legs. He makes quick work of cleaning me up but does it so gently because he knows I'm still sensitive.

Once he's back in bed, I curl up to his chest and begin to drift off. *I'm falling for Felix Karlsson hard, and it just might be my downfall.*

Chapter 28
Felix

Four days into this summer vacation with Antoinette, and I already know this week won't be enough.

We've managed to do a little sightseeing when we weren't wrapped in the sheets, giving each other countless orgasms. I won't lie, it was hard as hell to drag myself away from her in order to leave the house.

"What are you thinking about so early?" Antoinette asks as she wraps her arms around my middle from behind, resting her head against my back.

"How much I don't want to leave."

"Same." She sighs.

"Shall we walk the Cavtat Walking Trail today?" If I'm honest, this might be the only time I allow us out of bed for a while. I'm feeling . . . needy, and I'm not used to that.

To need a woman like I've come to need Antoinette is foreign.

It's scary, and I have lots of thoughts running through my head. But they would all scare her. It's too soon; we have too much at stake. I hear all the concerns, but the things I want to do for this woman defy logic.

"That sounds amazing. Fresh air, overlooking the bay." Her wistfulness is contagious.

"I'll make us some coffee while you get dressed. If I'm in that bedroom while you get naked, we'll never leave."

"If we don't do this trail, I will . . . I don't know . . . make you pay somehow. We can't spend the whole week in bed, Felix."

"Says you. I'd call that one hell of a vacation, darling."

"You're incorrigible."

"You like it." I can't help but smile.

"I'm getting dressed now!" she calls as she turns and heads back to the bedroom.

I more than "like" this woman. It's frightening how easy all of this is. Spending a week together was either going to show us we were good together or needed to call it quits. It showed me, at least, that I'd do a hell of a lot to keep her in my life.

Coffee poured into to-go mugs, both of us dressed, we set out to walk along the edge of the gorgeous bay.

"You know, you're good at this," Antoinette says a half an hour into our walk.

"Good at what? You'll have to be more specific," I joke.

"Not being humble, that's for sure." She chuckles. "No, the boyfriend thing. You're very good at it."

"I've only been a boyfriend a handful of times, but I'm glad you think so."

"What do you think we should do about work? Is there paperwork we can file with the FIA?" she asks, and I know I'm about to crush her.

"I think it might be better if we attempt to keep things how they have been. It's only three more months, and then we can look more in depth at how to approach this with our owners and the FIA. I think we need to make sure all of our bases are covered because there are always sharks in the water."

"So, we keep this hidden for longer?" I hear the doubt in her voice.

"Hey." I stop her and turn her to face me. "This has nothing to do with keeping us hidden and everything to do with covering all of our bases. I'm not ashamed of you or our relationship, but we have to be cautious. I won't let someone with a vendetta against one or both of us use our relationship as a stepping stone for their bullshit agenda."

"I don't love it," she says softly.

"I don't either, but I also don't want anything to derail your career. This has the potential to do much more than that."

"And what if I say I'm fine with the risks?" she asks.

"I'm not, Antoinette. You have the power to do so much good, and if being together somehow jeopardizes that, I'll never forgive myself."

"How very 'knight in shining armor' of you," she attempts to joke, but it falls flat.

"I'm serious. My career is fairly stable. Yours is just starting out. Add in that you're a woman, however fucked up it is that it is even a factor, and I won't let anyone have a reason to drive you from Formula 1. Just . . . give us some time—give me some time—to figure out how to do this, okay?"

Her eyes flick between mine. "Okay." Antoinette sounds anything but okay, but this is what has to be done.

I won't tell her, but I'm worried about Rocco pulling some shit. I'm worried that the other team principals will rally and find some obscure clause in order to oust her. I couldn't care less about my career. The owner could fire me for all I care, as long as she's safe from the blowback.

The thought stops me in my tracks.

I think I'm in love with Antoinette Bailey.

Even when I was with Steph, the thought of losing my job was catastrophic. There was never a time where I would have been okay with losing my job. Hell, things with Cierra had me scrambling to keep it however I could.

But as I look at this perfect woman in front of me, I know I'd lose it all just to stand by her side so she can succeed.

If that isn't love, I don't know what the hell is.

And the biggest shock of all, I'm not even scared shitless and wanting to run away.

"What's the look on your face about?" Antoinette asks with a furrowed brow.

"Nothing, just thinking about the future." *With you. Every single day until my dying breath.*

"Can we just . . . not talk about what happens once we leave here? I want to enjoy the last three days because I know once we get back to the real world, life will get hectic and I won't see you as much, and I just . . . don't want to admit how sad that makes me." She's rambling, but it's the truth in her words that I cling to the most.

"Anything you want."

We continue on our walk, hand in hand, talking about everything under the sun. We do all the corny "what's your favorite" questions, as well as talk about our pasts more. I learn she lost both of her parents a few years back. She had few friends when Brad made them move away from her hometown to isolate her. It makes me so angry that some asshole manipulated her this way.

I vow, as we head back to our rental, to look into him and make sure he's far, far away from my woman. He'll learn really quickly that I'm going to take matters into my own hands if he so much as breathes her way ever again.

"Hey, I have a crazy idea," Antoinette says as we reach the street our house is on.

"What's that, darling?"

"Do you need to be anywhere before you head to Zandvoort?"

"Not particularly. I'm supposed to head back to headquarters and do an all-call meeting, but it was just to touch base about the recent changes working the way they're supposed to. I can do that anytime after one of the practices. Why?"

"What if we extend our trip until Wednesday and fly straight to Zandvoort? I mean, if we can have the rental for more time."

"Four more days with my girlfriend? Where do I sign up?"

"Yeah?"

"Absolutely. Let me call the rental company and see what I can do."

Twenty minutes later, and a significant bump in the daily rate, I secured us more time in peace.

"I'm going to get my swimsuit on and jump in the hot tub. What to join?" Antoinette smirks over her shoulder.

"Do we work in Formula 1?" I ask, running up behind her and picking her up.

She makes me feel young again. Like I have a second lease on life. My relationship with my kids has improved. I'm happier. I'm taking not one but two vacations. I barely recognize myself.

It takes us entirely too long to get changed and into the hot tub. It might have been due to the orgasm I gave Antoinette.

It definitely was.

"Come here," I say, reaching out for her as she takes in the view. I curl her into my lap, and she rests her head on my shoulder.

"This feels like a dream."

"Which part?" I ask.

"All of it. The vacation, the job, you. I'm not the person who gets lucky like this."

"You really have no clue, do you?"

"Apparently not."

"You are the luck, darling. Everything you touch is exceptionally better than before. You have a way to get people to do what you want, and yet you're so kind about it that they *want* to go above and beyond for you. You turned a team that has no business being in the running for awards around, and now we're all chasing you. You made an old man rethink his priorities and actually start living his life," I murmur in her ear.

"You're not old," she hiccups through a laugh or tears; I can't quite tell which.

"I'm almost fifty."

"You're seasoned."

"Like a piece of meat."

"You said it, not me." Now she's laughing, and it brings a smile to my face.

"As long as I'm your piece of meat, then do with me what you will, darling."

"You're rather agreeable when you're relaxed."

"You say that as if you've never seen me relaxed before. If I recall, I'm the one who was supposed to be mentoring you on how to relax."

"And how's that going for you?"

"Great, never been this easygoing in my life."

"Somehow, I believe that. Which makes me disappointed I somehow fell for the 'oh, I'll show you exactly how to relax' shtick. It was just to get in my pants, wasn't it?" She looks up at me with a smirk.

"Now, darling, you know if that was the case, I would have fucked you a lot earlier than I did."

"I think I would have been okay with that."

"You deserve more than to be just a quick lay in bed, Antoinette. You know that, right? You deserve the world, and I sincerely hope I'm the man who can bring it to you."

She searches my eyes, hers glossy like they might flood with tears.

"You're sappy once you finally get some action," she deflects.

Antoinette can act like she's unaffected, but I see it in her eyes. I feel it in her touch. She's as far gone for me as I am for her.

But I'll give her time.

I'm a patient man.

Chapter 29

Toni

It's time to head to the Dutch Grand Prix.

Our time in paradise is over, and it's like I'm mourning what could be. Reality calls, and I'm not looking forward to it. This time with Felix has been . . . beyond words. I'm grateful that we even had the opportunity to spend so much time uninterrupted, thanks to the summer break rules.

Now, as we board our jet, the pressure of the job is catching up to me yet again. We decide to shut off our phones until we land to stay isolated just a little longer.

"Hey, we're still on Croatian time until we land. Don't start overthinking things now," Felix's voice says from behind me as I head to the back of the plane.

"It's not that simple, and you know it."

I plop down onto the chair, but before I can sink into my wayward thoughts, Felix is right in front of me, knelt down. There are perks to flying private, I suppose.

"Everything will be fine. I promise. We'll handle any challenges that come our way. We'll spend as much time as we can together."

"How do you know?" Weariness and unease are hitting my gut square on.

"Because we've been doing it for how many months now? Only three more months until the end of the season. In the meantime, I promise you I'm digging into things. I'll figure out exactly what we need to do so this stays drama-free."

"You can't guarantee that," I whisper, feeling my heart in my throat.

"I can promise that I'll do whatever I can to make things go smoothly for you."

"And what about you, oh Lord of the Grid?" I smirk, trying to bring levity to the conversation.

"I thought I was King of the Grid. Have I been downgraded?"

"You are a child, I swear." I chuckle at how ridiculous he's being.

"Darling, hear me when I say things will be perfect. I will make sure they are."

"Okay."

"Prepare for takeoff," an announcement on the overhead calls, forcing us to separate and buckle in.

"I am sad to be leaving Croatia. What an underrated little spot that was." I sigh as I lean my head back and close my eyes.

"That find was courtesy of Peirce Vanstone via Sydney."

"How come you didn't just find a place with a Vanstone? You know they'd comp our stay." I shift my head so I can look at him.

"For the same reason we're sitting on telling anyone about our relationship. Not that I don't trust Sydney, seeing as she already knows something's going on between us, but last year they had a privacy issue with Luka Tomic at their property in Austin, so I didn't want to take any chances."

It's unfair to Vanstone Properties, as well as Sydney, but I do understand where he's coming from. Renting a house for ourselves lessened the chances of someone seeing us together and then blathering to the media about it.

Before I realize it, we're at cruising altitude and being served drinks.

"So, hypothetically, what are we doing this winter?" I ask, changing the topic to one that's less depressing.

"What do you mean?"

"Well, my home base is Austin. Yours is Belgium. We both have work to do over the winter, so how do we make this work?" I ask.

"Hmm, great question. I suppose I assumed we'd travel? Trade weeks maybe?"

"What, like custody of our relationship?" I laugh.

"No! But also yes, a little bit. We both have things that we have to be at headquarters for, I assume, so I just was thinking we'd work around those as much as possible. And if one of us is stuck there working, the other would travel to them."

Sounds like a ton of work.

"It's not ideal, but at the moment, it's what we'll need to do. We can come up with a better plan for next year if we're still . . ."

"Together?" I add. It doesn't hurt any less that he didn't actually say it.

"Antoinette, I'm not saying we won't be. I'm just . . . getting tongue tied because I know you're stressed out, and all I want to do is take your worry away, but I can't. Next year, we'll figure out a better solution. I'll buy a house in Austin; I don't really care as long as, at the end of the day, I get to spend as much time with you as possible."

He takes my hand, intertwining our fingers and swiping his thumb along my wrist.

I think I'm already in love with Felix, and I'm scared that he's not on the same page. That I'd be dropping my whole life again to be with a man who doesn't love me like I love him.

But this is Felix. He isn't Brad, nowhere close to him, actually.

"I'm scared," I whisper, knowing that communication is the only way he'll understand where my head is at.

"I know you are. I am too, but I think this is worth it. It's worth figuring out the hard stuff for. It's worth going through the trouble of travelling more than we already do."

"Have I mentioned you're very good at this boyfriend thing?" I smile at him.

"Maybe once before." He smirks back. "Can you promise me something?"

"Anything."

"When things start to get overwhelming, or you feel like you're overwhelmed with things going on between us, promise me you'll talk to me? Don't hide, don't act like you're okay, just talk to me."

"I think I can do that." My eyes well with tears at how well he knows me already. He knows commitment freaks me out thanks to Brad. No matter what I do to try and move past it, there's still this shadow of doubt over my head. I'm not sure it'll ever go away.

Felix shifts in his chair, facing me more, before he cups my cheek. "I'm all in, darling. When you question that, tell me, and I'll prove it to you time and time again."

I choke out a laugh. "I'm going to be really bad at this."

"You're perfect at it."

"I'm going to freak out more than just today."

"I'm prepared."

"I'll fuck this up because, at some point, I'll freak out and push you away."

"And I'll be there to help you figure it all out."

"Why are you so, so, so good to me?!" I try to come up with a better word, but my brain is muddled.

"Because you're the woman who made me see there's more to life than work and winning. You're the woman who opened my eyes to true attachment and affection. Because you helped heal a relationship I had no clue how to repair. You helped a father reconnect with his kids when he thought all was lost. Please don't ever discount just how phenomenal you are."

Now, I really am crying. A couple of tears roll down my cheeks at his assessment of me. I feel wholly undeserving of it all.

"And you're crying. This isn't going at all the way I had intended," he whispers before kissing each tear off my face.

His words make me laugh. The lightness he can bring to any conversation is one of my favorite things about him. It's also because I'm not sure that anyone else gets to see that side of him. I feel like I've won the lottery, that I'm the one lucky enough to see it.

Around two hours later, we've landed.

I turn on my phone, and it instantly floods with hundreds of notifications.

"What the hell?" I murmur, trying to figure out what crisis is happening now.

"Fuck!" Felix yells louder than I've ever heard him.

"What?"

"Fuck." He tosses his glasses in his lap and scrubs his face. "Don't panic."

"I think I'm actually going to panic now, though," I say as fear thunders through my body.

"I . . . They . . ." He attempts to start his sentence a couple of times before he sighs and puts his glasses back on, grabbing both my hands and holding them in his. "I will fix this. Okay?"

"Fix what, Felix?!"

"Pictures got leaked. Of us. I'm not sure how. There are some of us in the hot tub at the house. Some of us holding hands while walking. Pictures, Antoinette, all over social media."

I stare at him, hoping he's joking. But then I remember the hundreds of messages on my phone, and I know he's not.

"What are we going to do? We have media interviews in two hours! We have a race to do. What are we going to do?" I hear the hysterics in my voice, but I don't think anything will calm me down at this point.

"I messaged Sydney already, saying we had flown in together. She just replied that there is media at the airport. So, what we're going to do is you're going to sit your gorgeous ass here, and they're going to refill the gas tanks and fly you back to Austin. Mason will take over your job duties, and Sydney will say you're sick, or taking a break since your privacy has been grossly invaded. I'm not sure yet, but we'll figure it out."

More hiding.

More questions about my capabilities on the job.

More questioning if I'm even fit to work in Formula 1.

A fucking nightmare.

"Do you hear me, Antoinette?"

"Stop calling me Antoinette!" I throw my hands up, grasping to the only thing I can in the moment.

"Fine. Do you understand that you're going back to Austin for this race?"

"No. I'm not going to do that. I'm not going to leave you and Sydney to cover up more shit."

"I'm not going to take that the way you wanted it to go. You will stay on the plane. You will go back to Austin, and either Sydney or I will call you later with an update. By the time you land, we'll most likely have some answers or at least a longer-term plan."

I'm so fucking mad right now I could rip someone's hair out.

"Fine."

He sags with relief. "Thank you."

Standing up, he grabs his bag and starts to head toward the door.

"And Felix?" I call out. "The next time you demand I do something with zero input from me will be the last time you ever talk to me again." I won't let myself get used by another man.

Felix turns abruptly and walks back to me. He grasps my chin, making sure I'm looking at him when he speaks. "I apologize for the tone and way I said that. I need you to be safe from all of this shit. I want you a million miles away when all the journalists decide to drag our personal life through the mud. I want you long gone when I take the beating and speculation. My goal is never to own you, just to support you. And I am so fucking sorry that this is happening." His words trail off as anguish seeps through his eyes.

Later, when I'm far removed from this situation and able to think a little more clearly, I'll see his words for what they are: fear.

We're both fearful about what's coming next for us.

No more sneaking around.

No more time to just be us, together.

For the foreseeable future, there will always be a camera not far from us.

And I'm crushed it's come to this.

Felix presses one last kiss to my lips before he walks off the plane into the lion's den.

Chapter 30
(Transcript)

Interviewer: How long has the relationship between you and Toni Bailey been going on?

Felix Karlsson: Any questions related to Zandvoort?

Interviewer: Were the owners of both Legacy and Empress made aware of the relationship before the news broke?

Felix Karlsson: So, no questions about race weekend?

Interviewer: Rocco, what do you make of this development?

Rocco Bianchi: Well, I am concerned about what it means for the other teams on the grid. Are they sharing plans? Devising a supercar together? How deep does this really go?

Felix Karlsson: Oh, get off your high fucking horse, Rocco. It's not the government, and we're not selling state secrets.

Rocco Bianchi: Might as well be. Why are you suddenly back on pace? Did Toni help you out when she saw how much her poor, second-rate boyfriend was failing?

Felix Karlsson: You shut your fucking mouth right now.

Rocco Bianchi: You know what? I don't think I will. How long before you start winning, Felix? Or did you hand over your winning formula for some ass?

Interviewer: Okay, I think that about does it for us.

Rocco Bianchi: No, I don't think so. I'm not done here. There are rumors that you treat your staff unkindly. Maybe some would go so far as to say that you've coerced them, just like you did poor Miss Bailey.

Felix Karlsson: Watch yourself, Rocco. You're crossing a line I don't think you want crossed right now.

Rocco Bianchi: Oh, I very much think I want to cross it. Don't have any answers? I have an employee who jumped ship and has some wonderful anecdotes he'd love to share.

Interviewer: Really, that's it for today.

Felix Karlsson: I'd love to hear what he's fabricated. I'll be sure to have my own team supply their version of the stories as well.

Rocco Bianchi: Bring it on, Felix. The King of the Grid is about to fall.

Chapter 31

Felix

My world is crumbling around me.

All I want to do is call Antoinette and make sure she's okay, even though I know she's not. Especially if she heard the shit Rocco was spouting in that fucking conference.

I sit in my computer chair and bring up the employee file of one Newman Fillom. If Rocco wants to play it this way, then I'll come bringing the canons.

My door slams open. Sydney marches right up to me and pushes my chest hard.

"I fucking told you not to hurt her."

"I didn't do anything intentionally!" Rationality isn't a friend to any of us right now; I know that.

"Fuck . . . Fuck! I know." She sighs before slumping in the chair in front of my desk. "What the fuck are we going to do? Toni's no doubt freaking all the way out, and I just know that asshole Rocco is tied to this somehow."

"I just pulled up the employment records of the guy he mentioned earlier."

"Good. We need dirt ASAP."

"Is she . . . is she going to be okay?" I'm not sure what answer Sydney could possibly have that I don't, but I realize I need reassurance too.

"God, I hope so. I honestly don't know. She doesn't trust easily, and even though you didn't have a part in this, her trust is still broken. Why'd you keep it hidden?" she asks me.

"It started off as something simple. Just helping her get used to the schedule and workload. Emails that couldn't be traced back to either of us. And it just . . . evolved." Rapidly, but I don't add that.

"And you went on vacation over break? I thought you went to Italy with the family," she remembers.

"I did. One week with them and one—and a half—with Antoinette."

"Does the family like her?"

"Aren't we supposed to be figuring out what the hell is going on? Who knew where we were going, and who the fuck followed us?" It's not that I'm against filling Sydney in with all the details, but we have bigger problems right now.

"Right. Sorry. Okay, well, Rocco seems too happy about this, so I assume he's connected, along with . . . what's his name?"

"Newman Fillom."

"Of course his name is Newman. Who else do we think?"

"I have no clue. You think there's more?"

"Well, did either of them have access to either of your phones? That's the only logical way I can see someone knowing where you two would be," she deduces.

"No. Hell no." I scoff.

"So there's more to it. More people involved. Who else have you pissed off?"

"Look around you," I grumble, suddenly more angry that my usual asshole personality is going to actively work against me right now.

Sydney cringes. "Yeah, that's not exactly a great help. Okay. What about Toni? Who doesn't like her?"

"Everyone loves her."

"Including you?" she asks with an arched eyebrow.

"Sydney . . ." I warn.

"Fine. Sue me for trying to get all the information. I want to make sure you're not dicking her around."

"In what world would I have ever 'dicked' anyone around? What the hell does that even mean?"

"Forget it. Let's focus."

"Yes please. Let's focus, Sydney."

"Enemies . . . mad people . . ." she mutters.

We gasp at the same time and say, "Brad."

"Fuck. Of fucking course he would pull some stalker shit like this. I bet he has a tracker app on her phone." I toss my glasses onto my desk, popping one of the lenses out, but I don't give a fuck.

Sydney and I sit there in silence as the gravity of the situation hits us full force.

"Antoinette's in Austin. Is she at her place?" I ask in a panic.

"Umm, I assume. Or at the office. Why?"

"Shit. Someone needs to find her now." I pull up my phone and scroll to her number I put in there on the pretense that I have every team principal's number. Nothing more, nothing less.

"What—" Sydney's cut off by the sound of Antoinette answering the phone.

"Where are you?"

"Hello to you too. What's happening?"

"Where are you right this second, Antoinette?"

"At the office, why?"

"I need you to hang up with me, and immediately trash your phone and get a new one. Also, don't go home yet. Is there someplace you can stay?"

"The Vanstone!" Sydney adds oh-so-helpfully.

"What the fuck is going on, Felix?" Antoinette sounds scared for the first time ever, pulling me out of my single-minded focus.

"Sydney and I think that there's more to this. Someone had access to where we would be, and no one has access to my phone. By deduction, we figured it's most likely Brad, especially since he's still bothering you."

"What do you mean he's still bothering her? Toni!" Sydney stands up.

I wave her off.

"Fuck. Fuck, okay. Umm, what do I do?" Her voice is so unsure, so small, I'd give anything to be there right this second to help her the best way I can.

"Get rid of your phone. I'll send a new one to the Vanstone. Head there right away, and we'll have you taken care of. Just please . . ." My voice cracks before I can catch it. "Go quickly."

My brain is flooded with every bad scenario that could play out. All the what-ifs. That Brad is banking on the fact that she'll retreat and be left alone with no protection. I have no clue if he'd turn violent, but I'm not risking Antoinette's safety for anything.

"Okay." She pauses. "Thank you."

"Please don't thank me." I laugh humorlessly. "Stay safe, okay? Call me the minute you get the new phone."

It's on the tip of my tongue to tell her I love her, but this isn't the time. I won't let the first time I say it to her be in a stressful situation that she could misconstrue.

I toss my phone onto my desk and stare at the door.

"If I could pick anyone for her, it would be you." Sydney's soft voice draws my attention.

"What?"

"The two of you. You're good for each other." The soft smile on her face tells me she knows it's much deeper for me than just seeing where things go. But she also knows I'm not the man to tell that to anyone except Antoinette.

"Can you make arrangements for her stay while I send a phone there?" I ask instead of addressing her statement. I'm not a sentimental man—except with Antoinette, I suppose.

Doing something—anything—doesn't lessen my panic, but it does make me feel like I'm being productive instead of sitting here, twiddling my thumbs.

"Done. And Felix?" Sydney asks.

"Yeah?"

"She's tougher than she looks. If she runs into . . . trouble, she'll be okay."

"It's not about her being tough. It's about her not needing to be around that scum any longer than she already has. She doesn't need to be put in that position. And I'm stuck here, watching fucking cars go in a circle."

"It's more like a windy J, actually."

"You're a smart-ass."

"I know, but you cracked a smile. We'll figure this shit out, okay? I won't let her get caught up in a witch hunt; you know that."

"I know."

"I won't let you get caught up in it either."

I stop shuffling things around my desk and look at her. "I can take care of myself."

"That's debatable. All I'm saying is that whatever Rocco's agenda is, I'm not letting him tear down two of my best friends."

"You consider me one of your best friends? Sydney . . . I hate to break it to you, but you should get better friends." I cringe to break the seriousness of her words.

"You're so annoying. If I didn't know you, I'd believe this Tin Man act of yours."

"Why the fuck is everyone saying I'm the Tin Man?" I ask, remembering Steph said the same thing.

"If the shoe fits." She shrugs. "I'll have her room set up in ten minutes, and then I'll start doing some digging into how this is all connected." She stands up to leave. "Sydney," I say, stopping her. "You don't need to stop your life to help us. Like you said, Antoinette is stronger than she lets on. And I have resources to figure this out. We can handle it."

"But you don't have to handle it alone. Beckett taught me that one, and trust me, it's a million times easier to lean on your supports than it is to stand on one foot."

"I . . . I don't think that analogy works."

"Whatever. Go get Toni a phone." She rolls her eyes and leaves just as quickly as she came in.

I've been a lone wolf in this world—by my own doing—for a long time. I've never asked for help, never saw a challenge I couldn't handle on my own. But that was before Antoinette. Before she got intertwined in a clash Rocco is determined to see through.

It takes me three minutes to order a new phone and have it sent to the Vanstone in Austin. I also paid a hefty fee to have them preload a few numbers in there, so Antoinette has access to a few people while we figure this out.

And then I wait.

And wait.

And freak the fuck out because I haven't heard from anybody yet.

I snag my phone off my desk and pull up the pictures from one of the ridiculous number of websites that did articles on us.

As much as I hate that whoever took these invaded a private time for us, I can't say I'm sad to have some permanent evidence that it happened.

Antoinette and I had been careful, only taking pictures of scenery or landmarks, never pictures with each other.

I now see how that approach was . . . wrong of me. I was the one who mentioned it and pushed for it. We could have had photos of our time in Croatia, photos that we could have remembered years down the road if we're lucky.

I fucked this all up.

My fears, stemming from my experience with Cierra, made me hide someone so special. Someone who never deserved to be tucked in the back recesses of our fake emails like some back-alley hook-up.

Like I'm ashamed of her.

Nothing could be further from the truth. Yet, on some level, I had to have made her feel that way.

New plan: figure out what the fuck Rocco's plan is then show Antoinette how much I want to shout to the world that she's mine.

Chapter 32
Toni

I've yet to process everything that's happened today.

When I walk into the Vanstone and announce myself at the front desk, I am promptly swept into the elevator and taken up to the top floor. Only then does my mind finally catch up with the situation.

The concierge is telling me about some perks or food—I honestly don't know because my head has that faraway feeling—and I'm not really hearing him.

"That's great, thank you," I cut him off as he starts another long-winded explanation of something. He pauses, tilts his head in acknowledgement, and leaves without another word.

I spin in a circle, taking in the huge space. Sydney went overboard, but then again, that's just how she is.

A package on the kitchen island catches my attention.

The familiar phone packaging makes my heartbeat speed up. The note on top has tears welling in my eyes as the weight of the day finally hits me.

I promise I'll fix everything. This has Sydney's, Daisy's, and my numbers in it if you need anything. After this race, I'll be right there with you, darling.

~ Felix

Inside the box is a brand-new phone already on. I don't hesitate, bringing up Felix's number and hitting the call button.

"Antoinette? Are you okay? Did you make it to the hotel okay?"

His rapid-fire questions do nothing to stem the onslaught of emotions about to break free.

"I'm here," I squeak out around the sobs caught in my throat.

"Oh, darling, I'm so sorry. Did something happen? Did you see Brad?"

I hear him shuffling around his office. "No, no nothing like that. I just think everything's hitting me." I hiccup, trying desperately to keep my meltdown in. I know Felix feels guilty enough as it is, even though it's not his fault.

"I wish I didn't have this fucking race to handle, otherwise I'd be on the first flight there." I can just picture him tossing his glasses onto his desk and rubbing the bridge of his nose.

"I'm fine, I promise." The lack of control over my leaking eyeballs would suggest otherwise.

"None of this is fine." He sighs.

I take a couple of deep breaths in an attempt to calm myself down.

"Do you really think Brad is responsible for all of this? I mean, following me? *Tracking* me?" It just seems so far-fetched yet completely plausible at the same time.

"Sydney and I both came to the same conclusion. I mean, who knew about us going to Croatia?"

"Sydney, Daisy, their husbands probably, and whomever you told. I don't have anyone else who would care." I say it carelessly, not thinking about how pathetic it really is. Just another reminder of the damage Brad caused.

If it was Brad, I'm just dragging Felix and his career through the mud because of a past mistake. Can I let him get caught up in this? I know it's essentially too late, but what if I can stop Brad once and for all?

If I have the chance to fix this all, to make sure that Felix's reputation and name aren't tarnished, I have to try.

"Just Steph knew about it on my end."

"So, Brad is the logical choice..."

"If he had a tracker or app on your phone, at least we've taken care of that, but I want to double-check that it was only him. Leave nothing to chance," he says.

"If it was Brad, I'm sorry you got dragged into all of this because of me." The tears start up again, but I tip my head to the ceiling to stop them from falling.

"At least I can call you whenever I miss you now."

A watery chuckle escapes me. "I don't hate that, if I'm honest."

"Are you sure you're okay?"

"No, but I think it's mostly just coming to terms with how much has changed in the last twelve hours."

"Understandable. Sydney said you have the room for as long as it takes to figure this all out and make sure you're safe."

I bark out a laugh at that one. "It's more like a very large apartment, not a room."

"Well, then you won't even miss your place for the time being."

"I need my clothes and hair shit. I don't know, probably a lot of other crap from my house, though," I realize, completely overwhelmed by the thought of just staying here until it's safe to return home. The indeterminate amount of time for all of this is not helping my freak-out at all.

"Let me handle all of that. Go run a hot bath, try to relax and not stress about anything."

"Felix . . . I can't just stay here until you or Sydney deem it okay for me to leave. I have a job; hell, we have some championships to win. I can't just do nothing."

"It's not forever."

"How can you promise that? Neither of us know what the fuck is going on!" I throw my hands up, exasperated the more we discuss this.

"I know," he says softly.

"I'm going to go take that bath in the hopes that I'll be calmer when I get out. I'm sorry for my reaction."

"Your reaction is quite tame compared to what I expected, darling. Call me when you're out of the bath, okay?"

"Okay," I whisper and hang up.

Hot water blasts out of the faucet, steam starts to fill the bathroom, and I sit on the edge of the tub, letting my mind wander while the water rises. Last year, Daisy shared her affinity for baths. She always says they're her place to think clearly. I sure as hell could use some of that right now.

It feels so good to finally strip out of the clothes I've had on since we left Croatia many hours ago, before I dip my toe in the steaming water. As I sink in deep, the warmth penetrates my stiff muscles, helping me descend into it more.

I take what feels like my first full breath since we turned our phones back on when we landed in the Netherlands and our little world seemed to fall apart.

After a couple of deep inhales, I try to make a mental list of what I *do* know about the situation.

I know that someone followed us and took pictures before spreading them all over the internet.

I know that the most likely person is Brad because Sydney and Felix are right—who else would have close enough access to me at any point to hide a tracker or app or whatever on my phone?

I know that Rocco has something against me and Felix—mostly Felix, I think. So, could he have a hand in things? It's not impossible.

I know that I'm more worried about Felix's career than mine. And I would bet money that he's more worried about mine than his. I'm not sure what exactly to do with that information, but it's something to keep in the back of my mind.

I can't go back to my home.

I can't go to the office to attempt to work.

I can't be at any races until we have a better handle on things.

I'm stuck here.

I suck in a breath and submerge myself in the water. I thought a mental list would help me find a direction to go with all of this. Instead, it has made my panic reach an all-time high. When my lungs start to burn, I scoot up and tip my head against the side of the tub.

I need to do *something.*

Rocco. My head is stuck on Rocco and something Felix said a while ago. He would have a ton of complaints against him or something like that. What if he's a part of this somehow? I can't imagine Brad coming up with something this advanced. Hell, I can't even believe he'd figure out anything relating to Felix. Even if Rocco isn't involved, maybe I can dig up something in an attempt to get him off of Felix's back. I have my work computer here, so maybe I can start looking into him.

The excitement of potentially bringing something to the table has me up, out of the tub, and wrapped in a plush robe before the water is even cold.

I race to the living room to grab my computer and stop in my tracks from the knock at the door.

I peek through, seeing it's hotel staff, and open the door.

"A package for you." he simply says, handing me the bag and walking away.

I make my way back to the living room and open it up. A card sits on top of what's inside.

I can't be there, so I made sure you had everything you'd need until I am and we can go to your house together. Please stay here. I'll worry about you less if I know where you are. If I missed something, text me, and I'll have it sent right over.

Missing you immensely,

-F

That reputation he has on the grid sure is nowhere to be seen around me, and it makes me damn near giddy.

I get to see this side of him. *I'm* lucky enough to see him when he sheds that skin and lets me in. It just may be the best feeling in the entire world.

Orgasms by him might take the cake, though.

Right now does not seem like the best time to be thinking about orgasms, in all honesty.

Sifting through one of the bags, I find a buttery-soft golden silk short and tank top set. Immediately taking off my robe, I slide into the most luxurious set of pajamas I've ever worn. In the next bag is a familiar logo, bringing a smile to my face. I stick my hand in and randomly pick a face mask to put on while I conduct some research.

An hour later, I've finally started getting somewhere. I found a handful of female employees who were laid off last year, but the reasoning all sounded a little suspicious to me. I emailed them all to see if they'd be willing to chat with me. I might have led them to believe there may be openings at Empress, but the good news is, if they actually do fit in well with the team and want to get back into Formula 1, I do have the capability for that to be true. So, I'm not actually leading them on. Not one hundred percent, at least.

My new phone rings beside me, startling me into slamming my laptop shut.

When I see who it is, and a video call at that, I can't keep the smile off my face.

"I see you found some of the goodies I sent," he says with the most genuine smile.

My mind goes blank for a moment, and all I can think is: *God he's gorgeous, and he's all mine.*

"Darling?" His voice pulls me from my daze.

"Huh?"

"You okay?" His brow furrows.

"Totally good. Yep, so good."

"Do you like the face masks?" He nods to the camera, and it's then that I realize I never took off the mask I put on over an hour ago. I got too caught up in researching once I had a direction to go.

Reaching up, I pluck it off my face and chuck it to the ground. "Love them. Super thoughtful."

His smile drops. "Hey, what's going on?"

"I . . ." Even though I've been able to push down the emotions of the day for the most part, they come bubbling to the surface again. "This day fucking sucks," I mutter, the tears threatening to spill over. I lean my head back and blink rapidly in an attempt to hold them in.

"I know, darling, I know. I wish I could just solve it all for you."

"And what about for you? This doesn't just affect me, Felix."

"Well, I'm not worried about me. I'm worried about you." *Exactly how I suspected he'd feel.* "If Brad is this reckless, then what else could he do?"

"So, I get to be locked up in this fancy hotel suite for the foreseeable future because you and Sydney deem it unsafe for me not to be? It's not sustainable."

"I know, and it won't be for long. Just for this race weekend until I can figure out something better."

"You can't put this all on your shoulders, Felix." I sigh, more and more exhausted from this roundabout conversation. It's not going to go anywhere because we don't have answers. That won't change in a weekend. I tip my head back and sigh again, still holding the phone up with one hand.

He doesn't speak for a few moments, allowing me the moment to freak out and calm myself down so I'm more rational.

"Did you go through all the bags?" he asks, confusing me even more.

"What?" I pull my head up and look at him.

"The rest of the bags, did you go through them?"

"Uh, no. I found these first, then saw the masks and decided to try and work a little bit." I won't tell him exactly what I was working on.

"I want you to put the phone down, and go look through the rest of the bags and find the vibrator." His command is exactly that—not a question, but a task for me to complete.

"You got me a vibrator? Who had to go buy that?" My voice goes high at the thought of someone having to shop for another person's vibrator.

"Go get the damn vibrator, Antoinette," he says instead of answering me.

Rolling my eyes, even though my pulse is pumping with excitement, I toss the phone down and race out to the living room.

In one of the last bags I check is a very discreet box that I would have passed over if I had actually looked through everything.

I grab a pair of scissors from the kitchen and open the box to find a vibrator similar to the one I usually carry with me when I travel. I test it, seeing that it's at least partially charged, and wash it quickly before heading back to the bedroom.

After all of that, I pick up the phone again with a smirk on my face. "You are a very horny man."

"I am a sucker for my woman, and I knew you'd probably be very stressed out about the situation. This seemed like a good trade-off since I can't be there right this second.""So, we're back to the stress-relieving orgasms?"

"If the dildo fits, darling."

I burst out laughing at his words.

"There's a smile. I was worried I'd really have to make a fool of myself to get one." He smiles at me through the phone screen.

If I wasn't already gone for this man, I think this moment would have done it. His quick humor combined with his posh tone is my kryptonite. He somehow knows the perfect moments to be serious but also the perfect moments to not be. To let me have a minute to catch up.

He's just . . . perfect in the most imperfect way.

Chapter 33

Felix

"Does it at least have some charge?" I ask, hoping this will distract her a little.

"Shockingly, it does." The amused yet shy smile on her face makes me breathe a little easier. Never have I wanted to quit my job so impulsively as I did today. Just so I could be by Antoinette's side while we figure all of this out.

Not when Steph was on the verge of giving birth, not when shit hit the fan with Cierra all those years ago.

But I can't just quit, so I came up with the next best thing, in a way.

"Good. I need you to get comfortable for me, darling. Set up the phone so I can watch your face." Thank God I'm back in my own hotel room for this.

I can't say I've ever had phone sex before, but there's a first time for everything, I suppose. And if I'm going to pull a stunt like this, I'm glad it's with this woman.

I watch as she shuffles down the bed, props up the phone on the nightstand, and shimmies out of her bottoms then flashes them to the camera.

"Felix Karlsson, I didn't think you had this in you." She smirks as she faces the camera.

"Nor did I, but it seems I do a lot of out-of-character things for you." Truer words were never spoken. In a matter of months, she's gotten me out of my shell and *feeling* again. She's a witch, a magician, and an enchantress all in one.

Her eyes soften, and her smile grows.

I would do an obscene number of things for this woman, just to see that look on her face directed at me time and time again.

"Move your fingertips across your skin—nothing too crazy, just skim your body," I say as I settle into the couch. I'm determined to make this all about her, not me.

She lies back on the pillow—her eyes fall closed, her lips part, and her fingers begin to roam her body.

"Good, darling, very good. Open your eyes and show me how you like your nipples touched." My voice is breathier than I intended.

"I think you know how I like them touched, Felix." The twinkle in her eye doesn't stop her from doing as I direct.

"I'm always eager to learn."

The golden top shimmers like water over her skin. It moves as she does and is hell on my imagination. I want to run my hands all over it, bite her nipples through it just to see the wet spot I leave. I wonder if it's as soft as her skin.

A raspy moan leaves her, her fingers tweaking her nipples. She's soft, working herself up and making me harder than stone.

"You're beautiful like this," I murmur, not wanting to break the spell.

"I'm really wishing this was you."

"Me too, darling, but we're improvising. Now, harder."

Her moans get louder the harder she pinches those rosy peaks of perfection. I reach down, squeezing my erection in an attempt to relieve some pressure, but it only makes it worse.

"Move that hand down to that little clit. Don't go too hard, just get yourself started."

I can see most of her body from the angle that she put her phone, and once I see her hand slide down her stomach to her clit, I have to close my eyes for a moment to regain control.

"Fuck," she curses. My eyes open to see her head tilted back, her mouth open, and her hand making circles on her clit.

"Are you nice and wet for me?" I rasp.

"So wet." Her hand moves lower, and I know she's testing how wet she is, drawing up all that delicious arousal I wish I could suck off her clit.

"Turn on that vibrator, darling."

I wanted to draw this out more, but there's no way in hell I can. She needs the orgasm, and I'm desperate to watch it. Impatient to see the rapture on her face, knowing I had some small part in it.

The subtle buzz hits my ears just before her gasp does. I'm speechless watching her.

The hand on my dick starts shifting along my shaft. I'm barely aware that I'm doing it.

"Felix," Antoinette moans, forcing my balls to draw up at the sound.

"Keep going." I clear my throat. "I want you to slide it inside yourself. Thrust it while you think about me doing the same."

Her eyes open as her head moves to face the camera. "I want to see you."

"This is just for you." I try, desperately, to keep my focus where it needs to be.

"Please," she whimpers. My eyes move down her body, watching as the little vibrator disappears inside of her.

"Darling . . ." I endeavor to stay the course, I really do, until the next words come out of her mouth.

"I need to see you. Need to look at you and imagine it's you inside of me and not some silicone replacement that doesn't do it like you do."

I'm ripping open my trousers before I register what I'm doing. My cock is in hand, and I'm repositioning the phone so I can still see her as she watches me pump myself hard.

It's not going to take much.

"God, yes," she pants as her wrist moves faster.

"Shit, get there. I'm not going to last, and I'll be damned if I come before you. Even on the phone," I grit through my teeth, trying to hold back my orgasm.

Just then, a shudder runs through her body like a tidal wave. Her muscles twitch, and her scream will probably get a noise complaint, but I don't give a shit.

"So sexy. So mine. Never letting you go," I mutter incoherently as she collapses back on to the bed.

She lifts the phone and brings it closer to her face.

"Show me. Come for me." Her command undoes me. I'm coming all over my hand and shirt that I carelessly left in the line of fire, but I couldn't care less.

I moan her name as the last twitches run through my body.

"Jesus, that was so fucking gorgeous," Antoinette whispers, making me laugh.

"Me coming is gorgeous?"

"So pretty it's ridiculous." The smile she gives me settles my soul. She's happy in this moment, and that's all I could really ask for.

"I will say it's never been called pretty before."

"Such a shame too. It curves upward just a little." She sighs. "Hits all the good spots every single time."

I can't help laughing at her assessment. I mean, she's not wrong, but I've never heard an analysis of my dick before.

"Hey," she says after a long minute.

"Yeah?"

"Thank you. I don't know how you figure out what I need before I do, but if I haven't said it before, thank you."

"No thanks needed, darling. I live to make you happy, to keep you happy."

I don't think I've ever meant words more before.

***

Zandvoort just finished up, and Legacy didn't have too bad of a race. At least we managed some points. Empress had both drivers on the podium even without Antoinette, which sufficiently pissed off Rocco to no end.

I immediately left the race, telling my second in command to handle all the debriefs. After flying a couple of hours, I'm now standing in front of the door, hesitating to knock.

"Are you just going to be a creeper out here or would you like to come in?" Steph asks as she rips the door open.

"I apologize; I got lost in thought," I say, stepping inside.

"To what do I owe the pleasure? The kids are both out if you were hoping to catch them." She cringes like that would be the only reason I'm here.

"I actually came to talk to you."

"Oh?" She walks us to the living room, where she takes the chair, and I take the couch opposite her.

"I have a plan . . . but it's crazy and impulsive."

"A plan for what, exactly? This media nonsense?"

"Yes and no. A plan for how to keep the trouble off of Antoinette, as well as a plan for the future."

"You're freaking me out, Felix."

I sigh. Pulling the band-aid off is the best option. "I'm thinking about retiring."

"What the fuck?"

"Well, I obviously want to discuss things with you. Pros and cons and such," I ramble. I'm not sure why I'm so nervous about this. It's been on my mind for a while, ever since I realized this thing with Antoinette is something *more*.

"Why would you retire? Because of the pictures?" Steph's brow is furrowed in confusion.

"Sort of. I need to figure out a way for Antoinette to not take the heat for any of it. For her reputation to stay intact. She has a whole career ahead of her. I'm forty-eight and have been doing this for too long already. What more do I have to prove? It's not like I can't get a role behind the scenes if I want to keep working," I reason.

Steph stares at me like she's trying to search for more. Then she says under her breath, "Holy shit, you're in love with her."

I look down, not wanting to fully admit it to her when I haven't gotten the balls to confess it to the woman herself.

"I—" Her mouth slams shut before she swallows. "Okay, so what do you need to discuss with me?"

"All of it." I throw my hands up and laugh. "I don't know if it's just impulsive, if I'm trying to do something that's impossible, or if it's a good idea. None of us are going to hurt for money," I add, in case that's something Steph is worried about.

She scoffs. "I'm not worried about the money. Jesus, both kids are moving out, and I'm downsizing as soon as possible. Plus, we've been smart with our money, both together and separately. I'm not concerned about that." She glares. "I'm concerned that if you do this, it still won't help Toni out in the long run."

"What do you mean?"

"Well, if people—the media—see you retiring as a fall-on-your-sword moment, Toni still gets shit on because she'll be the one who forced you out of Formula 1. Desperate people do desperate things all the time. How do you stop them from doing worse?"

"It's not like that, though," I cut in.

"I know it's not. Hell, anyone who knows you knows it's not, but that's not how it'll be perceived. I'm not saying don't retire if that's truly what you want to do, but don't do it because you expect the action to somehow save Toni. Sadly, she's going to have to figure out how to do that on her own. She won't have any merit if you jump in and do it for her. She's already in an uphill battle in this sport. Other team principals are threatened and looking for a way to take out their grievances on her."

"So, what do I do to help her?"

I feel . . . helpless. More so than I have all weekend while Antoinette and I have been thousands of miles away from each other.

"You help her on the back end. You help with a plan that *she* can implement—whatever that entails— and then you sit back and watch her destroy all the boys who said she couldn't do something."

"And if I decide retirement is what I really want? How would you feel about that? How do you think the kids would feel?" I've never done anything big in my life without getting Steph's thoughts and blessings, even after the divorce.

"I think that you've always done what's best for everyone else, or what you have perceived is best for everyone else. You never really think about what's best for you. If you've hit a point where this job doesn't feel like it's fulfilling you anymore, then I'm in full support. The kids will support you no matter your decision, and you know that. If you feel like you can still do more, win more because it's something that really matters to you? Then stay and kick it into high gear. It's not like you won't be a part of racing in some form even if you do retire."

She grabs my hand and squeezes it as I take in her words.

Do I feel that I have more to do with Legacy? Or do I feel like I can help the sport in other ways?

"I don't know what to do," I whisper.

"I suspect it's because you have a certain woman to discuss things with first." Steph smiles.

"This season has not turned out anything like I thought it would." I sigh, collapsing back into the couch.

"Same. But in a good way. A lot has happened already, and you're only halfway through."

"You just like Antoinette, and you like that the kids like her too." I smirk.

"First, the kids and I love her. She's an incredible role model, and she's brought you to your knees. Honestly, what's not to love? But also, you've grown a lot. In big ways. When's the last time you talked to Emilie?" She already knows the answer, but I understand her point.

"On the plane while I was flying here."

"And you had a great conversation, I assume. The way your relationship with her and Henrik has evolved in just a few short months has been a sheer delight to witness. They've always been on your side; you just never saw it. I think you don't need to make a rash decision about things right this second. Talk with Toni and see where you both want the future to go."

"Best thing you ever did was get your doctorate." I smirk.

"I did need to do something with all this brainpower." She nods.

"Thank you. For always being here for me. For dealing with me even when I was a grumpy asshole."

"Eh, you're not always an asshole. You can be fun sometimes." She winks. "Are you staying here tonight?" she asks, letting go of my hand and standing up.

"That was the plan, but I think I need to see about a flight to Austin."

"That's the spirit! Call me when you land and let me know if you need anything."

"I will." I stand up and head to the front door.

"Oh, and Felix?" I turn around to face Steph. "I'm really fucking happy for you."

"And I you. We should plan a dinner at some point."

"I would really like that."

I leave with no more real clarity for the massive invasion of privacy, but I do have something to think about at least. And the more I do think about it, the more I want to say "fuck it all" and throw all my weight behind Antoinette and Empress.

Chapter 34

(Transcript)

Interviewer: Quiet today, huh, Rocco?

Rocco Bianchi: I guess there are some people who are too good to do media interviews anymore.

Interviewer: So, Guardian places eleventh and seventeenth. What's your plan for Italy next weekend? Any changes you're hoping to roll out in order to better your results?

Rocco Bianchi: Oh, we have a lot up our sleeves. That's just not something I'm willing to tell you about.

Interviewer: Right. Well, you're quite a ways off pace of the rest of the grid, and according to the points, both drivers are almost at risk of being last in overall points for the drivers' standings. How do you hope to shift that over the back half of the season?

Rocco Bianchi: I'd rather discuss how a team principal is allowed to just not show up for a race.

Interviewer: Toni Bailey? I would think it's understandable, given the unfavorable press around her lately, that she wanted the focus to be on the race and not her life outside of it.

Rocco Bianchi: She's lying down on the job . . . literally, and I think she's a terrible excuse for a team principal. The FIA needs to look into her processes and see if she's all on the up and up. That goes for the whole Empress team, really.

Interviewer: So, let me get this straight. You're wanting the FIA to look into someone's personal life when she took a step back in order for the attention to stay focused on the actual race? What cause would the FIA have to investigate?

Rocco Bianchi: I have loads of ammunition I'm about to send their way. You'll find out soon enough, along with the rest of the racing world.

Interviewer: Last question: Did you make an agreement with one Newman Fillom to gather information about Legacy's car this year and, in doing so, poach him from their team? Did you also steal trade secrets about their car in an illegal way, therefore putting the entire Guardian team in jeopardy?

Rocco Bianchi: What blasphemy is this? You have no proof!

Interviewer: Guess you'll be finding out soon enough as well.

Chapter 35
Toni

It's been quite an interesting few hours.

The entire race weekend, I've been digging into Rocco. And right before the race started, I hit paydirt. Sydney gave me the name Newman Fillom to go off of in connection to Rocco, and it's been a rollercoaster since.

Somehow, Sydney got access to Newman's emails at Legacy—most likely thanks to Felix. I won't pretend to know how, but I'm not asking questions when it brought me what it did.

I found a not-so-well-hidden trail of emails between the two, very clearly outlining their plans to sabotage and steal Legacy's car plans. A very clear bribe of a job with Guardian for Newman as well. In his Legacy email. It's like they wanted to get caught. I mean, your old boss still has access to your emails, so why would you write this shit in there? It makes me thankful Felix and I went to such lengths with keeping our emails anonymous. Imagine how much worse our situation would be if those got out.

I shiver and shove the thought way down into the recesses of my mind. No need to dwell on that; it won't do me any good.

Productivity is the name of the game, possibly distraction too, but whatever you want to call it, it's something to focus on instead of the uncertainty surrounding my future in this sport.

My phone rings, and I pick it up without taking my eyes off another email between Rocco and Newman.

"Toni Bailey."

"So professional." I swear I can see Sydney smirking through the phone.

"Sorry, didn't even see who was calling before I answered." I scrub my hand down my face, feeling the exhaustion of the last few days.

"Next time, look please. Reporters are playing dirty, and I don't want you answering one of their calls and getting berated for no reason."

"Will do." Again, I know better, but apparently, I'm not on top of any part of my life right now.

"How's it going?" She changes topics.

I sigh. "Interesting, I guess. Found some dirt, but I'm not sure it's enough to use."

"Fill me in." I can hear her shuffling around as I dive into what little I know. "Interesting. So, we have them both on plans to sabotage, and if we can prove Newman was tampering with the balance, we have a lot to work with there. Plus, whatever clauses or NDA Felix put into Newman's contract can nail him down as well."

"But that would just land on Newman unless I can find a clear directive from Rocco," I say absentmindedly as I continue to skim emails. It's wild how many they've written to each other. Far more than Felix and I, and we're sleeping together. *It's more than that.*

"True, but it's a start—"

"Hold on," I mutter, rereading what I just saw. "Shit."

"What?"

"I think this just got way more complicated." I scroll through the email thread, seeing more and more damning evidence—a connection I would have never guessed.

"I'm attempting to be patient because I know you're reading emails right now," Sydney says.

"Rocco talks about the first time he tried to get Felix out of the job."

"The first time?"

"Seven years ago, when the media was tipped off about a relationship he was having with a coworker while he was still technically married." *Fucking Cierra. I cannot believe this all ties back to her.*

"Shit."

"Fuck." My head tips back as I try to wrap my head around all of this. "Why does Rocco hate Felix so much? It cannot just be because he got the Legacy job instead of Rocco."

"I honestly don't know. Probably the downside of not being in this world my entire life."

"I'll keep digging. When I figure out why he's going after Felix, I'll let you know."

"Just ask Felix," Sydney says.

I should. It'd be the obvious option, but telling my boyfriend that the casual ex he was seeing who destroyed his relationship with his kids is connected to Rocco, and her involvement with him was probably fabricated, is not something I want to do. If I can keep this information far away from Felix, I'm going to.

"I can't . . . He— I just can't." It's not my place to tell Sydney why Cierra being involved will crush Felix.

"I don't like this, Toni."

"I know, but I really don't have a lot to go on right now. I need more information, and then I can talk to Felix about it." A lie, but one I'm not going to think about.

The need to shield Felix from this is stronger than my anxiety about our pictures being leaked.

It's telling, honestly, and displays how deep in love I am with this man. Something I'm not willing to think about either because if I do, I'll fall apart.

Working, or whatever I'm calling this distraction, is the only thing keeping me from letting the darkness in. The one that was over my head for so many years with Brad. The one I can't let in again.

So, I need to figure out exactly what Rocco is up to.

"Well, I'm going to throw a little tip by way of the reporters and put some heat on Rocco, and see what comes of it," Sydney says before saying her goodbyes.

***

A knock at the door startles me awake. I look around, trying to figure out where

I am, when I see the hotel room I'm calling home. I also see a drool spot on the dining room table next to my laptop where I was working.

That exhaustion caught up to me, I guess.

The knock sounds again, and my heart drops. No one knows I'm here except Sydney and Felix. They're in Europe right now, so I know it's not them.

I creep to the door and peek through the peephole.

"What the fuck?" I mutter in disbelief, ripping the door open.

"Hi, darling." His smile hits me dead in the chest and all the emotions, all the stress of the past weekend, come flooding to the surface. Tears spring from my eyes as I try desperately to hold them back. "None of that." He wraps his arms around me, shutting the door behind him as I break down.

"I'm sorry," I gasp through my crying. I feel . . . stupid and immature, but I can't stop the tears.

"No apology needed. It's been hell the last few days." Felix grabs my hand and leads me to the bedroom. He peels out of his clothes, leaving only his boxer briefs in place, before doing the same to me. I'm dragged to bed before I realize what's happened. His arm wraps around my body, pulling me closer to him. "Just relax with me," he murmurs as his fingers scrap against my scalp.

"How are you here?" I hiccup, still trying to get my bearings.

"I left immediately after the podium. I needed to talk to Steph about some things, so I made a quick pitstop and then flew straight here. It's been dreadful without you."

"Such a charmer." I chuckle, my tears finally calming down to the point where I can think properly. "I'm glad you're here, however crazy it is that you just left without debriefing."

"Telling me how to do my job, darling?" I peek up at him and see the smirk on his face. His glasses sit slightly askew, and I know I'd do anything for this man. Even hide something from him to protect him.

"I would never. Seriously, though, how was the race?" We had limited time to talk, as is the nature of the beast with our jobs.

"Hectic. Busy. Annoying. Lonely."

We lie there in silence as I process his words.

"Thank you for letting Sydney, and me by proxy, have access to Newman's emails," I whisper, not sure if I want to even talk about this but needing him to know I'm working on things. I need him to know that he's not alone in figuring this shit out.

"She said she was hiring a P.I." He stiffens.

"Ta-da." I throw my top arm up like I'm showing him a magic trick. "I wear many hats at Empress." I smile, looking up at him, but it drops immediately.

"I said I would fix this, Antoinette. I need you to know that I will," he says with conviction.

"I don't doubt you. But I also need to help. We're in this together. Rocco isn't just attacking me, Felix; he's attacking you. You can't expect me to sit back and just let more shit happen." I lean up against his chest, imploring him to really hear me.

"This is about me. He just pulled you into it to hurt me. I can't let you get more caught up."

"Do you hear yourself? I appreciate you trying to do damage control, but it's already well past the time where I could just sit back and not be involved. If we're together, we're together in all things. I'm not going to just hope you figure things out." Anger takes the place of all the other emotions I'm feeling.

"That's not what I meant—"

"I know . . . I know." I sigh. "I just need your stubborn ass to include me. I can't just sit back and do nothing," I plead. "This is both of our livelihoods."

He cups my jaw, pulling me closer to him. "I know, and I apologize. I just need you safe. I can't wrap you in bubble wrap and hide you away."

"This"—I wave around—"feels pretty close to that."

"I'm not apologizing for this, darling. If Brad is involved, he's dangerous. I'm not risking your safety without knowing what he's up to. We can work on that together now that I'm here, but I'm not going to say I'm sorry. I would never have been able to work this weekend if I didn't know you were safe."

"This still feels pretty extreme," I push, needing him to understand he can't expect this to happen every time shit hits the fan.

"Dammit, Antoinette, don't you see? If I lose you, I lose everything. I cannot risk your safety or your career for anything. This isn't about locking you up; this is about protecting the one thing that means just as much to me as my children. The one *person* who has torn my world apart and left my rapidly beating heart on ground for all to see."

Holy romantic.

His eyes shift between mine. "You have changed me, changed my entire life for the better. You have no clue just how in love with you I am. I can't leave this to chance, darling."

I suck in a breath at his words.

"You love me?" I ask like a meek little girl and not the strong woman I've tried desperately to become.

He pulls me over him so that I'm straddling his torso, hand still on my jaw, then he brings me closer to him and tips our foreheads together.

"I love you more than I have words to express. I love everything you are, everything you have been, and everything you will become. And if I'm a lucky son of a bitch, I'll get to be by your side and watch it all happen."

I shake my head in awe, attempting to find the words to say.

But all I come up with is: "I love you too. And you better be by my side through it all." A watery chuckle escapes me. "God, I'm so in love with you."

Amazement washes over his features like he can't believe I could really love him too. "We're really doing this?"

"I think so," I whisper, afraid to break the spell.

His lips press against mine in the softest of kisses. "From now on, we do things together. No making decisions we think are best without consulting each other."

My heart twinges in my chest because I know I'm keeping Cierra's connection a secret right now, but I'm also not willing to bring it up when I don't have the entire picture. There's more to the story, and tomorrow, I'll do more digging and get more answers before I bring him into the fold.

For tonight, I'm going to enjoy some alone time with the man I love.

Chapter 36

Felix

The early rays of sun wash over my face as I watch Antoinette sleeping beside me. My fingertips brush over her skin softly, hoping I don't wake her up.

Last night, exhaustion won out for both of us. It's been a high-stress week, and we were both finally able to relax in each other's arms enough to get some much-needed rest.

I still can't quite believe she's mine. That she loves me. It feels like a dream, one I've only had glimpses of but no real clarity. But this? Antoinette? She's real, and my priorities are all jumbled now. Retirement is at the forefront of my mind. Not because I don't think we can handle this scandal—if anything, the united front will squash most of it before it takes off more—but because I don't think I can do another year like this. I can't travel almost every week, only seeing her a couple of days before the job takes over. I can't spend more hours working than seeing her.

"I can hear you thinking from here." Antoinette's voice is groggy but amused.

"Sorry to wake you, darling," I murmur, pressing a kiss to her bare shoulder.

"Probably need to get up anyway. Coffee?" She stretches, the sheet pooling at her waist giving me a delectable view of her breasts in her silk tank top.

"On its way," I say, still mesmerized.

"You're amazing." Her head rolls to face me. "Eyes up here, love." She smirks.

My gaze travels up to her face, where I unapologetically raise my eyebrow.

Room service interrupts anything I could say, forcing me out of bed and to the door. Once I'm back with coffee to bring Antoinette into the land of the living, we make a plan.

"I think we should figure out how deep this all goes," she says.

"Like look into Rocco more?"

"Yeah, like where this stems from, who all is involved. See what we can connect and come up with a plan to shut them up once and for all."

"And maybe write up a press release about us." I hold my breath, waiting to see how she reacts.

"Yeah?" Her entire body lights up.

"Cat's out of the bag already. We should at least say our piece and then leave it alone. If we turn it into a huge deal, we'll never be rid of the media."

"Very true." She takes a long sip of her coffee.

I force myself to roll out of bed and put on at least some pants. If we want to get things done before Monza, we need to do some research today. We have until tomorrow before we need to be on a plane for the race.

"Take your time," I tell Antoinette as I walk out of the bedroom in search of where I dropped off my work bag.

I find it by the front door—not shocking, considering I pounced on my woman before the door was even closed behind me. Getting myself set up next to her laptop on the dining room table takes no time at all, and before I can really dig in, Antoinette walks out in her silk sleep set that's bound to kill me the rest of the day. My dick stiffens in an instant, and I barely have control over my mind. It wanders to what we could be doing instead of this shit.

"Don't look at me like that. We have work to do." Her mischievous smirk makes my cock jump in my sweats.

"Then sit your ass down so I only have a view of your perfect tits and not that ass I've been dreaming about all morning."

"An ass man? I would have guessed otherwise."

"I'm an Antoinette man, darling. *You* are my kink, my kryptonite, my affinity."

"Damn," she whispers, pupils dilated. "We really aren't going to get a lot of work done if you keep talking like that."

"I love you." I smile before turning to my computer. "So, tell me what you have."

"Your ability to just move on is wild." She shakes her head. "Currently, I have emails between Rocco and Newman—thank you for access, by the way—detailing how Newman was sabotaging your cars at the direction of Rocco."

"Those assholes."

"Bribes are included in there. I'm honestly shocked by how much they both gave away within company emails." She shows me what she has flagged. My fists clench so tight my knuckles are white and start to hurt.

"All of this over some slight he thinks I had a part of. Just because he didn't get a fucking job over me," I growl.

After reading all the emails, I look up at Antoinette and see her biting her lip.

She is hiding something; there's more to this. I don't want to outright call her on it, so I decide to play a game only I know about.

I drag her chair to me, so her legs are in between mine.

"What are you—"

I cut her off with a kiss that has her moaning into my mouth. My hand slides down to her lower back, pushing her closer to me, as the other tangles in her hair and deepens our kiss. Her hips start grinding, telling me she's turned on and ready to go.

But my little independent darling is about to learn a lesson.

I grip her hip tight in my hand, stopping her from moving before pulling back from the kiss. "Not so fast."

Her pants fill the silence between us as her eyes shift back and forth between mine, trying to figure out what my plan is.

I shift her chair back so that she's facing her laptop once more as I stand up behind her.

"Keep digging, darling." My touch ghosts over her neck, causing goosebumps to pop up all over her body. It's tempting to kiss them all, but I'm on a mission.

She has more information, but she doesn't want to tell me, and I'm willing to work for it.

"So, it-it-it looks like . . ." she stutters before trailing off as my hands skim over her shoulders, down to those breasts that have been teasing me relentlessly.

"Keep going," I breathe into her ear.

"Rocco, umm, paid Newman to fuck with the . . . umm, the balance system. And he umm. . . *Oh god.*" Her head tips back against my stomach. My fingers are tracing circles around her nipples, soft enough that they turn to peaks like they're reaching for more contact. It's not enough for her, and she's struggling to focus. I fucking love it.

"What does he have on Newman?" I ask.

"I, umm, I don't know." Her voice is breathy, making my abs clench tight as arousal spikes my blood.

"We need to figure that out. You said he was supposed to get hired at Empress?"

"Umm, yeah, that looks like the original plan." Her moan has her struggling to finish her sentence, so I ease up on her for a moment. "Uh, Rocco said he saw us together in Canada and wanted to 'inflict as much damage as possible'. His words, not mine."

"What a fucking tool. At least he didn't find a way to mess with your cars."

"Actually, I think he did. Somewhat, at least." She perks up and scrolls through the document she's putting together. "I didn't see it before, but press asked about one of our wings early in the season, which was fucked, but we caught it before it actually affected anything outside of practice." She scrolls through the endless emails to a specific date as my hands knead her shoulders. I couldn't keep my hands off of her even if I wanted to.

"Here." She points at the screen, and I read the email.

David with Empress . . . point of contact . . . feed the press a line about a wing issue . . .

"Jesus, how far does this go?" I ask.

She freezes in her chair, and I know I have her. Moving her chair back, I lean forward, putting my shoulder on her stomach before lifting her up and fireman carrying her to the bedroom.

"Felix! We have work to do." She smacks my ass.

"This is work," I grunt as I throw her onto the bed, snagging her ankles and pulling her to me. "You are keeping information from me, and I don't like that."

"Felix . . ."

"No, now you have to wait until I've had my fill, then you can tell me." I feel feral, like I'm not in control of my body but also like I want to drown in her.

I want her dripping wet so I can taste her, use it to paint my body so she knows she has me completely. I want to drink her up until her voice is hoarse and she's so boneless she'll tell me what she knows. Only then will I allow myself a release.

She thinks this will be about me getting off, but that couldn't be further from the truth.

My eyes move over her entire body, unsure of where to start. I finally settle on that delectable neck, right where it meets her shoulder—the spot that never fails to have her whimpering. Climbing up onto the bed, I'm careful not to touch her. Once I'm hovering over her, I lower to that spot and kiss it. She moans, reaching up to cup my cheek when I pull back.

"Hands down, or I tie you up." It comes out harsher than I intended, but she does as I say. Her lips are parted, and she's breathing in heavy pants. If she had an ounce of apprehension in her body, I'd stop, but I rather think she likes this.

I pick up where I left off, starting soft before biting the area hard. Her hips jolt off the bed, attempting to find purchase, but are left empty.

"Please," she begs.

"Ah, darling, torture is the name of the game."

My lips brush against her breast, not touching her nipple at all, as my hand strokes along her stomach. It sucks in with her breath, and I swear I'm already about to combust.

I sit up on my knees, slowly hooking my fingers into her shorts before dragging them down her legs. She splays them open for me as soon as I toss her bottoms, exposing herself and her need to me like a perfectly wrapped present.

"Fuck, you are gorgeous." I close my eyes, attempting to regain control.

"Please," Antoinette whimpers.

"You beg so prettily. Makes me want to give in and give you what you want. In a way, I will, but it won't be what you're expecting." I suck a deep breath in through my nose, savoring her heady scent before exhaling. Brushing my nose along the bend in her thigh, I switch to the other side, licking my lips in anticipation.

"Felix, fuck," she barks when I graze my lips over her clit.

It's the straw that breaks me. I want her so fucking bad I can barely breath. I need her scent surrounding me as I lose myself in her pleasure.

The first lick up her pussy is like the best dessert I've ever had in my life. She's so wet that there's no resistance, only a smooth glide as I swirl her clit. Her hips damn near buck me off of her until I hold them down with my elbow. My hand puts gentle pressure on her lower stomach as my other circles her opening, my mouth refusing to move from her clit.

"Oh my God!" She squeals as I slide one finger, then two inside of her. There will be no slow warm-up today.

Sucking her clit into my mouth, I curl my fingers up and brush her G-spot over and over again as I press down firmer on her belly.

Her scream of pleasure and the pulse around my fingers signal her orgasm, but it's not enough. Not yet.

I continue the same ministrations. Even as she tries to push my head away. Even as she thrashes her head back and forth from the over-stimulation.

I'm not stopping.

Because I can hear it, the sound of how wet she is. I'm going to show her something completely new, and I'd be shocked if I don't come in my pants from it.

"I can't!" she screams as I pump my fingers harder. I moan on her clit, providing more vibrations, before popping off of it.

"Bear down, just a little," I tell her before going back to her clit.

I don't know if she actually hears me or if her body is just reacting naturally, but the moment she bears down, she floods me.

I work her through it, drinking up as much as I possibly can and giving her clit some much needed relief. She comes like a fountain, and I'd happily drink from her every fucking day of my life.

Pulling back is a hardship, but I need answers. I also need to stop my cock from leaking pre-cum, like it's currently doing. I kneel between her legs as she catches her breath. My hand squeezes the base of my dick hard, staving off my orgasm for the moment, but only just.

"What else do you know, darling?" I ask in a dark tone.

"What?"

"You're keeping something from me. Tell me." I put my thumb on her clit and apply the barest of pressure, but it does the job. She shifts her hips to get away from me before looking up at me with guilt in her eyes.

My chest locks up at the unknown, but her words release it almost instantly.

"Rocco and Cierra were working together seven years ago," she whimpers, closing her eyes like she's afraid of my reaction.

Honestly? I probably would feel the same in her position.

But I feel nothing.

Annoyance, sure, but utter betrayal? None.

I should feel betrayed. It almost ruined my entire career, but all I can think about is how all of it brought me to Antoinette. If none of it happened, I wouldn't have this woman in my life, in my bed. I wouldn't have just made her squirt for the first time, and I wouldn't be contemplating retiring just to spend all my days with her.

"Say something," she whispers.

"I . . . I guess I shouldn't be shocked," is all I can offer.

She peeks through her cracked eyelids before they pop open with a furrow of her brow. "You're not mad?"

"Oh, I am. But more so that Rocco's been messing with my life so much for so long. About Cierra, though? No."

For as much clarity as I have right now, Antoinette has as much confusion.

"We'll figure it out in a minute," I tell her before sticking my fingers in my mouth and sucking the taste of her off of them. Her eyelashes flutter as she moans. "You like that?"

"I have no fucking clue what just happened, and I shouldn't want more because I'm so damn sensitive, but God yes, that's such a turn-on."

It's like a fuse explodes inside of me. I'm shoving my pants down, releasing my cock that's begging to be inside of her.

"Fuck, darling, this is going to be fast. I'm sorry," I grunt as I line up and slide home easily. She's soft and pliable, and so fucking hot it's like she's scalding me in the best way possible. Combined with how wet she is? I'm a goner.

She reaches up, pulling me down on top of her, and kisses me like it'll be the last time. Within minutes, she's gasping into my mouth, tightening around my cock and making me lose my mind.

The orgasm hits me before I can even pretend to stop it. Grunting into her neck, I thrust a couple more times as I come down from the highest of highs.

Both of us are panting, trying to catch our breath for a long while. I hold her tight to me, probably too tight, but I can't find it in me to give her space.

Holding her is all I ever want to do from here on out.

"What the hell was that?" she whispers.

"That was something I've been dying to do to you for a while." I chuckle.

"I didn't think I could . . . I mean I know women squirt, but I thought it was like either you did or didn't. But like . . . what the fuck?" she mumbles, her head trying to grasp the extent of the pleasure she just felt.

"Your compliments are doing things to me."

"How was any of that a compliment?" She pulls back to look at me like I'm crazy.

I thrust my still-hard cock in her once more as I say, "Antoinette, you didn't think you could do that, but I showed you that you can. And you better believe I'm going to do it again and again and again." I thrust once more before kissing her hard.

"I think you're just going to kill me by orgasm." She sighs.

"Never, darling. I might make you pass out but never kill."

Her chuckle dies as I finally pull out, attempting to give her a reprieve. The serious look she gives me makes me sigh.

"You're really not upset?"

"Upset? No. I just think there's even more to it than we know." I pull her to my side. "I'm more worried about the possible Brad connection, to be honest." She stiffens but doesn't say anything. "I want to go through the emails more today and see if we can get anything else."

"Once we take a nap," she says. "And if you think what you just did was an incentive to not hide anything, I gotta be honest . . . it kind of just makes me want to do it more."

The bark of laughter that erupts from me is shocking. "So, you're a fan of me taking you right to the edge of what you can handle?"

"I don't care what you call it. I want more. Just not today," she adds with a slow blink of her eyes.

I kiss her forehead. "Rest, darling. The emails can wait."

Chapter 37
Toni

We haven't found a connection to Brad yet, and honestly, I'm glad. It just feels like one less thing to worry about.

We've been at it for most of the day, and I want to be done. We have to fly out tomorrow, so we're running out of time together without the pressures of the job.

"Come on, big boss man. The rest can wait." I stand up, pulling his hand as I do.

"Antoinette . . ."

"We have to fly out tomorrow, and I just want one last night of normalcy, whatever that actually looks like."

He stands up, scooping me into his arms bridal style, and walks off to the bedroom.

"Jesus, you are going to hurt yourself," I grumble.

"Are you calling me old? Because I thought I had made it clear I'm still very virile." He arches an eyebrow at me.

"I'm saying I threw out my back last month because I sneezed. This isn't about you being old; it's how our bodies can't do what they once could." I roll my eyes.

He tosses me onto the bed, prowling after me and finally lying next to me.

He stares at me for an unnerving amount of time, tracing my jaw, neck, and anything else he can reach. I get lost in the feeling, lost in his eyes and the promises they hold.

"What do you want in your life?" he murmurs.

"Like, grand plans?" I ask as he nods in response. "I want to feel like I'm truly living. Like I'm making a difference even if it's just to three people. I want to make sure I leave the world better than when I entered it, and I want a partner for all of that to love and support along the way." Cliché? Maybe, but it doesn't make it any less true. I try not to put tangible goals on my life—a fictitious dollar amount or title that means I've "made it". Plans change, goals shift, and I don't like boxing myself in , not anymore.

"You really have no clue just how special you are, do you?" he says in awe.

Clearing my throat, I reciprocate. "What about you? What do you want in your life?"

"If you had asked me before the season started, my answer would have been very different."

"What would it have been?" I'm curious what a man who seems like he has it all would have wanted in his life. I know better now, that it wasn't all sunshine and rainbows, but still.

"I would have wanted a better relationship with Henrik and Emilie. To be considered a good father. That's all I wanted."

My heart breaks for how much he's struggled with that, but it also heals in the same breath because I know it's so much better now.

"And now?" I ask, almost afraid of his answer.

"Now, I want you. I want to love you until my last breath. I want to support you as you dismantle what we currently know as Formula 1. I want to stand beside you as you change the landscape for all professional sports. I also want to continue to work on my relationship with the kids, but that's already so much better that I don't feel as dire about it anymore."

I stare at him, at a loss for words.

Besides my Empress family, I've never had anyone in my corner. It's been me and me alone that pushed for more. I was the only person I could rely on. It's strange to think that it doesn't have to be like that anymore, that it won't be.

"What does that all mean?" I ask, trying to wrap my head around his words. We both still work insane schedules. We both still don't have a ton of time outside of breaks to really be together.

Possibly the biggest hurdle to all that support is that we work for rival teams.

It's not like I don't know he'll support me from the sidelines, but openly? We still have to hide.

"It means I want to retire, from at least being the team principal at Legacy. I'm not sure if I can truly stop working, but maybe Sydney has something I can jump into." He smiles the genuine smile I can never get enough of as my heart pounds in my chest.

A whooshing starts in my ears as I process what he's saying.

"Retire?" I croak.

"What do I have to prove? This sport can be toxic, and generally, people don't know when to step away. If I have everything I could ever want in my life"—he pulls me closer to him—"then why do I need to work myself to the bone? It's not because I need the money. And time is a luxury I don't want to waste. Not with you in the picture."

"That's crazy," I say under my breath, mostly to myself.

"It's not so crazy; it's been in the back of my mind for a while. Steph is on board."

"So, you're going to retire just because of me?" I can hear myself getting a little hysterical. My head immediately goes to my situation with Brad. I don't ever want someone to give up who they are for me. I would never ask that of him.

"Not because of you. But because my priorities have shifted. I have nothing left to gain from staying at Legacy. At what point do I say enough is enough? In five years? Ten? Why not now? I can follow you around like a lovesick puppy who will sneak any attention I can."

I *hate* that I can't separate what he's saying from what Brad did to me. I know, logically, that this is not the same. I'm not forcing Felix to do anything, I'm not isolating him, but it still feels like I'd be pulling him away from his life just because my career at Empress has just started.

"It's too much, I know. Don't think about all of that right now. Just know that before I make any big decisions, we'll talk about it again, okay? We're in this together now." He stares at me hard. "If you want to be," he adds, uncertainty painting his words.

"Of course we're in this together," I say, although I'm not sure I mean it.

I press a kiss to his lips as a means to end the conversation and distract him. It works a little too well as we make out for a long while until a yawn escapes me.

"Get some sleep, darling," Felix whispers into the crown of my head and promptly falls asleep.

I'm not as lucky.

***

It's four a.m., and I can't sleep.

I slowly disentangle myself from Felix and go to the living area. I quickly change into some leggings and an oversized shirt.

Grabbing the key off the side table, I quietly head out the door and head down to the lobby. I just need some fresh air, some time to think. Felix saying he wants to retire threw me for a huge loop, and I just can't see it objectively yet.

I pull up my messages and send a group text to Daisy and Sydney, hoping I don't wake them up but needing to talk things through with someone. If they're asleep and don't answer, then I'll just talk it out with myself.

I cringe, knowing two buzzes instead of just the one probably woke them up. I pace up and down the sidewalk in front of the Vanstone but decide I need something different. The river runs nearby, so I head that way and walk along the river's edge.

Felix is not Brad.

I would never try to trap Felix the way that Brad trapped me, so why is this stressing me out so much?

My phone buzzes, halting my steps.

Sydney:

> Daisy's for sure asleep, so I took her out of the chat. What's going on?

Me:

> Felix said he wants to retire.

Sydney:

> Okay? And that's terrible?

Me:

> I don't know! Shouldn't it be? I mean, he's just going to give up the life he knows and, what, follow me around everywhere?

Sydney:

> I need you to take a deep breath. Felix is a big boy; he can absolutely make sound decisions on his own. He's been working for Legacy for years, and he's won championships with them. He has nothing more to win or gain by staying, and if he happened to find something more worth his time, why is that a bad thing? Especially if that someone is you?

Sydney:

> Also, if he does retire, how does he feel about a part-time job with Empress???

I burst out laughing, which I assume was her intention, but it's cut short when someone grabs me from behind.

There's no chance to scream before I'm being dragged backwards, hand over my mouth. I don't even realize my phone slipped from my grasp until much later.

Kicking and screaming gets me nowhere, just a tightened grip that's sure to leave bruises.

And then I get a whiff of whomever grabbed me.

Brad.

Chapter 38
Toni

I kick and attempt to scream harder now that I know who's behind me.

I didn't believe Felix when he said Brad was involved. I brushed it away, and now look where I ended up.

I slow my brain down and think about what I've learned in the few self-defense classes I have managed to take. *Rule #1: Fight like hell. Don't let them take you to a second location.* I stomp down on his foot hard enough that it startles him, causing him to loosen his hands so I can break free.

"What the fuck are you doing?" I yell as I spin around and face him.

He freezes like he wasn't expecting me to actually ask him. It takes a second, but he remembers himself. I watch while fear trickles in my veins as his face morphs from shock to hatred.

"I'm taking what's mine," he growls, stalking toward me.

I'm not sure what comes over me, but all the doubt, all the comparing of my situation with Brad to Felix's situation to me, becomes clear in a nanosecond. I rear back and punch him straight in the nose before kneeing him in the balls. I'm not taking any chances.

"Ow, fuck!" he yells, falling to the ground.

I barely register what happened. There's no pain, no realization that I actually hit someone. All I can think about is how ridiculous I've been the past few hours.

"*I* am not property. *I* am not yours to fuck with anymore." I walk toward him and put my foot on his dick, pressing down with all my weight as he squirms from the pain I just inflicted. I need to let this out, even if he doesn't hear me.

"You isolated me. You took me away from everything I knew, took my support system away, and made it seem like you were doing me a fucking favor!" I yell. "You don't get to come here after an entire year and act like you have any access to me or my life. You don't get to try and *take* me like you're some sort of kidnapper. You are a nobody. Do you hear me?" He doesn't reply, just whimpers as he covers his nose, blood streaming down. "Do you hear me?!" I scream, shoving my foot harder against his sorry excuse for a penis.

"Yes," he mumbles, eyes wide.

"Tell me what your plan was," I pant with exertion. I realize the events of the last few minutes are going to catch up with me quickly, and I need all the information I can get right this second.

He garbles something I can't make out before I realize my foot is preventing him from actually talking. I ease up but don't move my foot. This is an effective way to keep him where I want him while I get answers.

"Say that again."

"I said it wasn't my idea," he rushes out.

"What do you mean?"

"The plan was always to go after you and sabotage Empress. But you weren't accessible, so plans changed. But I was promised you!" he attempts to yell.

"You have two minutes to explain in great detail what the fuck you are talking about."

"I-I— Rocco, he found me one day, lurking around the Empress offices. He asked me some shit about how I knew you and asked me to go to dinner. It was fancy. He-he bought me some cool shit, and I agreed to help."

"Help what, exactly?"

"He said he wanted to take away his biggest competitors so he could finally win a championship."

Fucking Rocco is even more incompetent than I assumed.

"So, he went with sabotage? What was your plan?" I ask, my mind whirling a mile a minute.

"I was supposed to get back with you and get him documents of plans from your computer." I press my foot down harder in anger.

"Did you tell him I was this close to filing a restraining order and that there was no way in hell you'd be getting close enough to me to be getting anything off my computer?" I growl at the fucking audacity these dumbasses have.

"I-I-I thought you'd come back to me."

"In what fucking world?!" I yell, throwing my hands up. "You treated me like shit! You manipulated me. You're a textbook fucking narcissist who emotionally abused me for *years!* Where, in all of that, did you think this plan would fucking work?!"

"He promised me things. I wasn't thinking about if I could do it or not," he mumbles.

I pat my pockets before realizing I have leggings on and have no clue where my phone ended up.

"Yeah, no fucking shit. God, you really are that stupid, aren't you?" I shake my head, more at myself for ever falling for this prick. "Give me your phone, and then you're going to listen to me, got it?" He nods rapidly, handing me his phone while I still have my foot on his manhood. I must say it's a damn effective way to keep him immobilized.

I pull up the internet browser and sign into my email account. There's no way I'm trying to find my phone right this second, and Lord knows I don't know anyone's number off the top of my head.

From: AB (wannabebosslady@genericmail.com)
To: FK (Swedish_Boss48@genericmail.com)
Subject: Caught an asshole
I don't have my phone, so this is the best I could do because I don't remember anyone's fucking number. I'm by the river, just down from the hotel, and I have Brad. When you get this, can you come here?
No need to worry. I'm pretty sure I've got it handled.
I love you,
-T

Next, I call the police and briefly explain the situation. They promise police presence in minutes, so I know I only have so much time to say what I need to.

"Here's what's going to happen. You're going to give the police everything you have on Rocco when they get here. You will not keep anything to yourself, and you will fall on your damn sword, do you hear me?" He nods, but I'm on a roll. "You have no control in my life anymore. Your time to manipulate me, to make yourself feel like a big man, is over. The years I spent with you have made me second-guess every action of an actual good man. You did that. You made me think I wasn't worthy of true affection. You will not step foot near me if you ever get out of jail. You will not attempt to make contact with me. I spent years trying to make you love me, which is pathetic, by the way. You have made me doubt so much of myself, and that's done. You. Do. Not. Own. Me. Anymore. I am nothing to you. If I ever see you again, I'll do a lot more than smash your nose and your balls."

I'm calm, my tone is normal, and it's like this release throughout my entire body happens. I've spent too long worrying about this small man's opinions. No more.

"Do you understand me?" I ask.

He whimpers and nods in reply.

"Say the fucking words, Brad," I bark.

"Y-y-yes, I understand." He sniffles.

Shaking my head at him in disgust, I feel like I've come full circle.

And then I hear the clapping. A loud roar followed by hoots and cheers surround me as I look around. A crowd has gathered, and I didn't even notice. A few "you go, girl!" and "hell yes, tell him!" get called out, making me smirk. Then the sirens come.

Arms wrap around my middle and pull me back against a strong body. I tense for a minute before I register the scent of the man who has changed everything for me.

"Felix," I breathe.

"Holy fuck, I was so worried." His hot breath fans over my neck before he presses a kiss there.

I still have my foot on Brad, keeping him in place and not taking any chances. Commotion sounds around us as a couple of police file in. A few of the onlookers give the basic details as the police take charge of Brad so I can finally take my foot off of him.

I spin around in Felix's arms and bury my face in his chest. His rapid heartbeat somehow calms me even more. I'm here. He's here. We're safe. We have answers.

"What happened?" Sydney's out-of-breath voice comes from next to me.

"What are you doing here? Are you okay?" I pull back from Felix and grab Sydney, looking her over to make sure she's okay.

"Jesus, I am not the one you should be worried about right now. Why is Brad in handcuffs?" She hugs me tightly before pulling back and looking around to try and figure things out.

"Long story, and it can wait for now." I sigh, adrenaline quickly fading.

She nods and lets me go, but Felix takes her place just a fast.

And then the police come talk to me.

Chapter 39
Felix

I wake up and know immediately something is off.

"Antoinette?" I call out once I see she's not in bed.

"Toni!" I yell louder, jumping out of bed with my heart in my stomach.

My phone starts ringing, but I ignore it, walking through the entire suite before realizing Antoinette isn't here.

More ringing irritates me, but I pick up the phone. "What?"

"Is Toni with you?" Sydney asks, panic in her voice.

"No. What the fuck is going on?" I pull my phone away from my ear, seeing that it's almost five in the morning.

"She was texting me and then just stopped. I tried calling her, but there's no answer, which isn't like her."

"Shit. Do you know where she was?" I'm already hopping into pants and a button-up shirt I carelessly threw on the ground.

"No clue. She just SOS texted me and Daisy—" Her words halt unnaturally.

"Why did she need an SOS?" Terror hits me dead in the chest because I know this is about our conversation last night. It was too much, too soon.

"Felix . . ."

"Fuck. Okay. I'm going to go look for her."

"I just pulled up to the hotel. I'll meet you out front." She hangs up as I run to the door, not caring that I don't have a key to get back in. Sydney can figure all of that out once we find Antoinette.

Racing out of the lobby, I see Sydney pacing off to the side, the sun just beginning to rise over the horizon.

"How long ago did you she text you?" I ask, walking in a random direction.

"She stopped about twenty minutes ago; she couldn't have gotten far. I'm more concerned that it was dark and an accident could have happened."

"Don't even say that," I growl, all my emotions wreaking havoc with every step I take.

"I know. I know, but I'm just freaked out."

"What if we're going the wrong way?" I ask, immediately turning around and running into Sydney, who I realize is trying to keep up with me. "Shit, sorry. I'm going crazy. I'll slow down." Her rheumatoid arthritis has been more manageable, but that doesn't mean I get to run her until she's knackered because I'm scared.

"Let's stop and think. If she was upset or needed to think, where would she go?"

We both sit in silence while we think until we come up with the same answer.

"The river."

Wordlessly, we head toward the river, where we hear faint yelling. My pace picks up before I slow down again. Sydney waves me off, saying she'll be there shortly, and I take off at a sprint.

A woman yelling draws my attention first. I know that voice, and it makes me run faster until I find a small crowd surrounding the love of my life and the asshole stalker she has pinned to the ground.

"In what fucking world? You treated me like shit! You manipulated me. You're a textbook fucking narcissist who emotionally abused me for *years!* Where, in all of that, did you think this plan would fucking work?!" She's animated and fierce, but most of all, she's empowered.

I see it on her face as I watch her undress her ex with her words. She's letting out years of pent-up emotions. Years of being stuck under his thumb and saying nothing.

It's brilliant to watch. Like she's taking back her life the way she wants to.

I watch her take his phone, typing something out before calling the police. My phone buzzes. I check it and see an email from the love of my life, not three feet away from me. It makes me smile and rage, but most of all, I'm beaming with pride. She definitely has it handled, and I wouldn't dream of robbing her of this closure, no matter how badly I want to wrap her in my arms.

As she continues to tell him off, her words hit me hard. She's been struggling with differences between Brad and me. It's taken me a long time to break through some of her walls, but I underestimated just how much he altered the way she sees things.

Like a lightning bolt, our conversation from last night pounds in my head.

She wasn't comparing our relationships; she was comparing what Brad made her do with me giving up my job for her.

She thought me retiring meant she was doing the same thing to me that Brad did to her.

Clapping interrupts my thoughts, followed by police sirens. I can't sit on the sidelines anymore. I walk up to Antoinette and slide my arms around her stomach. She tenses for a second before leaning back on me.

It takes a while for the scene to clear and for Antoinette to speak with the police officers. She explains that she has more evidence on Rocco and will stop by the station later.

The entire time I'm by her side, guilt tries to strangle me.

I knew she had a hard relationship with Brad. I knew she was going to take a while to understand that things are different, that our relationship was different. But I kept pushing. I basically told her I was retiring, giving up my life as I know it for her, and I didn't stop to think about how she would perceive that.

Sydney pulls her to the side to discuss work for a moment while I pull out my phone and call Steph.

"Felix?"

"I need you to just listen for a second because I don't have a ton of time, but I need help."

"Okay."

"Antoinette's ex came after her today, attacked her, and made some pretty damning claims about Rocco." She gasps, but I continue because that's not the part I need advice on. "I told her I was thinking about retiring and following her all over the world while she's the team principal at Empress, and I think I freaked her out. Because Brad—her ex—isolated her from everything she knew.

I don't know if this makes sense, but how do I get her to see that I *want* to do this? I *want* to have less obligation so I can have more time with her, not so that I'm isolated."

Silence greets me, but I wait Steph out. She needs to process my very unorganized thoughts.

"First, is she okay?"

"I think so. She's a total badass and handled him like a fucking pro." The awe is still rich in my voice.

"Atta girl. As for advice, give her time to wrap her head around what just happened first. Then, you're going to discuss why the situation isn't the same. She isn't isolating you from your family or friends. She isn't forcing this on you. She needs to see that you want to do this for yourself, not for her."

"But I do want to do it for her," I say dumbly.

"I know, but you also want to do it because priorities in *your* life have changed. Toni being a priority for you doesn't mean you're doing it for her."

"So, I tell her that retiring would make *me* happy because it means I get more time with her."

"Basically, although I'm sure you'll find better words."

I bark out a laugh at that.

"Go take care of her, and don't stress her reaction to your retirement too much, okay? She's working through a lot, but I know she'll come around."

"Thanks, Steph. I'll call you later."

Antoinette is walking toward me, my phone call almost entirely forgotten as she walks into my open arms and collapses.

"Let's get you back to the hotel," I murmur, looking up and making eye contact with Sydney. She nods and starts to head back to the Vanstone.

"I have so much to go through to give to the police." Her voice is muffled by my shirt, her face still buried against my chest right where my heart is.

"We can worry about that later." I pull back enough to grab her hand and lead her the short distance to the main road. I know what just happened will hit her hard, and I know she won't want to be in public for that.

She's fine until the elevator ride. Her throat bobs a few times as she attempts to swallow back her tears, but it's useless.

I silently wrap my arms around her and let her cry into my shirt. I clumsily lead her to the room, where Sydney is waiting for us with the door open. It takes some time, but I get to the couch and sit down before pulling Toni onto my lap.

Sydney and I let her have her time to feel it all, everything that happened.

By the time she comes up for air, it's mid-morning.

"Can I order us some food? Or I can go and have it delivered," Sydney offers.

"I'm not hungry, but I know I should eat. And you both need to hear what happened." Antoinette sits up.

While we wait for room service to arrive, Sydney and I are filled in on what Antoinette learned from Brad.

Rocco is in far deeper than we realized.

"I also learned something else. Not from Brad." Antoinette hesitates before taking a deep breath. "Seven years ago, Rocco blackmailed Cierra. She released the photos and attempted to send Rocco the plans for your car at that time. They had dated briefly, and Rocco had some stuff on her that he used to get what he wanted. I only read Rocco's side, so I'm not sure how much Cierra was in it more than just being blackmailed."

My heart stops.

All this time. All the doubt, the fucked-up relationship with my kids. It was all because of a man who couldn't do better, so he thought he'd fuck with everyone's life in order to win. And for what? It's not like he isn't making good money. He's around luxury every single day.

"I'm so sorry, Felix. I should have told you when I learned about it, but I wanted to see how far it all went," she mutters.

"I—" I scoot her over onto the couch and stand up. "I need a minute."

The bedroom provides the solace I need.

It's hard to grasp what I've been told. Combined with my heart stopping for a while until I found Antoinette, I need to wrap my head around a lot right now. For seven years, I thought Cierra leaked the photos for clout. For seven years, I thought Cierra was simply there at the right time and place. Although our relationship didn't last, I didn't harbor any hatred for her, not really—just annoyance. For seven years, my relationship with my kids was nonexistent because I was so wrecked with guilt for betraying them.

And she was in on it the entire time. Not only that, she was helping Rocco for years. It wasn't just her being blackmailed; it was the fact that she went along with it all. It seems like it was her plan all along, like everything I went through with her, *for* her, was just a game. My whole life was a scheme to both her and Rocco, to fuck up without thought to any repercussions. Antoinette had told me about this, but I just assumed Cierra did it because she felt she had no other option. This, though? Dating him? Proves she was in on it the entire time.

But . . . if all of that never happened, would I have met Antoinette? Is it even worth dwelling on because it's in the past? Life, right this minute, is so damn good. Take out all the Rocco bullshit, and I'm happier than I've ever been. I have a purpose, a reason to live my life to the best of my ability.

She's sitting in the living area, probably worried about me.

I'm still hurt that Cierra chose the path she did and that Rocco took his vendetta against me so far, but it doesn't really change my life right now.

Determined, I walk out to the living space and find Sydney gone, a cart of food brought in and waiting for us.

"I'm so sorry—" I cut Antoinette off, cupping her cheek as I bend down and kiss her like it's the first time.

In a way, it kind of is. It's the first time I'm kissing her with a clear head. It's the first time I'm kissing her since we both put our exes and the past fully in the rearview mirror.

It feels like the first kiss to start the rest of my life.

Keeping our foreheads pressed together, I pull out of the kiss and soak her in.

"What was that for?" she whispers.

"For our future."

She pulls back, no doubt confused.

"The Cierra thing sucks, I won't lie, but she hasn't been a part of my life in years. Now that all the information is out in the open, I hope—I feel like—this is a new beginning. A fresh start. With the love of my life. And I kind of want to soak it all in."

"Felix . . ."

"I love you. My future is riddled by images of us together. I don't want to waste a second of our time together. Retiring means I get to do whatever the hell I want, and what I want is to help make all your dreams come true."

"How— I—"

"You don't need to analyze it right now. We can talk about it when life calms down a little. But I need you to know that I'm all in. Whatever that looks like to you, I'm all in, darling."

Chapter 40

(Transcript)

Interviewer: Seems we're lucky to have everyone today. Thanks for joining us.

Rocco Bianchi: Not a problem.

Interviewer: Now, Empress seems to be running away with the Drivers' this year. Amaro is the only one giving you a run for your money on the Constructors'. How are you feeling about that?

Toni Bailey: We feel great. The team is clicking; the drivers are happy. We just need to keep it up for nine more races.

Interviewer: And how are you feeling about your overall season so far, Felix?

Felix Karlsson: Pretty shitty, actually. No, honestly, it's been a challenge, and I've learned a lot this year. It's been hard, but the team is still working their asses off and will continue to do so. Johhny is feeling more comfortable in the car, so we'll see where the rest of the races take us.

Rocco Bianchi: It'll take you to the end of the line, that's where.

Toni Bailey: They're beating you in points.

Rocco Bianchi: For now. I've got more cards to play.

Marcus Prior: I'm so sorry for the interruption.

Interviewer: No problem. We're lucky enough to be joined by the FIA President Marcus Prior.

Marcus Prior: I actually need Rocco to come with me.

Rocco Bianchi: Why?

Marcus Prior: You're needed in a meeting with the stewards and the entire leadership board.

Rocco Bianchi: Absolutely ridiculous, that's what this is.

Interviewer: Well, that was certainly an interesting break. Anyway, what's your favorite aspect of Monza, Toni?

Toni Bailey: Well, personally, I love the history. We may not be the Italian team, but it's a blast to be surrounded by the die-hard fans. They show up rain or shine and have so much energy, even for practices.

Felix Karlsson: It's always enjoyable to go to races in the hometowns of the teams. There's a completely different dynamic, and even though we obviously want to win every race, there's a part of you that always hopes for a good race for the home team. Like Antoinette said, the energy, especially in Monza, is always exciting.

Interviewer: Wonderful. Well, we just got word. It seems that Rocco, as well as Guardian, is under investigation for a multitude of infractions, including the movement of personnel clause, non-compliance with the regulations of the car, as well as others. Any thoughts on that?

Toni Bailey: Wow, that's shocking. We'll have to wait for the outcome.

Felix Karlsson: Rocco's been underhanded for many years. I'm not shocked things have come to light this season.

Interviewer: Right. Well then, good luck this weekend, and I'm sure we'll be chatting more soon.

Chapter 41

Toni

It's been a whirlwind for a couple of days.

After the storm calmed down in Austin, I went to speak with the detectives and handed over all the files I had on Rocco and the whole . . . conspiracy. Then I hopped on a plane and flew to Italy like nothing happened.

I will say, Rocco getting pulled out by the FIA during the media conference was quite gratifying. A big thank you to Sydney for supplying all that evidence to them.

Now, I'm sitting in a conference room after Practice Two with Sydney, Daisy, Luka, and Beckett to discuss our ongoing progress as well as any changes we might need for next year.

"I really think we should bring her up. I know the team is solid, but Alejandro took forever to warm up. He's not on contract for next year, so it wouldn't be a huge deal to drop him and bring someone else in," Luka says regarding Remi Bouchard.

"But she's only been at the academy for, what , two years?" Sydney says.

"And she's crushing it. Seriously, she's not challenged, and she needs to move up," Luka adds.

"Then move her to Formula 2," Beckett chimes in.

"Guys, think about it," Daisy interjects. "First female president. First female team principal. First female driver. If we don't jump on it, we might miss the chance to make incredible history here."

"At the expense of the driver, though? What if she's not ready?" I ask.

"Toni, I promise you she's ready. She'll have a great support system here to help her adjust, and I'll be available as well. She knows me, and I've been subtly training her to be ready for this," Luka pleads.

The fact that he's pushing this so hard leads me to believe she is actually ready. But these decisions are hard.

"Except you're about to have a baby and will be out of commission for a while." I look at Daisy, who preens.

"What if I call Nate?" Beckett asks.

"For Remi?" Sydney tilts her head.

"Think about it. He knows Formula 1 better than most drivers. He can handle her physical prep, as well as make sure she's emotionally regulated for the job. Hell, he had to handle worse with me; he'll be fine with her."

"That's putting a lot of pressure on Nate, though," I add.

"Which he can handle. He's bored as fuck since I retired. Picking up random gigs here and there, like working with Alejandro for a short amount of time and traveling to keep busy. He wants to come back full time," Beckett says.

"He could come back for Alejandro again, though," Sydney says, tapping her finger to her chin.

"He's not going to do that," Beckett says darkly.

Interesting. Some bad blood there that I'm not aware of.

"If, and that's a big if, we bring Remi on, we need to put a lot of time into her development. There's a real possibility that our season tanks because of her adjusting. I'm willing to work with that because I think, in the long run, this is a good transition for the team, but I want to make sure it's not too soon. And Toni would be the one putting in the work," Sydney says.

"And Nate," Beckett adds oh-so-helpfully, making me smirk.

"I'm fine with a rocky season," I tell her. "And if Luka says she's ready, I trust his judgement."

"You shouldn't," Beckett mumbles.

"What was that? Couldn't hear you, Mr. Retirement. At least I have an actual job, not one my wife made up for me," Luka jokes back.

"Oh, and you didn't get your job because of my wife?" Beckett starts to laugh.

"Jesus, the testosterone in here is feral." Daisy sighs.

Sydney and I look at each other, decision made on both our ends.

"I'm in." I smile.

"We're going to be making Formula 1 history," Sydney says.

"Wouldn't be the first time." She nods at my response, a brilliant smile on her face.

"Then let's do it. I'll start the paperwork; you can give her a call."

"Fuck yes!" Daisy fist pumps from her chair.

"I'll call Nate," Beckett says, ignoring Luka's continued taunts. For men in their late thirties, they act more like frat boys than frat boys themselves sometimes.

Everyone gets up, the meeting adjourned, but I pull Sydney aside.

"I know it's not final, but can I share with . . ." I look down, already knowing the answer.

"Hey, I heard through the rumor mill he may be retiring soon anyway. Tell him; he knows to keep his mouth shut." Sydney smiles, but I'm hung up on the rumors.

"Where did you hear that?" We've been too busy to discuss my response to him genuinely wanting to retire.

"From Felix, obviously."

"Then I've got to see a man about a rumor." I try to keep my tone light, but Sydney sees right past it.

"Don't give him too hard a time. He's a man in love; they say dumb shit sometimes when they don't know how to express themselves."

I nod, but Felix isn't the problem here. I am.

I pull out my phone as everyone else files out of the conference room. I have big things to say, and even though we don't have to do this anymore because of the leaked pictures, it's a nod to something bigger for me.

From: AB (wannabebosslady@genericmail.com)
To: FK (Swedish_Boss48@genericmail.com)
Subject: Do you have time to chat?
There's a little spot behind the Amaro offices on the grid that's secluded.

Meet there? Five minutes?

 Miss you already, even though it's only been a couple of hours.

 -T

I suck in a deep breath and then head to the spot.

My pace is quick to the point that I'm almost sweating, but my pulse instantly calms when I see my man in his usual uniform of slacks and a button-up Legacy shirt, finished off with his black-framed glasses.

"Hi." I smile.

"Hello, darling."

"I have two things I want to talk to you about. Well, more tell you about, I guess," I ramble.

"Hey, come here." He pulls me to him in a hug that releases all the built-up tension in my shoulders. "You can tell me anything; you know that."

"I know." I take a deep breath and proceed to word-vomit my thoughts. "If you want to retire so we have more time together, more flexibility, I think I would really like that. I just didn't want you to end up feeling like me when I was with Brad. Even though I know I would never knowingly put you in that situation. I don't want you to think you have to give up anything to be with me, though. And then there's your family, so I know you can't be with me all the time, you know? But I've been thinking about it, and I think if you really want to, I'm in support of your decision."

God, that was a mess.

"What's the other thing?" he asks, not saying a word about anything I've just said.

"Umm." I'm thrown off but pull myself together enough to switch topics. "We're going to sign Remi Bouchard for next season."

His smile is my favorite one. The one that says he's so damn happy, that says he's thrilled for something I've done even if I don't see it as a big deal. It's the supportive one, the one I've never gotten from another person.

"I am so fucking proud of you. And Sydney, for that matter."

Out of nowhere, my chin starts to wobble and my eyes fill with tears.

"Hey, no tears unless they're happy." He swipes at my cheek, brushing them away.

"I am happy, I think. It depends on what you think about my earlier ramblings." I hold my breath as he cups my jaw with both hands, tilting my face up to his.

"I already have my written notice done. I was just waiting to make sure it was okay with you before I sent it. I honestly can't think of a better way to spend my retirement."

"Sydney's going to poach you." I laugh through my happy tears.

"Might as well make her pay me to follow you around everywhere." He smiles.

"You're sure about this?"

"Never been surer of something. I've lived life the way I was supposed to; now, it's time to live it the way I want to. And that's by your side."

"I know we've already labelled it, but we're doing this? For real?"

"If by 'this' you mean spending the rest of our lives together and being happier than anyone could ever be, then yes, darling, we're doing this." He leans down and presses a kiss to my lips, sealing the deal.

Chapter 42
Felix

Monza was the best race we've had all year. Antoinette killed it, per usual, taking first and second, but we snuck in with a third place to round out the podium.

Shit hit the fan with Rocco. The FIA investigation was just the beginning, and a lot of other information is coming out from others who didn't feel safe to speak up earlier. He's not only out of the sport, but it looks like he'll be arrested and sued soon as well, thanks to the women who came forward about his unwanted sexual advances, one of them being Cierra. Although, I'm not sure how that works with all the countries he pulled shit in. Not my problem anymore, thank God.

Now, I'm on a plane heading to San Francisco to meet Emilie and Steph to move my daughter into her new apartment. I asked Antoinette to come—Steph even agreed—but she said this was family time and that she had meetings she couldn't reschedule because of everything she's missed. We understood, but next time, her ass is coming with me.

In time, she'll realize she is family, but I think that'll take some time to sink in.

But we have time, and I can't fucking wait.

The flight is uneventful. I spend it going over some specs for next season; even though I've already sent in my notice, there's still things to work on. The owner of Legacy wasn't shocked, and he'd already had people lined up to interview. He said watching me in the media conferences was very telling as to my feelings about Antoinette, especially when the pictures were released, so he was expecting it if not this season, then next.

The drive to the hotel is short, luckily, and once I'm finally there, I find Emilie and Steph sitting in the lobby waiting for me.

Em jumps up and hugs me. I'll never get over the feeling of having her openly talk to me and be so affectionate.

"I'm so excited you were able to come. The apartment is so nice," she gushes like I didn't painstakingly find options I approved of before sending them to Steph for her and Em to choose from.

"I can't wait. Are we doing dinner and then calling it an early night so we can move everything in tomorrow?" I ask as she pulls back. We have movers, but according to the women in this family, we still need to set things up and make it look like "home".

"Yes please. That flight was so damn long." Steph sidles up next to us. We go up to the suite and drop off my things before heading to the restaurant in the hotel.

Dinner starts fine, nothing out of the ordinary, but out of nowhere, things hit me.

My daughter isn't my little girl anymore. She's grown and about to do amazing things with her life. She's moving out and living on her own, and I'm suddenly very worried about what that means.

Clearing my throat, I attempt to bring up my myriad of thoughts.

"I just want to tell you that I'm proud of you. This is a big change, a big step, and I'm honestly at a loss as to when you grew up. But I know you're going to do great things at school and in life."

Emilie is silent, and I peek over at Steph to check if I fucked up, only to see her eyes glistening with restrained tears.

Shit, I messed up.

My thoughts are halted by the sound of Em's chair scraping on the floor as she launches herself at me in the biggest hug.

"Thank you. That means . . ." She gulps. "It means everything."

I wrap my arms around her and hold tight. She may be growing up—grown—but she'll forever be my daughter, the little girl who continues to change my life.

I finally release her, kissing her cheek, before she goes back to her seat when

Steph clears her throat. "So, fill us in on all things Toni."

"Oh yes!" Em claps and leans forward like I'm telling her a huge secret.

"Nothing major, I suppose. You know all about the Rocco shit, so we're mostly dealing with the fallout of that."

"But what about the two of you?" Emilie asks.

"We're good—great, actually. I put in my notice yesterday."

Em's eyes widen comically as Steph's lips roll inward in a poor attempt to hide her smile.

"What does that mean?" Em asks.

"It means, at the end of the season, I'm retiring. And then I'll travel with Antoinette. So I won't really be done with the sport, just the title."

"Oh my God! You love her!" Emilie squeals so loud most of the restaurant looks over at us.

"Em, chill," Steph tells her.

"Sorry, sorry. This is just so exciting. Are you going to get married?"

"That's up to Antoinette," I tell her honestly. I don't care if we get married or not, as long as I'm with her for the rest of my life. I don't need a piece of paper to tell me she's the love of my life.

"I'm really happy for you, Felix. Toni is the best addition to the family." Steph smiles at me.

I reach over and grab her hand, squeezing it in thanks for dealing with me over the decades. She's the reason our family isn't dysfunctional. She's the reason the kids are so well adjusted. And I couldn't thank her enough for that.

"We'll have to double date," I throw out there.

"You could have a double wedding!" Emilie adds.

"Jesus, Em, please don't go bothering Antoinette about wedding planning when there isn't one on the horizon at the moment." I take off my glasses and rub the bridge of my nose. Steph finally laughs and doesn't stop for a couple of minutes.

"No, really, I am happy for the two of you, but you will absolutely have this one"—she points to Emilie—"hounding you about a wedding now."

"And what about you?" I grill her right back.

"Oh, I send her wedding dresses all the time. I'll get her to cave too," Em says with a grin.

The rest of dinner is spent discussing the plan for tomorrow, as well as school. Shortly after, we're up in the suite, telling each other good night and preparing for a restful sleep.

Except for me.

I'm restless, lying in bed. I wish I could have convinced Antoinette to come, but I understand why she didn't.

A wild idea crosses my mind. I'm pulling my phone out before I register how dumb this may be.

From: FK (Swedish_Boss48@genericmail.com)

To: AB (wannabebosslady@genericmail.com)

Subject: Fancy some nostalgia?

Never let me agree to you staying home again. Lying in bed alone is miserable.

What are you wearing?

Your perpetually horny and lonely man,

-F

I click send and hope to God she doesn't just open it and laugh at me.

From: AB (wannabebosslady@genericmail.com)

To: FK (Swedish_Boss48@genericmail.com)

Subject: I'm down for a good time

I do have a job to do still, just saying. Not everyone can shirk their responsibilities because they're almost retired.

I'm in that silk set you got me, the black one—no panties.

Never let age stop you from dirty emails,

-T

From: FK (Swedish_Boss48@genericmail.com)

To: AB (wannabebosslady@genericmail.com)

Subject: God, I miss you

Jobs are overrated. Just quit and be my concubine.

… You're not allowed to wear that without me there again. I'm practically drooling picturing you in it. I want to suck on those gorgeous nipples through the silk, leaving obscene marks on the fabric.

Take your shorts off and tell me what you'd want me to do to you if I was there.

Hard as stone, and the hand isn't cutting it,

-F

From: AB (wannabebosslady@genericmail.com)

To: FK (Swedish_Boss48@genericmail.com)

Subject: Going straight to it, eh?

I'm too expensive for your blood, sorry, F. And I don't remember us being in a relationship where you tell me what to do.

I think that's my job, but I'll be nice, for now.

I'd want your hands all over my skin. Maybe your tongue too, but I'd definitely want you to do that thing again with your fingers and your hand on my stomach … Fuck … I'm so turned on.

Take your clothes off.

And now my hand isn't cutting it either. Glad I have some battery-operated assistance, though,

-T

From: FK (Swedish_Boss48@genericmail.com)

To: AB (wannabebosslady@genericmail.com)

Subject: Woman, you're going to kill me

Never tell me you're too expensive for me again. I'd bankrupt myself ten times over for you. As I recall, you like it when I'm in charge.

I'm stark naked for you already, darling. What more do you need?

Yeah, I'd like to do that move more as well. Maybe next time, with my dick instead of my fingers . . .

Already too close to coming,

-F

My phone rings abruptly in my hand. A video call.

"Hello, darling." My voice is ripe with arousal.

"You're cruel. Show me," she responds, eyes hooded, and the faint sound of buzzing makes my pulse thrum in my veins.

I span the camera over my body, hand already stroking my cock, wishing it was her instead.

Antoinette groans. "I should have come, but I didn't want to intrude on family time. And I really can't miss these dumb meetings."

"Next time, when I tell you that you are welcome here, don't be stubborn. Show me that pretty cunt."

"Jesus, the mouth on you." She spans the camera down her body so I can see her circling her clit with the vibrator I bought her. I smirk at that. She isn't using one of hers; no, she's using mine.

"I'm not apologizing. I seem to recall you liking my mouth on you quite a bit."

"You seem to like mine just as much."

"Fuck yes, I do," I moan, squeezing my dick so I don't come immediately.

"This is going to be comically quick," she pants.

"Good because I can't hold on much longer. Slide that vibrator inside, darling."

"Oh God," she breathes.

"Just like that. So good for me. Now tap that little clit. Yes, just like that." She better come in the next minute because I'm about to make a huge mess on my stomach.

"So close."

"Just imagine it being my cock, sliding deep and hitting your G-spot. Imagine it's me kissing and biting your neck." My breathing is getting shallower, and I will myself not to close my eyes. I don't want to miss anything even if it means I lose my shit.

"Yessss." Her back arches as she drops the vibrator and cups her pulsing pussy. It's all the view I need to erupt in my hand.

"Goddamn, you look so pretty right now," I moan through my strokes as she refocuses on the camera.

I come in a rush of feeling, and it's over too quickly.

"I did not have phone sex on my bingo card today." Antoinette sighs happily, pulling the phone up to her face.

"I did not either. Can't say I'm mad about it, though."

"It's a good thing you have a suite with ample space between you three." She grins, still recovering.

"True, darling, true." We both sigh as we come down from the high. "I couldn't sleep. Not without you," I murmur.

"Same. But I did rent a little condo for Azerbaijan and Singapore, so hopefully, this is one of the last times."

"Thank you for doing that. I can't imagine sleeping without you for any extended amount of time after this."

Silence stretches for a moment before she speaks again.

"How's she doing?"

"Em is really excited. Steph is holding her shit together so far, and I'm . . . a little sad, to be honest. She's all grown up."

"She is, and she's a wonderful young woman. She texted me yesterday about how happy she was that you were coming and how sad she was that I wasn't."

"Yes, I got read the riot act about it today. Seems you're fast becoming the favorite in the family."

"I'm not. She needed her mom and dad there to help with this huge life change. I would have just been a distraction."

"Hey," I tell her so she'll look at me again instead of going off into space. "You are a part of our family now. You're never a distraction. I think they love you more than they love me." I smile.

"That's a lie. I'm just the new shiny thing." She laughs.

"Well, you sure are wet and shiny right now."

"Jesus, that was terrible." She chokes on her laughter. "Seriously, never again."

"Listen, I just came so hard my brain cells are having a hard time working. Blame yourself for that terrible joke."

She sighs. "I love you and your terrible jokes."

"I love you and your incessant need to put everyone before yourself."

"Whatever. I'm working on it." She yawns.

"As am I, darling, as am I. Get some sleep, and I'll meet you in Azerbaijan."

"I love you."

"Love you too."

We hang up, and I finally fall into a dreamless sleep.

Chapter 43

Toni

A month later, we're in Mexico, and Empress has the chance to win it all. Both the Drivers' and Constructors' Championships can be won today if Sawyer wins and Alejandro just gets in the points.

Life has been good lately. We've got our lineup for next year, Rocco is officially in jail—as is Brad—and my balance in life feels good. Really damn good, actually. Felix is a huge part of that success.

I peek over at the Legacy pit wall and see the man I love relaxing in his chair, watching me with a small smile on his face.

A blush creeps up my neck. I have to look away in order to not do something crazy, like run over to him and kiss him.

We may technically be "out" as a couple, but we don't show that on race weekends.

"You ready?" Mason asks after he checks in with Sawyer.

"Honestly? I think I am. You?"

"No." He chuckles. "I'm scared shitless, but Sawyer is confident, so I'm running with that."

"Good. We've got this. And if we don't place where we need to, there are still races left to make it happen. There really is no pressure," I tell him.

"Sure, boss lady, no pressure at all."

I smile at the nickname. What was once a joke turned into reality, and it's still a little bizarre. I came into this season panicked and on the verge of a mental breakdown.

And then Felix came into my life.

I not only gained a boyfriend but an entire little family. Emilie texts me almost daily. She sends me clothing links and random memes she thinks I'd like. Henrik emailed me the other day to ask advice about working for a corporation, and Steph and I grabbed lunch once when we were finally in the same place.

It's been a life-changing season.

But the time for reminiscing is over. It's time to focus on this race and win the damn thing.

***

With seven laps left, we're exactly where we need to be. Sawyer has a twenty-second lead, and Alejandro is sitting pretty in fifth. What I'm more excited about is Legacy being in second and third. I know Felix has made peace with this season, but it's still nice to see some validation at the end of the season.

Communication between Sawyer and Mason sounds in my headphones. There's an excitement, a knowledge that we just need to keep it clean for six more laps, and then . . . we win it all.

It's surreal, to be honest, and I'm not sure it's actually hit me yet.

Five more laps.

I can feel the excitement mixed with the anxiety from everyone around me. The stress that something will happen to ruin this, the pure elation that this could be it.

Four laps.

Mason reaches over and grabs my hand. My leg bounces as I watch Sawyer.

Three laps.

My heart is beating out of my chest. It feels real now, and I have no clue what to do with myself.

Two laps.

Everyone is standing around me, but I'm frozen in place, staring at the screen like somehow everything is going to fall apart still.

Final lap.

I hold my breath as Sawyer speeds down toward the checkered flag.

He did it. Holy shit, we *did it!*

I'm frozen in place as Mason congratulates Sawyer. It's only when he taps my shoulder do I realize I need to talk.

"Sawyer, incredible job. You earned every ounce of this championship. We're so incredibly proud of you."

"Thank you so much. I'm so thankful to be a part of this team and so grateful for the opportunity you've given me. A big thank you to the entire team. A full team effort today, and we fucking did it!" he yells, making me smile, as cheers take over the area.

And then everything hits me at once. Tears fill my eyes as my smile stretches across my cheeks so much it hurts. My hands cover my cheeks after I toss my headphones down, and I just sit there, in awe of what we've accomplished this year.

My chair spins, shocking me until I see Felix staring at me with nothing but pride on his face.

"I am so fucking proud of you." He cups my cheeks over my hands and pulls me in for a hard kiss.

The tears I've been desperate to keep in fall without my permission. The dam breaks, and I don't even care if it looks unprofessional.

It's my first full year as a team principal, and we just took the whole damn thing.

"Oh my God, we did it." I pull back, wide-eyed, looking at Felix.

"Yeah, you fucking did, darling!" He has to yell to be heard over the crowd, but the smile on his face is louder than the noise.

I pull him in for a hug and take a minute to just *feel* everything that is happening. This is something I didn't ever think would happen, let alone in my first year. It's been hard and stressful, but it's also been the best year of my life.

Felix pulls back, kissing me one more time before disentangling us.

"Go celebrate. I'll see you after the awards. I love you." He kisses me one more time and then spins on his heel to go celebrate a great race for his team.

The next fifteen minutes are a blur of congratulations and celebrations. If you ask me in a month what happened, I'll tell you I have no clue. But I'll remember the feeling forever.

Standing against the barriers, waiting for the awards to start, I feel a hand slide into mine.

I look up to find Felix standing next to me.

"I should be telling you congratulations as well. What a turnaround." I smirk at him.

"Amazing what a car does when it's not being sabotaged every single race." His wry smirk tells me how he really feels.

Johnny and Pavel get announced first, and then they announce Swayer. Mexico is fun because they have a lift under the winner's car that propels them both up to the stage. When Sawyer appears, his excitement and emotion are infectious.

I watch with tears in my eyes, hand in Felix's, as my entire team cheers on Sawyer. When his national anthem plays, the glossy sheen in his eyes has my tears falling.

Then the United States anthem plays for the winning constructor of the race, and my excitement reaches a fever pitch.

Once the champagne is sprayed, all bets are off.

Felix grabs me around the waist and spins me around, dipping me as he kisses the hell out of me.

The crowd starts dispersing, but Felix continues to kiss me like we have all the time in the world, and I guess now we do.

A throat eventually clears, making us pull away from each other to see it's a PR woman with an awkward smile on her face.

"Apologies. The media conference is starting soon, and they're requesting you both."

"Of course, we'll be right over," Felix says, completely unaffected while I'm as red as a tomato with embarrassment.

"Oh my God, this is why we can't be together during races," I mumble into his shirt.

"And why I can't wait to fucking retire." He sighs.

"I love you." I pull back with a smile.

"I love you too, darling. Now, let's go give the media some headlines."

Chapter 44

(Transcript)

Interviewer: What a win today. Congratulations all around. How are you feeling?

Toni Bailey: Overwhelmed, honestly. And thank you. It's been a whirlwind year, and this is by far the best possible outcome. Sawyer and Alejandro really did some incredible things that made all of this possible. Every employee, crew member—a big credit to them because none of this is possible without them.

Interviewer: With such an incredible year under your belt, how do you feel about next season? How can you possibly improve on this?

Toni Bailey: I think the goal for me and our team is to not look at it like improving, as much as making the best team possible. Making the best car possible. We'll see where that takes us, but if we have a good team together, then any issues that arise are that much easier to fix.

Interviewer: I hear that there's going to be some changes in the driver line-up as well.

Toni Bailey: Yes, we're actually quite excited to have Remi Bouchard joining Sawyer next season. We're so thankful for everything Alejandro has done with us this season, and we know he's going to do amazing things wherever he lands.

Interviewer: So, women at all levels?

Toni Bailey: Best people for the job at all levels, actually. But yes, we're very lucky to have Remi join us and to challenge what Formula 1 has always known. She has incredible potential, and I can't wait to see what she does with it.

Interviewer: Very good. And what about you, Felix? It's been a hard season for you guys overall, but you have rallied lately, and the end of the season looks to be on the up and up.

Felix Karlsson: Yes, while we're disappointed by some people's actions, we're happy with where we're at currently and where we'll be for the remaining races.

Interviewer: Any news on personnel changes for the next season?

Felix Karlsson: Actually, yes. Abu Dahbi will be my last race. I'm officially retiring and passing the reins off to Rick Luther. I can't imagine a better person than Rick to take over.

Interviewer: Wow. Well, the sport sure will be different without you. Why the sudden shift?

Felix Karlsson: My priorities have changed. I feel that I don't have anything to prove in Formula 1 anymore, and being with my partner as much as possible is more important.

Interviewer: Oh, well, congratulations on the relationship.

Felix Karlsson: You'll still be seeing me around. I'll be following the love of my life as she travels for races and decimates you all again next season. It'll be interesting to see it from the sidelines.

Toni Bailey: Felix, be kind.

Felix Karlsson: Darling, that was kind.

Interviewer: Well, we're looking forward to seeing how Legacy does in the remaining races, and again, Toni, congratulations on a truly incredible year.

Epilogue

Felix

I'm in my final meeting on my final day at Legacy.

And I'm ecstatic.

There's a badass little woman waiting for me at the condo we rented, naked, and I can't get out of here fast enough. I've already said my goodbye, already wrapped up my work, so this is just the last formality.

"Felix, thank you for everything you've done for Legacy. It won't be the same without you, and I'll strive to keep up the level of excellence you've set," Rick says.

"You'll do just fine." I shake his hand before standing up and waving to the group. "I'll be seeing you around from the other side." I wink.

Chuckles trail behind me as I walk out of the office one last time.

I've never been more secure in a decision. I'm done, free and clear to spend my days spoiling the shit out of a woman who deserves it more than anyone I know.

Face masks, massages, anything she wants or needs—it's now my job to make it happen.

I practically sprint to our condo, not far from the track, and barrel in, locking the door behind me.

"Oh, darling," I call out, stalking my way to the bedroom.

The sight that greets me nearly brings me to my knees.

Antoinette, naked, the vibrator I got her circling her nipples as she arches her back on the bed.

"Took you long enough." She smiles.

"Had I known you were going to get started without me, I would have skipped the entire thing. You feeling needy, darling?"

"So needy. I think you owe me a couple of orgasms for taking first today."

A bark of laughter leaves me as I unbutton my shirt.

"Did I ruin your nearly perfect season?"

"You did." She pouts, moving the vibrator down her stomach.

"Poor thing, how ever will you recover?" I quickly strip out of my pants and boxer briefs, kneeling in front of her and taking the vibrator from her hands. "One rule from here on out." She arches an eyebrow at me. "If you need an orgasm, you come to me. Your vibrator is my teammate, not the thing that gets you off. You don't touch this pretty little pussy anymore unless I tell you to." I press the silicone tip to her clit, causing her to moan.

"Do you hear me, or are you already too far gone in this one, darling?" I smirk.

"I hear you," she gasps as her hips thrust.

I have this moment where I'm flashed forward three years from now, and we're in this same condo after Antoinette just won her third title and I get to do this exact same thing. This is my life now. I get to do this whenever the hell I want to with no obligations outside of pleasing my woman.

It's mind-blowing, truly. I've never been in a position where I could put my full attention on a woman, not even Steph, and it's like there's a brand-new world that just opened up to me.

It's addictive already. I'm not sure Antoinette knows what she's signed up for.

There's no reason to waste more time; my fingers find her drenched and pulsing, so I know she's right on the edge. Sliding two inside of her, I keep the vibrator on her clit as she goes off almost immediately. I let her ride it out before dropping it and surging up on my knees. Quickly wrapping her legs around me, I thrust in to catch the last of her orgasm around me.

It feels like Christmas and my birthday all rolled into one. Like a vacation to the greatest place you can think of. It's what I imagine being high would be like.

"Jesus," I groan, tipping my head back as I grip her hips hard enough to bruise.

"Oh my God." She pants and clenches around me once more.

Once we calm down a little, I collapse on top of her, holding most of my weight on my forearms.

"How the fuck did I get so lucky for this to be my life?"

"You're very poetic right now." She smiles.

"I just realized that I'm the lucky man who gets to keep you happy at all times. I get to travel with you and be waiting for you when you come home. Give you all the orgasms you can handle."

"My very own house husband."

"Call me whatever you want to, darling." I give her a shallow thrust, making both of us moan.

"I feel like this is a dream."

"All real," I tell her, although it feels like one to me as well.

And then she jolts me out of my reverie by begging.

"Move please."

I call upon all my stamina to not fail me now.

Then I pull out and thrust deep.

The longer I keep pace, the wetter she's getting, and it reminds me of something I promised her. Pushing myself up to my knees once more, I press on her lower belly as I thrust, but I know my angle's off, so I snag a pillow and wrap an arm around her middle to lift her hips. Now that they're elevated, I thrust again and know I've hit the right spot when she gasps, eyes wide open.

"Get ready, darling," I warn, planting my hand back on her belly with pressure and thrust hard. It doesn't take long, the orgasm she already had helping me out here, until I hear the sounds I'm looking for.

"Holy shit." It finally registers what I'm doing.

"Just like with my fingers, bear down just a little— Ah!" What I didn't account for is just how phenomenal it would feel on my dick. It's like she's pulling me in and pushing me out at the same time—a dichotomy I can barely think about because, in a matter of seconds, she's coming. I pull out and circle her clit as she rides it, making a mess of our bed. The moment she's done, I slide back in and ride her hard, chasing my own release.

I come with her name on my lips and her hands in my hair.

The decision to clean up later is an easy one, considering we have to change the sheets completely, so I pull out and collapse next to her, dragging her with me.

"I— That— I have no words," she says against my chest.

"Good. Let's me know I've done my job right." She smacks my chest, but I'm serious; I want her tongue tied and exhausted.

My fingertips draw aimless shapes along her body as we soak in our new reality.

"I talked to Sydney while you were gone."

"Oh yeah?" I ask.

"She wanted me to convince you to sign onto Empress."

"Doing what, exactly?"

"She doesn't care. Told me that you can make up a title, create your hours, whatever you want."

"Might give me an excuse to be able to see you whenever I want, even when you're at work."

"That's not what she's talking about." Antoinette laughs.

"Could fuck you in your office."

"Felix!"

"Finger you in the cool down room when you're stressed."

"Jesus, forget I mentioned it. I'm taking it off the table." She sighs.

"Too late. I sent her the signed contract before I got here."

"What?" She sits up, staring at me.

"She sent me a contract after talking to you. I came up with a title and told her I'd agree if I only worked part time and it didn't take me away from you." I won't tell her that I plan to send the salary Sydney offered me straight to Luka and Daisy for their charity work. They can disperse it however it's needed.

"What's the title?" she very astutely asks.

"Foreign relations." A nod to my made-up email address that only Antoinette would actually pick up on. It seemed fitting.

She bursts out laughing. "You are the most ridiculous man I've ever met. Did

Sydney pick up on your little play there?"

"She did not. She asked and then promptly said forget it because she knew it was something to do with us. I think she thinks it's sexual." I smirk.

"Now she's going to be looking at me like I'm a freak in the bedroom."

"Well, darling, the bed sheets say that isn't a lie."

"You're enjoying this too much."

"Too right. But I just secured a reason to be able to be around you 24/7 and gave you some powerful orgasms, so overall, this is a win of a day."

She rests her chin on my chest, looking up at me. "I love that this is going to be our life."

"I love you." I give her the only response I can.

I wasn't looking for love. I sure as shit wasn't looking to date anyone, but this woman wiggled in without effort, destined to be mine.

And now I'm holding on tight and never letting go, prepared to spend the rest of my life building her up and watching her conquer the world.

She kisses my nose, then my lips, before snuggling into my side.

This is the best version of life I could ever dream of.

Acknowledgements

To my lovely writer besties, J and Michelle: Thank you for helping me stay the course. I think imposter syndrome would drown me if it weren't for you two.

To my beta, Annalee: Thank you for taking the time to read Balance and make it the best it could be!

Amy, thank you for helping me edit this and making it SO GOOD!

Nina, there aren't words to tell you how much I love having you in my corner. You aren't just my editor; you are a friend and I'm so thankful for you!

Hubs, during the writing of this book, life has been hard. You've been incredible helping me navigate things and helping me figure out how to have more balance in my life. You are the best human and I'm so lucky to have you.

Dear readers, none of this is possible without you and I can never thank you for the incredible support. I wouldn't be here without you, and I am so grateful you took a chance on me!

Also By

The Catalyst Series

The Beginning

Meet the women of The Catalyst Series a decade before the series takes place!

The Detour

Bea and Riggs

The List

Penelope and Andy

The Case

Larkin and Theo

The Vacation

Jane and Pierce

Bluebell Falls

Second First Impression

Ainsley and Ledger

For the Thrill of It

Willow and Oakley

What You Broke

Rina and Arlo

Redefining Strength

Roxy and Lennox

Qualifiers of Love Series

Serendipity

Sydney and Beckett

Fuse

Daisy and Luka

Be sure to join my newsletter to stay up to date on new releases and all other things me!

http://www.samanthamthomas.com

If you enjoyed Balance, please think about leaving a review! I would be so grateful to you!

Review Here